HOW TO SURVIVE THE APOCALYPSE

Through the concealed is the literal translation of the **Apocalypse**. That Greek word also means the unveiling, disclosure of knowledge and the uncovering.

Source: en.wikipedia.org/wiki/Apocalypse

SHEMA'YAH BEY

PARADISE PUBLISHING GROUP

This book is a work of fiction. Names, characters, places, and incidents are products of the author's imagination, or are used fictitiously. Any resemblance to actual events, or locales, and/or persons - living or dead, is entirely coincidental.

Grateful acknowledgment to: Queen! for coming to the rescue, GM (Hazel), Vonda, Ra Herakthy, Thomas & Judy, Charles Pitts, Jr. and my Spirit Friends.

THE RITUAL
HOW TO SURVIVE THE APOCALYPSE
Book TWO of THE RITUAL Series

Written by Shema'yah Bey

DISCLAIMER:
Reader Discretion Advised

Cover artwork is courtesy of Josh Hild

Emailed to: TheRitualTVShow@gmail.com

Printed in the United States of America

ISBN: 978-1729230268

First Edition

1 2 3 4 5 6 7 8 9 10

We had to pay a lot of souls for you…

- Ida May Bouché

BOUCHÉ (pronounced: Boo-Shay)

1
NO WORRIES
New Ulm, Minnesota

Three bounty hunters found themselves on the wrong side of the law. They got stopped on the unforgiving highway of 15 North in New Ulm, Minnesota. The sun's glare added to their frustration. Those bounty hunters had been transporting a powerful weapon to New Orleans, Louisiana. Their so-called 'weapon' had a name. They called her Paradise Montoyier (pronounced: *Mon-toy-yea*). Her soothingly sweet southern voice evoked the feeling of eating pink cotton candy at midnight. Paradise replaced her signature Indian braids with a bun; but, then quickly settled for a long pony-tail. She had naturally thick hair. She also had caramel skin, a centerfold body, and a runway model face. However, the government wasn't interested in her booty, or her beauty.

Their sights were set on her magical abilities. Quiet as kept, Paradise had no intention on sharing her supernatural skill set.

Moments before Paradise and her crew approached highway 15 North, the Holy Ghost told her to do something of extreme importance. That unseen force instructed her to anoint their vehicle with divinely infused water.

"*Use the ancient Lemurian water ritual,*" said the divine voice inside of her head.

Ancient Lemuria, also known as the lost Land of Mu, existed thousands of years ago. Lemuria's location is currently known as the Pacific Ring of Fire. Paradise followed the spiritual command. She uncapped a bottle of water, inhaled deeply, and whispered over the cool liquid. Then she doused the bounty hunters' Cadillac Escalade with that divine elixir. Her daylight ceremony helped the bounty hunters avoid arrest.

The arresting officers were two Minnesota State Troopers. When they approached the bounty hunters' parked vehicle, their bowels loosened. Knowingly, or unknowingly, they encountered a force beyond scientific understanding. Paradise invoked that supernatural force moments before those troopers arrived. The Spirit of Fear told them to unholster their guns. Without hesitation, or mental reservation, they followed the unspoken command.

"*I got a bad feeling,*" thought the stocky state trooper.

"*I feel it too,*" thought one of the bounty hunters.

That particular bounty hunter had a bad case of the bubble guts. Her upset stomach increased when that unexplainable presence made its presence known. The Spirit of Fear caused the taller trooper to question his top-of-the-class police training. He thought to himself, "*This doesn't feel right. We need to let these people go …*"

His fear had been confirmed when everyone involved heard the troopers' disturbed dispatcher on the walkie-talkie say, "The suspects are considered armed and dangerous. Proceed with caution."

"WATCH OUT!," screamed the stocky state trooper.

The taller trooper jumped out of the way. To the bounty hunters' surprise, those state troopers returned to their vehicle. A parade of unmarked squad cars had been in pursuit of a dirty white cargo van. When the dispatcher said, "Proceed with caution", her warning pertained to the violent occupants inside that fast moving van. Those bandits robbed the New Ulm Bank, abducted the bank manager, and were asking for the taller trooper by name. The bounty hunters were free to go, because the hostage happened to be the stocky trooper's wife.

The female bounty hunter remarked, "That was close."

"Take your turban off," commanded Blurry to the female bounty hunter.

Eighteen hours ago, the woman who wore the turban had been hired by the very impressive bounty hunter called, 'Blurry'. They met one another at the International Bounty Hunters' Convention in Minneapolis, Minnesota. Blurry's government name was 'Bernard Jackson'. He had dark chocolate skin, award winning muscles, and a bald head. His newly appointed apprentice looked like a slimmer version of Jill Scott. Jill Scott happened to be the very popular soul singing songwriter from Philadelphia, Pennsylvania. Unbeknownst to either Blurry, or his new trainee, they shared the same last name. Her name was Taka El-Kadir (pronounced: *Tah-Kah El-Kah-Deer*) Jackson.

Inside the truck, Taka sucked her teeth and begrudgingly complied with Blurry's command. For the safety of everyone involved, Taka carefully removed her bright red turban and her star and crescent pendant. Taka had long, flowing dreadlocks with auburn tips.

Two years and one week ago, Taka abandoned Philadelphia for the nightlife of Las Vegas, Nevada. Three days after graduating from the Las Vegas Private Eye/Detective School, she attended the International Bounty Hunters' Convention in Minneapolis, in search of a job. But, she didn't have any luck securing a position. As she walked dejectedly through the crowded convention center, she saw Blurry first. He looked out-of-sorts too. Blurry's business partner, and best friend, was the scheduled keynote speaker. Yet, his present whereabouts were unknown.

Concerned, Taka gently inquired, "What's wrong brother?"

"Oh, wow ... is it that evident?," he replied.

"*It really is,*" nodded Taka.

Blurry inhaled deeply and in unison they exhaled slowly. Taka softly caressed her left ear and caringly said, "Woo-sah brother, woo-sah."

That classic relaxation sound caused Blurry to smile. Taka smiled too. She closed her almond shaped brown eyes, and inhaled slowly to hear Blurry nervously ask, "Now what…?"

"Your breath," said Taka curiously.

Caught off guard, Blurry self-consciously asked, "What about my breath?"

"It's so minty," she said playfully.

Relieved, Blurry shook his head, smiled again, and removed something from his suit jacket. Taka smiled, shook her head and extended her right hand.

"It's wintergreen. And I've been chewing these mints all night," Blurry said, half joking, half serious.

Though her hand is now fully extended, Taka still respectfully asked, "May I?"

"What's your name?", queried Blurry as he handed over the tin of mints.

"It's Taka," she said comfortingly.

"Bernard Jackson," he proudly stated.

Taka looked stunned. Her hands moistened. She gulped, stepped back, and accidentally dropped the tin of tiny mints. That unexpected sound caused those nearby bounty hunters to duck for cover. They restored their composure when the event manager stated, "Move along. There's nothing to see here."

"What's wrong sister? You look like you just seen a ghost," Blurry said astonished.

When Taka spoke, the tone of her voice was downcast - her concern evident. "You said, "Jackson"... my last name is Jackson. I really hope we're not related."

"No worries," said Blurry confidently.

Blurry felt what Taka felt, so what they felt had to be true. Taka looked toward heaven, puckered her full shea butter lips and stepped onto the metaphoric limb. She returned her gaze to Blurry, inhaled deeply, and sheepishly said, "I know you feel it too."

"I do," Blurry said happily.

Frustratingly, Taka emoted, "I don't know what you're smiling at. 'Cus I don't do that! That's just nasty!!"

Blurry quickly shot back, "I said, "no worries". We're not related."

Blurry told Taka he had been adopted around the age of eight. His foster mother, who was Ms. Wanda Jackson, raised him in Harlem, New York. Mom-Jackson took great care of Blurry. So, to show his appreciation, he requested a legal name change from the court in New York.

The Judge honored the nine year old's wish, and Blurry's name went from Bernard Harold Washington, to Bernard Harold Jackson. Blurry was in his early 30s. Taka was in her late 20s. In addition to being close in age, they were also close in height. In three inch high heels Taka stood six feet three inches tall. Blurry stood six feet three inches tall without shoes. While they had only just met, they had the look of the classic Hollywood handsome couple.

"Yo, Blurry, we need an exit strategy," said Lulu.

"I got you Lu," assured Blurry to his brother from another mother.

Lulu was the reason Blurry and Taka were in trouble. Lulu's birth name is Luis Taylor Tapia, but everyone calls him Lulu Fortune. Lulu was of mixed stock. His mother came from the Dominican, Republic, and his African-American father hailed from the 'BX'. The BX happened to be Bronx, New York. When he spoke, his afro-latino accent was easily detected.

Life hardened Lulu, so he appeared older than his age. Nevertheless, he had a cover-model look. If, it wasn't for his deformed right ear, visually, he'd be considered a god. Lulu suffered permanent hearing loss in that once good, but now deformed ear. In truth, the mutilation was the result of his half-brother, Lex's failed attempt to murder Lulu when he was a little boy.

It's worth noting: Lulu was born three months premature. So, the hearing in his left ear was compromised at birth. He wore a tiny hearing aid to help resolve his hearing complications. Thanks to modern technology, his hearing aid was virtually undetectable to the untrained eye.

According to the eye-witness testimony of Hanna, a jogger in New Ulm's Mueller Park, Taka and Blurry kidnapped Lulu. However, Hanna's smartphone footage contradicted her testimony, as it failed to represent the truth. Nonetheless, she forwarded her video and skewed point-of-view to the New Ulm Police Department. They, in turn, directed her information to those Minnesota State Troopers. The tight knit community of New Ulm - whose buildings looked like the Glockenspiel in Munich, Germany - had been an old German settlement for years. The desk sergeant who reviewed the video, accepted Hanna's statement and thought to himself, "*Those two assailants need to be arrested for carjacking too.*"

So, he ordered an APB, police lingo for an 'all-points-bulletin'.

Blurry figured they had a thirty minute window to escape. Lulu figured they had at least an hour before those troopers realized they'd let Blurry and Taka escape.

"We need to do a threat assessment so we can determine our options of escape," Blurry suggested to Lulu.

"What about the APB?," Taka said inquiringly.

"That's the least of our worries," Lulu told Taka.

"You're extremely quiet," Blurry said, taking notice of Paradise.

Paradise remained quiet because her thoughts were on the APB. The desk sergeant was unaware that Blurry and Taka didn't kidnap Lulu. He didn't know that they were actually assisting Lulu into the truck, because Hanna - the young German jogger - failed to report that she witnessed Lulu asking Blurry for help.

Lulu needed the assistance because he was assaulted ten minutes before Blurry and Taka arrived on the scene. Lulu's assailant set his modified stun-gun to kill. When Lulu landed face-first, everyone involved assumed he was dead. But, it wasn't his time to die. Lulu awoke within a minute.

In an effort to determine what direction the kidnappers had taken, he strained in his hazed state to focus on the skid marks left by their vehicle. According to the tire tracks, they were headed toward the Cottonwood River in Flandrau State Park.

Lulu had knowledge that Paradise had been snatched. Her kidnappers were five German nationals. They were dressed like militarized New Ulm cops. By the way they moved, Lulu figured they were mercenaries.

Lulu didn't have the strength to stand. So, he crawled on his belly groping for his car keys. When Lulu and Paradise were stopped, they were separated. Being assaulted at gunpoint had caused Lulu to throw away his keys.

When Hanna arrived on the scene, Paradise and her kidnappers were gone. Hanna heard Lulu grunt. She stood nearby watching him struggle, yet she never approached him. He followed Hanna's gaze, shook his head, and frustratingly said, "Coñaso! Tres ruedas pinchadas!" In Spanish, he'd said, "Damn! Three flat tires!"

One of the attackers slashed the tires of Lulu's rental car with a utility knife. Lulu looked pleasantly surprised when he discovered the black truck. The rescue vehicle had New York license plates. Hanna watched the muscular black man step out of the Escalade. Though she attempted to retreat into the nearby woods, her pregnant bulldog - Athena - refused to move. So, Hanna yanked the growling dog's chain nervously commanding, "Lass uns gehen, Athena! Beeil dich! Schnell!

Schnell!" That's German for, "Let's go, Athena. Hurry Up! Quickly! Quickly!"

Lulu grabbed the muscular black man's hand.

"You alright?," laughed Blurry.

"Help me up," barked Lulu.

Lulu returned his attention to the atmosphere inside the truck. Paradise remained unusually quiet, which disturbed Blurry and Taka. Her eyes were closed. So, they figured she was pretending to nap. It wasn't until Lulu cleared his throat, that Paradise opened her eyes, looked out of the window, and softly said, "Every shut eye ain't sleep."

2
GREEN BOOK
Lafayette, Minnesota

Paradise didn't need a global positioning system (GPS) to know they were headed north. She shook her head when the GPS announced "Rerouting." To help calm her nerves, she twirled her thumb around the tip of her right index finger. Though the terrain was far more rugged, Blurry purposely took the wooded trails instead of the major roadway, as there were several checkpoints on the roads surrounding the city of New Ulm.

Every major artery was being monitored by a local, state, or federal agency. The local police focused their attention on rerouting traffic. The focus of the State police was the capture of Blurry and Taka. The Federal Bureau of Investigation (FBI) drilled down their efforts on those bank robbers. And, Homeland Security was there too, along with Virginia Gregory, the United States' National Director of Intelligence. They got involved because of the domestic terrorist element. Ms. Gregory looked like the 40-year-old version of Katniss Everdeen, from the movie, Hunger Games. It's worth noting that Virginia, the brunette bombshell, had the coveted body of a lingerie model.

When the state troopers let Paradise and the others go, Lulu spotted National Director Gregory's convoy headed toward Flandrau State Park … the same park Lulu, Blurry, and Taka recovered Paradise. The domestic terrorists that assaulted Lulu, and kidnapped Paradise were actually five German nationals. They died in that state park, killed by a countless number of blackbirds after Paradise prayed the self-defense prayer. She later learned that Lulu had prayed the same prayer around the same time. Their collective invocation caused hundreds of blackbirds to appear out of nowhere. Those raging birds flew over the German kidnappers' getaway cars. Squawking their last breath, the swarming drove of birds dropped from the sky causing mayhem. Both vehicles flipped, and the SUV crashed into a tree, exploding upon impact. The vehicle Paradise was in was badly mangled having wrapped around a tree near the Cottonwood River. Paradise managed to escape through the opened trunk. She removed the duct tape, held back her scream, and fled into the wooded area.

Immediately, Lulu asked, "Paradise, are you okay?"

Agitated, Paradise responded, "I'm okay Lulu." She then posed the question, "What's the deal Blurry? We're a long way from New Orleans."

To which Blurry quipped, "I'm working on it."

Blurry responded to another text message, fiddled with the GPS, and cleared his throat.

"Po-Po got it on lock," announced Taka, pretending to be a thug.

"This ain't the time for Gallows humor," tempered Lulu, referring to the dark, ironic satire used by executioners, police, and firemen about grim, deadly, and hopeless situations.

Knowing they weren't 'there' yet, Blurry injected, "Our situation isn't hopeless."

"I know that," Taka said soberly. "I was attempting to be funny."

"*Turn right,*" instructed the GPS.

As Blurry followed the computerized command, Lulu looked confused, and Paradise looked upset. Taka broke through the justified question, "What are we doing on this abandoned road?"

The GPS led them to a farmhouse just off an abandoned road. There were animals roaming freely about, and the farmhouse appeared to be isolated as the threesomes had not seen any other farms for miles around. No one got to answer Taka's question, because they were distracted. Someone in another vehicle was flashing their headlights at them. Paradise squinted.

"Who's that fat white man?," asked Taka curiously.

"I don't know. I've never seen him before," said Blurry.

The fat white man appeared to be in his 60s. He drove a muddy blue pick-up truck. Blurry drove up to his truck slowly. Lulu removed the gun from under his seat. He placed it on his lap. Taka removed a box cutter from her leather jacket. Paradise nervously tapped her finger on her left knee. That's when the Spirit of Irritation decided to pay Paradise a visit. It touched Lulu's and Taka's soul too. The red-faced fat man *turned-up* too; he unholstering his revolver and placed the 44 Magnum (gun) on the passenger seat. He rolled down his window, furrowed his brow and coldly said, "Pull around back." Afterwards, he spat a mouthful of partially chewed tobacco onto the muddy driveway.

His irritated, gray-mouthed German shepherd barked uncontrollably. "Settle down!," he demanded authoritatively. Immediately, the dog obeyed and became silent.

The gray haired fat man put his truck in reverse. Blurry followed behind him slowly, Lulu released the safety on the gun, and Paradise calmly questioned, "What are we doing here?"

"That's a damn good question," chimed in Lulu, speaking to Blurry.

"He's our ticket out of here," said Blurry.

Taka was confused. "I thought you didn't know him," she said.

"I don't. But, trust, he's our 'green book',"

In a skeptical tone, Lulu followed up with, "Yo Blurry, all jokes aside, how do you know him?"

To which Blurry nonchalantly responded, "I don't know him. He's Bo's uncle."

"Bo? … 125th Street Bo?!," questioned Lulu combatively.

"Calm down Lu. Here he comes," said Blurry.

Under her breath Taka inquired, "What's a 'green book'?"

The fat man, along with his dog, approached Lulu's side of the truck. Lulu rolled the window down slowly. The fat man spat on the ground again, wiped his mouth on his flannel shirt sleeve, and dryly said, "Who's Blurry?"

"I am," nodded Blurry.

In his thick Minnesota accent, the fat man commented, "Bo never said you was black."

"Is that a problem?," Blurry asked in a raspy Harlem tone.

"It is," the fat man stated coldly. "But, I understand you saved Bo's life."

Blurry confirmed. "I did. What's your name sir?"

"No names. Now, hold on," said fat No Name.

Lulu, Taka, and Paradise remained quiet. No Name removed a brand new smartphone from his muddy overalls, and dialed out, engaging the device's face-to-face video app. Once the video connection was made, he turned the face of the phone - which revealed Bo's nervous face - to Blurry and agitatedly asked, "Is this him?"

"Yeah, that's him," Bo said to his uncle.

No Name terminated the video call. He looked at Lulu, Paradise, and Taka with a scowl. Paradise flared her nostrils. Taka raised her chin. Lulu furrowed his brow.

No Name cavalierly said, "Get out of the truck. If you gals got to 'go', y'all can squat behind that there tree." Taka's defiant response? An angry, "I ain't squatt'n behind no damn tree."

"You better check your boy Blurry, before I check him," Lulu remarked heatedly.

Blurry's firery retort clarified, "He's not my boy. But, he is our 'green book'."

"What the hell is a Green Book?," whispered Taka to Paradise. Paradise remained silent.

Having lost his patience, No Name blurted out, "Are y'all getting out, or what? We don't have all day!"

Lulu looked at Blurry, nodding a silent communication: "*It's okay. We need to get out of the truck.*"

They stepped out of the truck slowly. Lulu put the gun on safety and stuck it in his waistband. Taka held onto her box cutter. The German shepherd stood guard for No Name. She protected him as he stepped inside the muddy blue pick-up truck. No Name carefully removed the State of Minnesota Inspection Sticker from the windshield. Then, he stepped out of the pickup truck, slammed the door shut, looked at Blurry with disgust, and spat again. Blurry never flinched. No Name felt their vibe. So, he calmed himself by inhaling slowly. He quickly removed the phillips-head screwdriver from his back pocket, and began removing the license plates from his vehicle. As he waddled his way toward the Escalade, Lulu asserted himself with a stern directive. "Don't touch my truck."

"Very well, do it yourself," shrugged No Name to Lulu.

No Name handed Blurry the screwdriver and boldly said, "Consider Bo's debt paid."

Blurry gave the phillips-head screwdriver to Lulu, who replaced his New York license plates with No Name's Minnesota plates. No Name tossed the inspection sticker scraper onto the ground. Paradise picked it up and handed it to Lulu, who nonverbally said, "*Thank you*" with a nod.

"*You're welcome,*" nodded Paradise in acknowledgement.

Lulu carefully removed his State of New York inspection stickers. No Name adjusted the driver's seat so he could squeeze his rotund body into the Escalade. Using double-sided tape, he stuck the State of Minnesota inspection sticker onto Lulu's windshield. He then commanded Blurry and Lulu, "Step back."

Lulu, Taka, and Paradise looked at Blurry disgustingly. He felt their metaphoric daggers and whispered, "Green book."

No Name drove the truck a few yards away. He hitched the horse trailer to the back bumper of the Escalade. Meanwhile, Taka, Paradise, and Blurry followed behind Lulu. They approached the truck with a sense of urgency in their steps.

"Get in," ordered No Name. Taka and Paradise reached for their respective door handles. They flinched when he said, "Not you. I was talking to my dog."

"I'm a hurt you, him, and that dog," whispered Lulu to Blurry.

Blurry grimaced before he mouthed, "Green book," to Lulu.

Blurry opened the back door and the dog jumped in. No Name barked, "Get inside the horse trailer. It's clean.

Lay behind those bales of hay. Use the blankets if you have to. And, don't get up until we cross the state line."

"Ain't nobody using them horse blankets! They're probably infested with smallpox," said an irritated Taka to Paradise.

They stepped inside the horse trailer begrudgingly. No Name got out of the truck, locked the horse trailer, and returned to the driver's seat. When he drove off the property, Lulu whispered to Blurry, "You know we can't trust him."

"I know. I got a backup plan," Blurry said reassuringly.

"Will somebody tell me what's going on? And, what the hell is a green book?," said Taka in a frustrated whisper.

The phrase 'green book' saved Blurry from getting choked out by Lulu. When they were teenagers, Blurry's foster mother told them scary stories about the South.

"My parents were sharecroppers under Jim Crow. Around 1956, they fled backwoods Alabama for Harlem, New York. When I was a little girl, Papa introduced me to Mr. V. H. Green. He was the mailman who authored the green book," recalled Mom-Jackson.

The Negro Motorist Green Book, served as a survival guide for coloreds, negroes, and blacks. That very important travel guide was printed during the Jim Crow era, which existed from 1936 to 1966. Jim Crow laws served as legal racism under the term, 'separate but equal.'

"White folk had 'sundown' towns every place you looked," Mom-Jackson told the teenage Blurry.

"What's a 'sundown' town?," asked the young Lulu.

"After sundown, black folk couldn't be on the white folk's side of town. So, Mr. Green created a travel guide to help us survive. His precious gem helped numerous black families avoid embarrassment, harassment, and death. The 'green book' also contained the names and addresses of eateries, gas stations, and sleeping facilities friendly to our kind," Mom-Jackson recounted.

Blurry called their escape plan, Project Green Book, in honor of Lulu and two unnamed South Carolinians - one negro and one white. Both lived during the Jim Crow era.

Lulu had a fancy vehicle, and so did the unnamed negro in his time. However, because of the era, the negro needed to rent a white man to drive across town. The unnamed white man met the black man on a barren dirt road. The white man got inside the vehicle, sat on the back seat and cavalierly said, "Hey uncle, take me across town."

The black man wore a chauffeur's cap to appear more official. When they approached a 'sundown' town they'd switch roles. The black man would climb into the trunk, and curl himself into a ball. The white man then closed the trunk, sat in the driver's seat, and drove unmolested through the town.

3

AGENT BRUNO

Sioux City, Iowa

Paradise, Lulu, Taka, and Blurry arrived in Sioux City, Iowa. They'd gone through the State of Minnesota in peace. No Name encountered two checkpoints. But, the police never inspected his horse trailer. They simply nodded, "*Move along, there is nothing to see here.*"

No Name complied with the order, thought about Bo, and his fate. Bo had red hair, green eyes, and extremely pale skin. He worked as a realtor in a tiny office in Upper Manhattan. Blurry sent two goons to Bo's place of business. Bo knew the goons were coming, because Blurry had sent him a text in advance. Bo instructed his secretary to take the day off. She gathered her things, smiled goodbye, and walked out. Within twenty minutes, those goons were inside Bo's office. They came from what's known as Alphabet City, located in Lower Manhattan, New York.

"What do you want?," asked Bo, pretending to be nervous.

"Run that phone son," said the seasoned thug.

"Here take it," offered Bo, as he removed the smartphone from his belt clip. "I don't want any trouble."

The younger thug was Puerto Rican, and had the happy face. He snatched Bo's phone, and scrolled through his pictures. Happy face showed Bo the picture on his smartphone, aggressively asking, "Yo, who-dis?"

"*Wow. These guys are really good actors*," thought Bo.

"Here, hold this," said the goon with the prison muscles.

Bo took the New York Times newspaper from the goon's hand. The goon, also known as Ex-Con, looked at Happy Face.

"*Thanks for your cooperation, because things could-get real messy, real quick*," nodded Happy Face to Bo.

Happy Face became Happy Face thanks to a utility knife. Happy Face's scars traveled from the corners of his mouth up to his ears.

"Hold it correctly," ordered Ex-Con.

Bo complied. He held the newspaper firmly and pointed to the date. Happy Face wore a politically incorrect Obama mask. Ex-Con wore the appropriate Richard Nixon mask.

Their uniform of choice was motorcycle gloves, dirty blue jeans, and black hoodies with no print.

"Take the picture already," directed Happy Face.

The Ex-Con was confused. "Yo, how do you work this stupid phone?," he asked.

Ex-Con handed Bo the smartphone. Bo opened the camera app, pointed to the camera button, then gave the phone back to Ex-Con.

"You better not smile," said Ex-Con to Happy Face.

Bo thought, "*We're even Blurry. Consider my debt paid in full.*" Blurry and Bo were retired U.S. Army Rangers. Blurry had saved Bo's life a few clicks outside of Kandahar, Afghanistan. Thereafter, Bo would go on and on about how he'd do anything for Blurry. On more than one occasion, Bo even promised to somehow repay his debt. But, Blurry never needed his help … until now.

"Did you take the picture?," Happy Face asked Ex-Con. "Cause if you did, I didn't see it flash."

Bo's impatience was clear. "It flashed. Now, what?"

"Call your rich uncle," instructed Ex-Con.

"Which one?," Bo wanted to know.

"The one in the midwest," said Happy Face.

Bo was puzzled. "How do you know about him?"

"We know everything baby," boasted Ex-Con.

Bo looked confused. He retrieved his rich uncle's telephone number, and after tapping the FaceTime button had the phone snatched away by Happy Face. In protest, Bo furrowed his brow. In response, Ex-Con revealed his concealed gun. Bo got the message, sat back, and calmed himself. After the phone's second ring they heard, "Hey favorite nephew, how are things in New York?"

That greeting was quickly met with, Happy Face saying, "If you want to see your nephew alive again, you're going to do as you're told."

During his delivery, Happy Face abandoned his Spanish accent, replacing it with a believable Italian accent. He sounded like he was from Staten Island, New York. Bo's uncle laughed uncontrollably. This disturbed everyone involved. They were expecting a different response. Ex-Con pointed his gun at Bo, who held the New York Times in front of his chest. His uncle stopped laughing, and could be heard spitting tobacco before he bellowed, "Bo, what the hell is going on?!"

"Do what they ask," Bo replied stoically.

"The HELL I WILL!," shouted Bo's uncle.

"Is this a joke?! … you're a got-damn Army Ranger … you're a trained killer! … you're not a pacifist," ranted the uncle with great disgust. "Aw, hell nephew, I can beat the man in the monkey mask," he said insultingly. Having collected himself a bit, Bo's uncle settled down and got to the business at hand. "So, what's the real story?"

"In less than an hour, a man called Blurry will be at your house," Bo said.

The uncle didn't remain settled for long. His agitation revved up. "What does he want? … whatever it is I ain't buying! … and, what kind of name is Blurry?"

"He needs to get out of town. No questions asked," Bo advised.

"I'm not going anywhere and I'm not doing spit," Bo's uncle declared.

"If you don't take our associate to his destination, your favorite nephew is dead," Happy Face replied.

Uncle's response was indifferent. "As far as I'm concerned you can kill him."

In shock, Bo screamed, "What?"

"You can kill him for acting like a punk," uncle remarked coldly.

Bo flinched, but recovered quickly. His reaction exposed the dejection he felt. Bo got choked up as he told his uncle, "If I turn up missing, contact Agent Bruno … "

"Whoa. Nobody is killing anybody! Obama and Mr. Nixon, there's no need for anybody to turn up missing. My nephew knows I can be a little hot-headed at times. I apologize. I'll take your associate wherever he needs to go," uncle said somberly.

Ex-Con terminated the call, and kept Bo's smartphone. Bo didn't know how to play it, so, he didn't protest. After 4, or 5 hours, Happy Face and Ex-Con walked out of Bo's office. There was no need for bloodshed because of the text Blurry sent Ex-Con. Happy Face smiled when he read the numeric code, '9 13 19 1 6 5', which correlated to specific letters in the English alphabet. Translated, the numbers meant 'I'm safe'.

In the event that Bo turned up missing, his uncle had no intention of contacting Agent Bruno. He feared Agent Bruno would trace Bo's last call. So, he agreed to take Blurry wherever he needed to go. Bo and Agent Bruno were friends. Bo sold Agent Bruno his home on Ocean Drive West in Brighton Beach, Brooklyn, NY. The agent paid $959,000 for 2 bedrooms, 2 ½ baths, and 1,400 total square feet. After closing their successful business transaction, the two became friends. Bo had no clue his uncle fled New York because of Agent Bruno. And, Agent Bruno had no clue that Bo's uncle was still alive. From Agent Bruno's perspective, Bo's uncle disappeared without a trace.

Agent Bruno was employed by the FBI. He worked in the Special Victims Unit. His office was located in Midtown Manhattan, NY. Bo had no clue his uncle was a reformed pedophile priest. So, when his uncle heard Bo say, "If I turn up missing, contact Agent Bruno …," he figured his life was over.

Bo's uncle sexually assaulted Agent Bruno in his youth. When young Bruno's mother acquired knowledge of the crime the church had Bo's uncle relocated. As part of his 'disappearance', the uncle resigned from the church, changed his name, and deliberately gained weight. Using his severance pay, he moved to Minnesota and purchased a horse breeding farm.

If Agent Bruno knew of the uncle's whereabouts, he would have flown to Minnesota and gotten away with murder. Bo's uncle wasn't prepared to die. So, he agreed to drive the Presidents' associate out of the State of Minnesota. Neither Bo, nor his uncle knew that Agent Bruno did 'wet-work' for a three-letter agency operating out of Langley, Virginia. Wet-work meant Agent Bruno worked as a domestic assassin for a Section Chief named Dixie May Johnson. Dixie May's husband was the senator from the great State of Georgia. Her husband and Paradise's deceased grandmother, affectionately known as Madame Montoyier, had a one-time business arrangement. Madame Montoyier's magic helped him get elected into office. Because that one-time arrangement took place when Paradise was only two, or three years old, she had no knowledge of her grandmother's business affairs with Dixie May Johnson and her husband.

Dixie May was so pleased with Madame Montoyier's work, she went to her husband to recommend that he hire her fulltime. Madame Montoyier refused their offer. In retaliation, the senator threatened to harm her daughter, Nina, and her granddaughter, Paradise.

Madame Montoyier returned the threat, through her lawyer Mr. Avi Weinberg. The senator feared Madame Montoyier's counter abilities, and withdrew his threat. Madame Montoyier subsequently withdrew hers as well. And from that point forward 'Dixie May' never attempted to recruit Madame Montoyier again.

In Sioux City, Bo's uncle parked near Love's Truck Stop. He waddled to the back of the horse trailer and with some concern asked, "Now what …?"

"Keep your voice down," whispered Blurry.

Paradise, Lulu, Taka, and Blurry sat on a bale of hay. The floor of the horse trailer was too hard to endure. Lulu removed the smartphone from his pocket. Before turning the phone 'on', he inserted the SIM card and battery. After it beeped, he scrolled through and selected the surveillance app. That app identified the location of all the surveillance cameras in the area.

Lulu did a few calculations in his head. From Paradise's perspective, his bachelor's degree in mathematics was paying off. He graduated years ago, with a 4.0 GPA, from New York's Hunter College. Within a manner of seconds, Lulu triangulated their position in relationship to the nearest satellites. In the process, he discovered every blind spot. A blind spot is a specific area wherein surveillance cameras are unable to operate, or 'see'.

Based on this, Lulu told Blurry where to tell No Name to park. No Name followed Blurry's instructions, driving them into one of the area's blind spots. Blurry handed Lulu his personal burner phone. Burner phones were cell phones used once or twice in a single day. After the second call, the burner phone was disassembled, wiped clean, and thrown away. Lulu used the phone to tap the local taxi app.

"Enter the horse trailer slowly," Blurry instructed.

No Name followed the directive accordingly, moving a few bales of hay as he entered. Unsure of how things would play out, he questioned, "How am I going to get back?"

"Here's two hundred dollars," Blurry said. "A taxi driver will meet you at Love's Truck Stop. He'll be there in twenty minutes. You better hurry. You have a little over a mile to walk."

No Name took the money, spat on the floor, and sarcastically commented, "You're about $5,000 short ... this here trailer is a 1995 Featherlite."

Lulu's response was stern. "You can come back for the trailer. That money is for the taxi driver. He'll take you and your dog home."

Irritated, No Name snapped, "What about my license plates?"

"They'll be in the trailer, with the inspection sticker, if you come back," said Blurry.

When he heard the word 'if', No Name assumed they knew about Agent Bruno. Because he feared being murdered by the agent, No Name re-adjusted his attitude to a state of calm. The last thing he said, "I didn't see you and you didn't see me."

In unison Taka, Paradise, Lulu, and Blurry nodded, "*We agree.*"

No Name stepped out of the horse trailer as slowly as he had entered it. Leaving the trailer door cracked, he returned to the Escalade, opened the driver's side door and let his dog out. He closed the door gingerly, took a deep breath, and walked away - never looking back. From the horse trailer window, Taka watched the two trot away.

Curious, Blurry asked, "Do you see him?"

"They're headed toward the truck stop," said Taka.

"*Good*," nodded Blurry.

Taka turned to Lulu. "What's our next move?"

"You and Blurry wait inside the trailer. Paradise come with me," Lulu said purposely.

They followed Lulu's command. He opened the trailer door, poked his head out cautiously, and motioned the following 'communication' to Paradise, "*Okay, team leader, you step out first.*" Paradise raised an eyebrow.

Lulu stepped out the horse trailer with an attitude that said, "*No matter what happens, never panic.*"

"You said, they said, they'll be here," said Paradise anxiously, covering her mouth as she spoke. She did this just in case they were being filmed. Lulu covered his mouth too. They learned the technique from the people who trained them.

Lulu provided the assurance Paradise needed, while refocusing her attention. "They'll be here. Now, help me unhitch this horse trailer." When they were done disconnecting the trailer, the two moved on to the next task. Lulu tenderly asked Paradise to, "Help me change these plates."

As Paradise squatted, she noted Lulu's eyes shifted elsewhere. She followed his gaze, and locked onto what had caught his eye. On the edge of the safe zone, they discovered a teal passenger van. The vehicle's occupant had parked on the side of the road in a blind spot, outside of the surveillance cameras' range.

"Wait here," said Lulu.

Paradise was wary, "Where are you going?"

Lulu announced, "Project Green Book is over. I'll be back."

4
PHONE CHECK
Omaha, Nebraska

Casually, Lulu walked toward the teal passenger van. Paradise waited with baited breath for his return. Lulu cautiously approached the vacant vehicle. He smiled when he discovered the letters 'VPJ' scribbled on the dusty window. Lulu looked through the passenger's side window. He tested the door handle to find it was unlocked. Without hesitation, he opened the door. Then, he sat inside that van like he owned it. He opened the glove compartment, removed the keys, and sat on the driver's seat. Paradise smiled when Lulu pumped the brake lights three times. With the vehicle flashers 'on', he drove in reverse, and beeped the horn. Taka and Blurry stepped out of the horse trailer. They shared Paradise's thought: that Lulu stole someone's van. He stepped out of the van, opened the trunk and said, "Taka, can you help Blurry take the items out my truck and put them into the van?"

Taka's face was flush with concern. Looking at her, Blurry nodded, "*I don't know what he's up too. But, help me anyway.*"

"Okay," Taka replied to Blurry.

Taka helped Blurry lift two pieces of samsonite luggage into the van. Taka looked at Lulu and asked, "What do you have in here? Bricks?"

Lulu didn't trust banks so he stored his money in several suitcases.

In a terse tone, Lulu directed his response to Paradise. "They're not bricks. And, I didn't steal this van, if that's what you're thinking."

Paradise didn't respond right away. She watched Taka and Blurry rearrange Lulu's luggage. She followed Lulu's gaze. It directed her attention to the 'VPJ' written in the dust on the window. She smiled, he winked, and Blurry said, "Hey, I saw that."

"You saw what?," Paradise said slyly.

Lulu wiped those letters away with his right hand. Paradise remained silent, walked to the horse trailer, and opened the door. She put No Name's inspection sticker and license plates on the floor of the horse trailer. Paradise then closed the door locked it.

Out of curiosity, Taka asked, "What does 'VPJ' stand for?"

Paradise heard Taka's question, but pretended to be deaf. She proceeded to retrieve the Flintstones lunchbox from the back seat. Since Lulu was deaf in his right ear, he had the perfect excuse for not answering.

Blurry shared his observation aloud with Taka, telling her, "It means something significant, because those initials are also on Lu's license plate."

Lulu looked at Blurry and urgently said, "Come on, let's go!"

Blurry and Taka sat on the back seat, while Paradise rode 'shotgun'. And though Taka was upset because Paradise ignored her question, she gave thanks for the tinted windows.

"We need a status update," Lulu informed Blurry.

"You first Lu," said Blurry.

"What does VPJ-621 mean?," injected Taka.

"I'm responsible for getting Paradise to safety," said Lulu.

"We know that Lu," said Blurry.

"It's my license plate number," Lulu said defensively.

"We know that too," countered Blurry and Taka in unison.

In addition to being the number on Lulu's license plate, VPJ-621 was also a code that stood for a secret order, which Paradise and Lulu had joined. But, Lulu wasn't prepared to share that information with Taka, or Blurry. The name of their mystical order was 'Le Vingt Premier Juin'. They pronounced it "Ley Vahn Pre-Me-Ay Zhew-Ahn." That meant the '21st of June' in French.

Paradise's grandmother had been a ranking member in that occult sleeper cell. All of the members in the 21st of June were required to speak the German language. They needed to understand it to help them survive the fourth Reich. The fourth Reich represented the fabled rise of the Nazi Party. The 21st of June believed the Nazis' planned for Nazi rule behind enemy lines. According to their intel, the Nazis' were scheduled to rule the world with political elasticity. Their political stretchiness appeared through Islamic terrorism, suicided bankers, and European unions. Their inside joke had been, "Jihad, along with radicalized Islam, got its start in Germany."

The word 'occult' means 'hidden' knowledge of the paranormal. A 'sleeper cell' is a secret group of individuals, or agents. The secret agents live amongst the targeted population, and lead normal lives until activated by the sleeper cells' leader. The 21st of June worked off the books as counterinsurgents. Those militarized mystics were organized by the paranormal branch of the military.

Lulu was abrupt. "It's just a license plate number."

"You know I don't believe that," Blurry said, looking at Paradise. "But, I'm-a-give you a pass."

"*I'll tell you what it means when the time is right,*" nodded Lulu.

"How did you know to text Bo?," Lulu asked Blurry.

"After witnessing Paradise's magic trick," Blurry said.

Paradise was curious and wanted to know, "What are you talking about?"

"Po-Po let us go. I know they let us go because of whatever you said over that bottle of water. So, I figured I needed to step my game up," Blurry confessed to Paradise.

Lulu redirected the conversation back to his question. "And, you texted Bo?"

"Yeah, I remember he told me he had family in Minnesota," said Blurry to a concerned Lulu. "But, I texted the Diaz brothers first."

"Happy Face and Ex-Con from the lower East side," noted Lulu.

"Yeah, I reached out to those two knuckleheads and told them it's time to *put'n-dat*-work! 'Cus, you already know… they-down-for whatever. So, I sent them up to 125th Street," Blurry mused cryptically.

"As they should," responded Lulu.

"And that's IT?," Taka demanded.

Blurry clarified. "No. There's more. I texted Bo and told him that two of our 'employees' were headed to his office." Going on, he added, "I had to give Bo a heads-up. 'Cus you know he suffers from that PTSD and that would've been a disaster." Bo's Post Traumatic Stress Disorder was caused by a bomb explosion. The bomb lay roadside, disguised as a crushed Coke can.

Concerned and perplexed, Paradise sought something deeper from Blurry, "But, that doesn't explain why Bo Diaz helped us."

"Bo Diaz. That's funny," chuckled Blurry as he replied. "It's Bo from 125th Street and the Diaz brothers work for Lu and I, and they trooped to Harlem from the Lower East Side of Manhattan on the subway."

Paradise remained dissatisfied. "Well anyway, whoever they are, why did they help us?," she asked, again pushing for more.

"No shade ... but, they didn't help you. They helped me and Lu. Like I said before, the Diaz brothers work for Lu and I. Truthfully speaking, they didn't even know Lu was involved. Bo helped me because I saved his life during our second tour in Afghanistan.

"I wasn't looking for any type of repayment. Nor, was I expecting some reciprocal gesture from Bo," Blurry explained. "But whenever we spoke he would always say, "I'm forever in your debt"."

Digging deeper still, Taka had her own set of questions. "How did you know his uncle would help us? Wait, let me rephrase that ... how did you know his uncle would help you?," she asked.

"I didn't know who was going to help us. But, I knew Bo would keep his promise," Blurry said to an extremely impressed Taka.

"Why do you call him Bo from 125th Street?," said Paradise.

Blurry went on. "Bo's people are filthy rich. The majority of their assets are rooted in Midtown Manhattan real estate. When Bo joined the military, his parents disowned him. So, after our second tour in Afghanistan, he moved to 125th Street. Rightfully, or wrongfully, he used his real estate knowledge to gentrify Harlem."

Gentrify means Bo's people are coming into the hood, and displacing the lower-income residents. Keep in mind... The influx of opportunistic property developers, along with the taxman, will always force those undesired families to leave their homes. Blurry flipped the topic of conversation.

"It's your turn Lu … where did this van come from? And, where's that tow truck taking your Escalade?"

"Man, you don't miss anything!," Lulu shot back half jokingly.

"How do you think I survived Kandahar?," said Blurry.

Lulu pointed to the sky as a reference to God.

"*True that!,*" nodded Blurry in reverent acknowledgement.

"The Escalade is on its way to Omaha," said Lulu.

"Nebraska?," asked a shocked Taka.

"Yeah, it's about an hour and a half from here," Lulu said. He also advised, "When we were in the horse trailer, I texted someone too."

"How did they know where to be?," inquired Paradise.

"I texted them the Sioux City's mile marker on I-24," said Lulu casually.

"From what I recall, you only used your phone once and that was forty-five minutes into our road trip. So, how would they, or you, know where we would be?," said Taka inquisitively.

"Let's just say, I have an advanced skill set," said Lulu.

Dumbfounded, Taka asked, "What does that mean?"

Lulu played deaf. So, Taka looked to Blurry for the real answer.

Blurry also side-stepped answering Taka by teasing Lulu. "After all these years, you still struggle with being a nerd?"

Clearly agitated, Lulu snipped, "Yeah, whatever. Do you want to know how I got the van, or what?"

Lulu used an algebra formula in his head to determine the place and time of their arrival. The unknown person, who left the van, deliberately parked a football field away from Lulu's mile marker. Lulu calculated their rate of speed, time, and distance. But, he feared being called a nerd. So, he allowed them to believe whatever they wanted. Lulu inherited his smarts from his parents. His African-American father, Rygiel Fortune, had been a College Professor at New York University. Lulu's mother, Josefina Tapia, was a math genius from Dajabón, in the Dominican Republic. Lulu's parents never married because Rygiel had a wife. The reality is that Josefina only slept with Rygiel to get a passing grade for the course. Unfortunately, one thing led to another, and their lives took a turn for the worse.

The scandal forced Rygiel into early retirement. Their secret tryst also caused Rygiel to suffer a bitter divorce, in part, because it had produced an unwanted child - Lulu. For Josefina's participation - she received an unwanted child, life on welfare, and an addiction to heroin and crack cocaine.

"I sent a text to the people that hired me to protect Paradise, I explained the situation, and they said to leave the truck," Lulu explained to Blurry, Taka, and Paradise.

"And, they left you this van," Blurry said skeptically.

Taka was skeptical too. "That's one JANKY story, Lulu."

Brushing their doubt aside, Lulu was unfazed. He authoritatively stated, "There was nothing broken in what I said. But, now it's time for a phone check."

Paradise was quick to say, "Don't look at me. I don't own a phone."

Lulu, Taka, and Blurry handed Paradise their burner and smartphones. Paradise opened the back of the smartphones, removing their batteries and SIM cards. They didn't protest because they were officially off-the-grid, rendering them untraceable through normal means.

5

OFF THE GRID

Sioux City, Nebraska

Although Lulu, Paradise, Taka, and Blurry were officially off the grid, they made one stop - against Lulu's wishes - in South Sioux City, Nebraska. Paradise and Taka needed to use the bathroom.

Before they approached the Scenic Park Campground, Paradise tossed their disassembled phones into the Missouri River. When they entered the campground, Lulu and Blurry employed their tracking skills. That meant Taka and Paradise used an advanced bounty hunting technique, to enter and exit the bathroom without being detected.

"I'm pretty sure there are surveillance cameras on this campground," Lulu said observantly to Paradise and Taka.

One one hand, the ladies cared, but on the other, they could have cared less. They really needed to use the bathroom. After they honored their biological function, Paradise exited her stall, to hear Taka quietly utter, "Ut-oh … " Paradise didn't need telepathy to know what Ut-oh meant. She empathized, "Heavy, or light?"

"Heavy," Taka sighed.

"Hold on. I'll be right back."

After she washed her hands, Paradise snuck out of the bathroom. She came back in under a minute. The two took care of business, and several minutes later, Taka and Paradise discreetly emerged from the bathroom. They returned to the van, having used the advance bounty hunting techniques they'd been taught. As Lulu exited the campground, Taka expressed her appreciation to Paradise with a simple, "Thank you." However, being inquisitive, she went right back into being an inquisitor. "What else do you have in that bag of tricks?"

"You can call me Felix the Cat," Paradise said playfully.

"Who?," Taka said curiously.

"You're welcome. But, you need to thank Lulu," suggested Paradise.

In an attempt to deflect their praise, Lulu chimed in, "Thank me for what?"

Taka and Paradise were thankful because someone had stocked the van with three unopened bags of sanitary napkins.

Taka backtracked a bit. "Who's Felix the Cat?," she asked.

No response.

"The question that needs answering is who kidnapped Paradise?," Blurry told Taka. "And, what was their motive for doing so?" Looking at Paradise, Blurry racked his brain. "If it is Sector Seven, like we suspect, what do they want from you?"

In order to draw a conclusion, it was necessary for Blurry to speculate. "Lu, why do you think the National Director of Intelligence was in New Ulm, Minnesota? Out of all the places in the world, she was in New Ulm! Yo, Lu … we both know there ain't no-such-thing as a coincidence."

"Oh, I agree. Her appearance wasn't a coincidence," said Lulu.

Blurry's mind was racing as he spoke to Lulu. "What's the National Director's connection to Paradise and Sector Seven? Is there a connection between the two? Personally, I suspect there is for two reasons: number one, her office is in Langley, Virginia. And, number two; you saw her convoy race toward Flandrau State Park. That's the same park we rescued Paradise from." Taking his observations further, Blurry reflected. "You and I have been bounty hunting a long time. And, like I just said, we both know there is no such thing as a coincidence. Just like the letters 'VPJ' that were written on the window of this van, AND are the same letters on your license plate ... those aren't coincidences."

"And your question is …?," sought Lulu.

"My question is … are we dealing with a real life Alternative 3 situation?," asked Blurry.

"A what? Y'all lost me at Felix the Cat!," said Taka.

Speaking from his gut, Blurry shared his 'take' on the situation. "In my opinion, their end game is Alternative 3." His observation caused an immediate hush inside the van, and prompted him to thoughtfully repeat his question, "Is this a real life Alternative 3 situation?"

Something Paradise's mother, Nina, once told her caused her to reflect. She'd told her, "When they come, you CAN'T let them take you." She spoke those words to Paradise in French, when she was about ten, or eleven years old. Nina was emotionally disturbed, and struggled with mental illness most of her life.

There wasn't anything queer about Nina. However, when she spoke, she sounded like the sweetest French fairy. Her unaltered voice had always been extremely light and airy. Once, her husband, Alonzo C. Mingo, endearingly told her, "Nina, you're just like those mythical creatures. You're magical. And you're voice is so light and airy. Oh, Ma Douce, you're my beloved French speaking fairy." The phrase, 'Ma Douce' means 'My Sweet' in French.

Alonzo was her Hollywood handsome husband. They were a beautiful couple, who created a beautiful child. Paradise was considered a combo-kid. That meant Nina and Alonzo could never deny her because she looked like both of them. Nina had smooth cinnamon skin, the stereotypical wavy black hair, and pretty white teeth like her grandmother, Isabella 'Madame' Montoyier. Because they share similar physical traits - blue eyes, a muscular build, and tan skin - the actor, Michael Ealy, most closely favors Alonzo in appearance.

When Nina told young Paradise, "When they come, you can't let them take you," her intention was to warn her daughter. The statement pertained to the real life Alternative 3. Around 1977, British television aired a program called, '*Alternative 3.*' The fictionalized story only aired one time in the United Kingdom. The broadcast focused its attention on the English 'brain drain'. The term referred to the disappearance of extremely smart people without a trace. The intellectually challenged weren't exempt either. The goal of the third alternative, or Alternative 3, was to populate the planet Mars and to use the Moon as their transfer station. The second alternative, or Alternative 2, the 'powers that be' was to construct underground cities to house government officials. The first alternative, or Alternative 1, dealt with drastically reducing the human population.

"When I was ten, or eleven, my mother said, "Paradise, stay away from Alternative 3." Instructively, Paradise added, "She also told me the elites were preparing for a great catastrophe."

Taka looked shocked. Blurry looked intrigued. And, Lulu remained silent. Though skeptical, Taka's curiosity propelled her to bravely ask, "So, we're talk'n slaves in space? And, what kind of catastrophe … ?"

"Climate change," Paradise said nonchalantly. "I never believed in Alternative 3. But, my mind changed when one of the Germans said, "Nehmen Sie die Frau, die durch das Tor." Paradise spoke it in German.

"What does that mean? And, your captors were from Sector Seven right?," asked Taka noisily.

Paradise provided Taka with the translation. "It means, 'Take the woman through the gate'."

"The masked German had bad breath," Paradise recalled, wincing from the smelly memory. "But, it didn't stop him from whispering, "Sektor Sieben Hexe," eerily in my ear. My immediate response was, "Je ne suis pas une Sorcière!" Don't know if he heard me clearly. My response was somewhat muffled, because my mouth was taped at the time. In English, he said, "Sector Seven Witch!" And, in French, I told him, "I AM NOT A WITCH!" That sorry son-of-a-bitch obviously understood something he didn't like, because he tasered me in the neck, and I blacked out," Paradise said.

Amazed, Taka asked, "How many languages do you speak?"

"Why, are you write'n a book?," quipped Paradise jokingly.

"I sure is," said Taka playfully.

Paradise smirked, "This is weird."

"What's weird?," Taka asked curiously.

"I never had friends before," Paradise confessed with a startling sincerity.

Simultaneously, Blurry, and Taka raised their left eyebrows, cocked their heads, looked at Paradise, and in unison asked, "What do you mean you never had friends?"

However, Paradise was unresponsive, her thoughts had moved on. At that very moment in time, she found herself reminiscing … reflecting on something her estranged godmother had said, "I know you're lonely. But, great leaders don't have friends."

Her godmother was Ida May Bouché. Aunt-*tee* Ida, as Paradise affectionately called her, had been Paradise's mother's adopted sister and best friend. Aunt-*tee* Ida and Nina parted ways when Nina confronted her on Paradise's thirteenth birthday. The confrontation was over Ida's adulterous relationship with Nina's husband, Alonzo.

Blurry snapped his fingers to get Paradise's attention.

"Hey, where did you go?," he asked, curiously.

Drifting back, Paradise responded, "I'm still here. I was raised speaking French by my grandmother, because she refused to speak English to me. My *Aunt-tee* Ida taught me how to speak Haitian Creole. And, I learned '*Laissez les bons temps rouler*', and other colorful Louisiana Creole words from my father."

The ever inquisitive Taka, couldn't resist. "What does 'Lazay Lay Bon Tom Roulay' mean?"

"It means, 'Let the good times roll'. My Mom-Mom forced me to study the German language with her," Paradise added.

"Your who?," Blurry said teasingly to Paradise.

"What, are you twelve? 'Mom-Mom' means grandmother … even I know that," Taka said defensively.

"I know. I'm just bust'n her stones," chuckled Blurry.

"Well anyway! Mr. Avi Weinberg taught us German. He was Mom-Mom's lawyer and my trust fund manager. He never liked me, and I never liked him. Avi Weinberg stole my money, caused my homelessness, and he put a 'hit' on my life. Life is crazy. But, I'm still standing! Sometimes you've got to laugh to keep from crying," Paradise relayed, with a hint of introspection.

What Paradise had shared was jaw-dropping. Taka and Blurry were stunned. Lulu, however, continued to drive as if everything was okay.

Sektor Sieben (Sector Seven) was an elite group of exiled Nazis. They built their headquarters in the jungles of Argentina. Some of the founding members had ties to the mid-1850s, and mid-1890s Airship Mystery. The German nationals involved lived near Sonora, California. They flew in cigar-shaped airships powered by a fuel called suppa. German bankers backed their secret organization. The name of their secret order was the Sonora Aero Club and Prussia's rumored NYMZA. Those same German bankers financed the American railroad.

In the book 'ORIGINS' by W. Bosley, NYMZA is NJMZa. NJMZa is the acronym for Nationalistiche Jagdelugzeug Mashinens ZahlungsAmth. Here's the English translation: 'Nationalist Hunting Flying Object Machines Payment Office / Department.' A looser translation of NYMZA is the Nationalist Pursuit Exploration Airship Program Office. Ancient Egypt's fringe of the fringe called the otherworldly NYMZA the 'Nameless Ones'.

Now, back to Sector Seven… they helped the 'Powers-That-Be' create a Breakaway Civilization. Sector Seven also protected the Nazis' Alternative 3 spaceship builders. With the help of the NYMZA scientists, and the development of deep-space medicines, 'Sector Seven' had every intention of returning home. It was their belief that their Aryan ancestors had come from the planet Mars. So, they set a course to build a super race of Nazis called 'UBER MEN'. Those 'Uber Men' were created to rule interstellar space, and to destroy the so-called Jews, blacks, and any other useless eater.

It's also worth noting: a retired German butcher named Charles Dellschau started painting fantastic images of the Sonora Aero Club's airships in 1899. According to Dellschau's paintings a German National name [Homer] 'Trump' was an influential member of the Sonora Aero Club. He was so influential, his German Club members, named one of their mid-1850s airship the 'Aero Trump'.

In the early 1860s a physician name Solomon Andrews invented an airship called the 'Aereon'. Solomon demonstrated his airship to President Abraham Lincoln's War Department during the height of the Civil War. According to published reports the War Department didn't need an airship. So, it's assumed Solomon Andrews returned to Perth Amboy (NJ) with his flying machine and no deal. But, it's worth noting circulating rumors declare Solomon's 'Aereon' as Washington DC's first black project.

In 1903, the Sonora Aero Club ended their relationship with NYMZA. It's also alleged those 1903 Sonora Aero Club members established their own Breakaway Civilization, left Earth's orbit, and flew to Mars purportedly using Tesla technology. Who was Tesla? Oh, let's see ... he was an inventor, electrical and mechanical engineer, physicist, and futurist. He was best known for his work designing the modern alternating current (AC) system for electrical supply. The thing that made Nikola Tesla truly enigmatic was his knowledge and ability to tap into the ether for electricity. Tesla died on January 8, 1943.

Three weeks after Tesla's death, German Professor, John G. Trump, reportedly said, "There's nothing to see here," which suggested that Tesla's papers on how to build a death ray, time travel device and spaceship to Mars were considered fake news, and therefore, were not meant for public consumption. It's worth noting, that Professor Trump worked for the FBI's Office of Alien Property. In this particular case Alien meant Foreigner and not Extraterrestrial (ET). Now, check this out... in the book 'Wall of Light' by Arthur H. Matthews, its reported Nikola Tesla came from the planet Venus. His mother gave birth to him on a spaceship and he was raised by Earthlings (human parents) in Smiljan, Croatia. Is it true? Who cares?

According to the story, the 1903 Breakaway Civilization helped professor Trump's nephew, Donald J. Trump, become the 45th President of the United States. Now, peep this… according to Ingersoll Lockwood's 1896 Sci-Fi / Fantasy book 'Baron Trump's Marvelous Underground Journey', Baron lived in Trump Castle. He also had a time machine, which he used to travel to modern-day Russia. While in Russia he met the 'Don', who's the Master of all Masters. In 1900, Ingersoll published another book entitled, 'The Last President'. According to Ingersoll a man name Trump, who lives on 5th Avenue, in New York City will be the [Last] President of the United States.

In early May of 2018, the United Kingdom's online newspaper the Daily Mail reported, "Donald Trump says he could launch a SPACE FORCE alongside other branches of the military to fight extraterrestrial wars - Trump made claims in a speech to the Black Knights US army football team."

"Blurry in addition to being a U.S. Army Ranger and bounty hunter, what else did you do?," Paradise asked.

"I worked for the United States Department of Defense (DoD), as an assistant librarian. In addition to studying OOparts, I had a temporary fascination with the former Secretary of Defense, Robert McNamara. Back in 1962, he allegedly told JFK, it appears our nation has two space programs … a regular space program and a secret space program," Blurry proudly informed Taka, Lulu, and Paradise.

Prior to his honorable discharge, Blurry's military clearance exceeded 'Top Secret' status, allowing him unrestricted access to OOparts, occult manuals, and other military grimoires. The term, 'OOparts' stood for 'out-of-place artifacts'. And, the grimoires (pronounced: *grim-wahs*) were occult books containing magical spells and invocations used by the military.

The term 'breakaway civilization', refers to a group of people, or a rogue nation, that achieved energy independence, field propulsion, and/or space-time weapons. The Nazi scientists from Sektor Sieben, who folded, or twisted, time and space were called, Wizards.

The Wizards discovered an easy way to counter-rotate time and space. Imagine time and space as a twisted dish rag. The 'twists' are electrified plasma that literally can open a portal, or gateway, through the heavens (space). After the heavenly gateway opened, Sektor Sieben's modified men traveled long distances through space in a short period of time. In other words, the German Nazis, Swiss Nazis, Dutch Nazis, Irish Nazis, South African Nazis, and American Nazis allegedly discovered an easy way to literally 'BREAKAWAY' from planet Earth.

Taka wondered aloud, "What are OOPARTS?"

"Where did that come from?," questioned Paradise.

"I don't know. It just flew out my mouth," Taka mumbled.

Blurry attempted to explain to Taka that, "OOparts are 'out-of-place artifacts'. Most of them are fakes. But, occasionally, you'll come across something like the Greeks' Antikythera, an analog computer, which dates back to 150 BC. It was used to predict astronomical positions and eclipses for astrological purposes, and in the conception of calendars," said Blurry to Taka.

6
ASTRAL POLICE
Kansas City, Missouri

As Lulu approached Kansas City, Missouri, he thought about National Director Gregory. Taka thought about Felix the Cat, and Paradise thought about finding something to eat. Blurry? He questioned how much time they had left. From his, and Lulu's perspective, everybody gets caught sooner, or later.

"*It's just a matter of time,*" they thought to themselves.

National Director Gregory had been considered a White Hat. The 'hidden hand', or 'powers that be', that were behind the government, assisted with her installation as the National Director of Intelligence.

The White Hats had been at war with the Black Hats for thousands of years. Among other things, the White Hats were adept at cracking computers as a means to identified security weaknesses in computer networks and computer systems. White Hats worked hard to fix data breaches. Their Black Hat counterparts were computer hackers who stole data, planted computer viruses, and installed malware. They too were diligent. The Black Hats worked equally as hard to locate those data breaches.

Secretly, National Director Gregory praised the White Hats in the United States, and Israel for their deployment of the Stuxnet computer virus. That cyber warfare weapon was a 'viral worm' that was used, around 2010, to sabotage, then destroy Iran's nuclear weapons program.

Curious, Blurry asked Lulu, "What do you think National Director Gregory is up to?"

"Another Zero Day," Lulu said with a straight face.

"All come on Lu," said Blurry.

Unable to resist her own curiosity, Taka entered the discussion. "What's Zero Day?"

"Our President …"

Taka abruptly finished Blurry's sentence saying, "Obama?"

Blurry confirmed Taka's remark, with a quick, snappy, "Yes." He followed up to say, "Well anyway, he authorized the three letters to create the viral worm called Stuxnet. With the Israelis' help, that computer virus destroyed a key part of the Iranians' nuclear enrichment program. Problem was that the virus spread beyond its designated target."

"So, that's Zero Day," Taka surmised.

Needing to know, Paradise questioned, "How does that apply to me?"

"Yeah Lu, how does that apply?," asked Blurry.

"There's a documentary called, Zero Days, which is about the Whites Hats destroying the Black Hats' ability to use Stuxnet. What I'm trying to figure out is whether Virginia Gregory is a White Hat, or a Black Hat. And, did she have anything to do with Sector Seven snatching Paradise and trying to dead me," said Lulu.

Befuddled, Taka asked, "Who's Virginia Gregory again?"

"She's the National Director of Intelligence," said Lulu.

"She's supposed to be a White Hat. Rumor has it she's a ranking Druid in the Order of Bandrui. She's a follower of Badb Catha. Some say, she was initiated into that magical order by the Morrigan herself," Blurry said informatively to Taka.

Frustrated, Taka lamented, "Here we go again."

"What do you mean?," said Paradise caringly.

"This is just like Felix the Cat ... I have no clue what Y'ALL BE TALK'N ABOUT!," Taka shouted.

"You're funny," said Paradise.

Taka calmed down a little, but was exasperated, "What's funny about that? I'm hungry. I'm irritable, and I'm tired of not knowing what Y'all-Be-Talk'n About."

Thinking Taka should just chill, Blurry playfully blew a "Woo-sah," her way.

But, it was too late. Taka had had it. In rapid succession, she angrily blurted out, "Woo-sah my ass! … what's a Bad Cat? … what's a Morrigan? ... who's Felix? … and, what's the Order of Dru Hill?"

Though she was tickled, Paradise kept a straight face. "Dru Hill was an R&B music group from Baltimore."

Taka caught on, and in a pissy tone of voice said, "Everything ain't funny Paradise."

"Okay. Okay," Paradise said, trying to soften things up. "I'll be serious. In Baltimore, Maryland, there's a wooded area called Druid Hill Park. In ancient Celtic religion, the priests who practiced magic were called Druids."

Feeling better, Taka joked, "Like the Boston Celtics, Celtics …" "Oh, now you got jokes!," Paradise said light-heartedly. "We're not talking about basketball Taka." She continued. "You wanted to know about that Badb Catha. Her name, Badb, sounds like you're saying 'bAave', pronounced with a hard 'A' - like the word 'grAve'. And that 'Cat' word is actually pronounced 'Cath-Tha'."

Taka started off slowly, "B-a-d-b …" But, by the time she finished dragging out "C-a-t-h--t-h-a," she sounded like she'd just gotten off the 'short bus'. Even she had to ask, "Did I sound like I was on the short bus?"

Paradise eased Taka's embarrassment. "A little, but don't sweat it. Like I was saying, according to the ancient Irish legend, Badb Catha appeared in the form of a Battle Crow. She beset her enemies with fear and confusion. Her wailing cries fortified her favored army to be victorious in battle. Badb Catha is death, and she's rebirth.

She continued by telling Taka that, "In the book, Celtic Lore and Spellcraft of the Dark Goddess: Invoking the Morrigan, you will find the recipe for Protection Powder. Since I don't do dark magic, that particular spell isn't for me. Plus, it's Celtic magic. Celtic magic belongs to the Irish, or Celtic people." In a clear, prophetic tone, Paradise stated, "We're the Originals. As copper-colored Americans we use the divine sciences that WORKED for our ancestors."

As delicately as she knew how, Taka said, "No disrespect Paradise, but, you don't look all black."

Paradise acknowledged that. "I got some mixtures going on." But, in the same breath, she gave proud recognition that, "During this lifetime, my core essence is African. And, my DNA can be traced back to the land of Khem."

Feeling some-kind-of-way, Taka felt the need to put her people on the map too. "Like I said before, no shade intended. You say your people are from ancient Egypt. Well, my mom had her genealogy done, and the origin of her bloodline was pinpointed to some village in Ghana, West Africa. Now, my father, his people were Igbo. And, the Igbo are known as the 'uncreated people'. Have you heard of the Igbo before?"

With sensitivity and regard, Paradise replied to Taka's question. "I have," she said. She then impressively informed Taka that, "The so-called 'uncreated people' were the recent topic of discussion on C-Span, featuring Nigerian Professor, Catherine Acholonu, author of a book called, <u>They Lived Before Adam: Prehistoric Origins of the Igbo, The Never-Been- Ruled.</u>"

Blurry could relate. "I read that book in the DoD library," he said. "Professor Acholonu researched the Ikom Monoliths of Cross River State, Nigeria. She argued that the inscriptions on those stones were made by a lost civilization of ancient Nigerians. The professor called their common ancestors the Niger-Benue. They were part of the human species called, Homo Erectus. The Niger-Benue was a sub-family of the Nigerian tribes. That means the Nigerians existed before Adam and Eve were created."

"In Surah 15, Ayat 26, of the Holy Qur'an, it is written, "... and WE did certainly create man out of clay from an altered BLACK mud"," said Taka to Blurry, instructively.

Excited, Taka turned to Paradise. "You know what's crazy about that? I remember reading about this brother from South Carolina. His lineage was traced back to 338,000 years ago!"

"Yeah," Blurry said to Taka. "His Y chromosomes, or the genes he got from his father, were traced back to the Mbo. The Mbo were sub-Saharan Africans who live in a small village in western Cameroon. The results of that brother's ancient DNA were published in the American Journal of Human Genetics."

"I bet you read that in the DoD library too!," Lulu teased.

"Don't hate. You're not the only genius in the van," Blurry said to Lulu, competitively.

Trying to tie up her loose ends, Taka attempted again to get answers. "So, what about the Morrigan? … and, Felix the Cat?"

"What about getting something to eat?," Paradise asked.

"Rumors say, National Director Gregory was initiated into the Order of Druids by the Morrigan herself. The Morrigan is a Celtic goddess," said Lulu.

"What bag? Do you mean this metal lunch box," aloofly said Paradise to Taka.

"Yes, I'm talking about Fred and Barney." humorously said Taka.

"Oh, I don't have any food in here. If, that's what you're thinking?"

"I wasn't…"

"All I have in here, is good and bad memories."

"Why the Flintstones and not Felix the Cat?" said Blurry teasingly.

Paradise flared her nostrils, inhaled deeply, and turned around. She looked at Taka and reassuringly told her, "I'm gonna touch Blurry's hand. But, I am not flirting with him."

Blurry looked at Lulu first and Taka second, then he turned his attention to Paradise, who quietly said, "Let me see your hand."

"Why?," Blurry asked cautiously.

"Don't be ascared," said Taka playfully.

"Never that," said Blurry stoically.

He extended his hand and Paradise grabbed it, calmly saying, "I didn't appreciate the Flintstones joke Mr. Bernard Harold Washington, from the Community Group Home in Harlem, New..."

In a jerking motion, Blurry snatched his hand away from Paradise. He flinched at what just happened. And, his witnesses, Taka and Lulu, were also visibly shaken by the experience. To say Blurry was disturbed is putting it mildly. He couldn't contain, or control, his outburst. "My court records are sealed. So, how the HELL does she know my government name?!"

"Don't look at me," said Lulu seriously.

"I didn't tell her either. 'Cus you and I met Paradise at the same time, remember?," Taka confessed.

"How'd you do that?," Blurry demand.

Paradise explained, "God allows me to see things. It's a blessing and a curse."

"So, you be probing peoples' minds without their permission?," Blurry asked.

"No. It doesn't work like that for me. I get glimpses into their past, present, and future," Paradise said. "But, it only works when I'm nervous, or very upset. I got the gift from my mom. But, after looking into your world, I now understand why she wore gloves. She used to say, *"Paradise, Tant de Problèmes, Tant de Problèmes.*"

In her usual fashion, Taka had to know - had to ask, "What does that mean?"

Paradise's vision revealed that Blurry had been 'sheep dipped'. Sheep dipped was a reputed military term. It supposedly referred to the military's ability to disavow a person even though that person still worked for them.

But, Blurry never spoke of this to either Taka, or his best friend - Lulu.

"Hey Paradise, ..." Taka said nervously.

An aloof, "Huh?," was Paradise's response.

"Huh! *Nuth'n.* Where did you go?," Taka asked curiously.

"I didn't go anywhere Taka ... I'm present," said Paradise, followed with her own curious remark. "And, what does *what* mean?"

Eager to know, Taka asked an attentive Paradise, "'Taunt-Day-Problems', what does that mean?"

Paradise was reminiscing. "My mother used to repeat it all the time. "Tant de Problèmes. Tant de Problèmes." It means, 'So Many Problems, So Many Problems'," Paradise said sadly.

Having checked that answer off her need-to-know list, Taka gave up a quick, "Wow, That's deep," before rebounding onto the question that had really plagued her. "Ok, now who's Felix the Cat?"

Irked, Paradise snapped, "You're wearing me out with this Felix the Cat thing!"

Unfazed, and unrelenting, Taka flipped the snippet, "Well?"

"Okay ... alright. In 1953, Felix the Cat cartoons began airing on American television. Felix was a black cat, with big eyes, and a giant grin. Later, around 1959, he began carrying something like a big, vintage Luis Vuitton bag." Paradise explained.

"Oh …. he was gay?" interrupted Taka.

"I don't think so," Paradise said. "Well anyway," she continued, "That big bag was called his Magic Bag of Tricks, and at his behest, the bag would magically transform itself into whatever Felix desired, or required." Paradise went on to illustrate her point. "Here's an example of how the Magic Bag of Tricks worked: imagine Felix in an apple orchard and he wanted to eat an apple. But, the branches of the apple tree were so high the fruit was beyond his reach, and Felix didn't have a ladder."

Taka's imagination was fired up. In an excited, almost child-like manner, she said, "Don't tell me … he pulled out a ladder?"

"No, Taka. Felix did something more amazing. He whispered an unspoken word, and opened his Magic Bag of Tricks. It released an escalator. Not a ladder. No steps … a freakin escalator!! Felix rode that moving staircase, ascending to the top of the tree. He grabbed an apple and then descended to the ground smiling. When Felix bit the apple, the escalator retracted and disappeared back inside the magical bag." said a delighted Paradise.

"I wish I had one of those magical bags. I could get us something to eat," said Taka longingly. "And, thanks for telling me. It was worth the wait."

Having enjoyed telling the story, Paradise satisfyingly said, "You're welcome."

However, Paradise hadn't told them everything. She never described in detail how the magical bag looked. While she mentioned it looked, "something like a big Luis Vuitton bag", that was her way of providing a general description. In fact, Felix' Magic Bag of Tricks looked like an old-fashioned doctor's medical bag, except the bag was neither black, nor leather.

Additionally, Felix's magical bag was made from mystical materials. Countless thin threads of anointed gold were woven into the bag's canary yellow fabric. The color yellow had been chosen because it is the color that represented the Archangel Raphael in Hebraic lore. The Archangel Raphael guarded the Eastern Gate. That unseen gateway separated the physical world from the spiritual world. Ancient Hebrew mystics asked their God to send the Archangel Raphael to heal their sick.

And, there was another bit of information that Paradise intentionally failed to mention: Felix' magical bag possessed a supernatural glyph. This same mystical symbol was used to form the bag's decorative pattern. The ancient Magi called that powerful symbol 'The Astral Police Cross'. The magi were Persians. Ancient Persia is modern-day Iran. The magi were skilled magicians, astrologers, and priests. When humans dealt with the unseen world, the Astral Police were responsible for watching their ethics and morals, and for protecting their astral body. The word 'astral' means forces from the non-physical world, or the resemblance of a star.

In French, Madame Montoyier told Paradise that the Astral Police were unseen forces commissioned by the Higher Authority (God). A few weeks before Madame Montoyier's death she said, "IS-AH-BELL-LAH, they don't come because you don't call them ..." She relayed that French message in her soul penetrating voice.

Madame Montoyier's unforgettable presence complimented her heart of gold. But, whoever crossed her often paid with their life. Madame Montoyier wasn't afraid to ask God to punish her enemies. And yet, she wasn't a stranger to turning the other cheek. However, she was extremely selective on who received that courtesy. When Madame Montoyier lived, she had a youthful appearance. She had bowed legs, cinnamon smooth skin, and pearly white teeth.

Inside the van, Paradise pondered a question Madame Montoyier had asked her about the Astral Police. In French she'd asked her, "*When they come do you know how to send them back?*"

Without realizing it, Paradise said out loud, "I remember Mom-Mom."

"Who you talking too?," said Taka to Paradise, curiously.

"You ain't nutt'n-out are you?," said Blurry.

Paradise responded apologetically. "No. I'm not going crazy. It just slipped out."

"Oh yeah, one more thing about Felix the big eyed, black cat. In my opinion, he represented Bastet," Paradise told Taka.

"Who?," Lulu inconspicuously whispered to Blurry.

"Fix your hearing aid Lulu, 'cus I heard that. Bastet was the ancient Kemite, or Egyptian goddess, who appeared in the form of a black cat. Originally, Bastet was the lioness warrior goddess of the sun," said Taka impressively.

"Well Taka, it's safe to say you're no longer on the short bus," Paradise said playfully.

Taka's response was a light-hearted, "Ha, ha … NOT funny."

"We're here," announced Lulu.

"I said New Orleans, not Kansas City," Paradise said in jest.

"Oh, now you got jokes," said Lulu to Paradise.

7

DO YOU JUMP?

Kansas City, Missouri

As they headed to New Orleans, Louisiana, Lulu made a pit-stop at a used car lot in Kansas City, Missouri. He pulled into the lot, and waited with Blurry, Paradise, and Taka inside the van when the short Black man greeted them. He was the owner of the used car lot. His most notable features were a chipped front tooth, a scared face from chicken pox, and a 'George Jefferson' haircut. George Jefferson, was the central character in the popular 1970 TV sitcom, The Jeffersons. The series was about the day-to-day life of a black man, who was the successful owner of a chain of dry cleaners in New York City.

Lulu spoke briefly with the rugged faced black man. Paradise noticed that Lulu gave the man she mentally named 'Kansas City George' the secret handshake used by members of the 21st of June. After Lulu explained the situation, Kansas City George could be heard saying, "It has a full tank of gas. When y'all get to St. Louis, stop by the Spiritualist Church of God. Ask for my cousin, her name is June Spade. She'll fix y'all something good to eat. And, she'll provide y'all with a safe place to stay."

In acknowledgement, Lulu nodded, "*Thank you.*"

Blurry helped Lulu transfer the luggage from the van into the used car. Kansas City George kept Lulu's van, waved to Paradise, and watched them drive away. The 21st of June was the code name for their secret order.

The '21st' was created to help their kind survive the Fourth Reich, or Nazi takeover. Their edict proclaimed: We are here to deploy, to defend, and to win our battles with the aid and assistance of supernatural forces. Every member swore an oath to God, and was prepared to sacrifice their lives for the sake of the Order, and its mission. If a member needed anything, within reason, they received it. The founders of the 21st of June were three brothers from Shreveport, Louisiana. Paradise's grandmother served as a high-ranking member in the organization. And, naturally, it was her grandmother who introduced Paradise to the 21st of June. Lulu's induction was the result of his maternal grandparents, Lola and Jose Rafael Correa Tapia.

Inside the van, Paradise looked at Lulu and thought,

"I hope this June Spade is a good cook."

Paradise looked surprised when Lulu said, "I hope June Spade can cook."

"I hope she can cook too, 'cus I'm starving," said Taka.

"Yo Lu."

"What's up Blurry?"

"I hope you're planning to jump into another car ..."

"... 'Cus this one's just a little toooo tight," Taka chimed in.

Kansas City George had replaced their van, with a blue 1993 Ford Festiva.

"Speaking of jumping, my grandmother was a 'jumper'," Paradise said lightheartedly.

"What's a Jumper?," questioned Taka.

"Like the movie, Jumper?," said Blurry nosily.

"More like Dr. Safwat El Amin," said Paradise.

"Who?," Blurry and Taka asked in unison.

"The doctor from Cairo, Egypt."

"Never heard of him," said Taka.

"I have," said Blurry proudly.

Taka was smug when she said, "Damn, you spent a lot of time in that library!"

"*Yeah whatever,*" nodded Blurry dismissively.

"Alright y'all two," said Paradise diplomatically.

Taka quickly checked herself. Her, "Hey Babe, I didn't mean to hurt your feelings," reflected it.

Blurry blushed. Lulu stuck his fingers in his mouth, gagged, and pretended to vomit. Paradise shook her head and asked, "Do y'all want to hear the story or what?"

"I'm sorry girl. I'm listening," said Taka.

Blurry didn't try hide his skepticism. "Are you implying your grandmother knew how to teleport?"

"I'm not implying. I'm stating a fact from what I've seen and heard," said Paradise boldly.

"What do you mean "teleport"? As in not needing a plane, train, or automobile to travel from one location to another?," Taka asked.

"I'm saying she could disappear and reappear just like Dr. Safwat," Paradise informed the group.

"What do you mean she could disappear and reappear … before your eyes? What kind of trick was that?," asked Taka.

"It wasn't a trick."

Blurry cut in, and derisively asked, "Can you do it?"

"Yo, what the hell Blurry!," said Lulu, forcefully.

"I never said I could do it! And I don't know why you're feeling some type of way."

"I can't do it because my mother wouldn't let my grandmother teach me," Paradise told Taka with a straight face. "So, you can untwist your face Blurry, because I watched my grandmother disappear and reappear before my eyes."

The look in Blurry's eyes was unmistakably 'saying',

"I find that hard to believe."

"I can still see my Mom-Mom reappearing in the kitchen and shouting, "Ne Le Tuez Pas!"," said Paradise to Taka.

Taka was confused, and questioned what she just heard. "What does that mean? And, when did she disappear?"

Paradise explained. "She was shouting, "Don't kill him! Don't kill him!""'

Still at odds with what he'd heard, Blurry commanded, "You're all over the place … stay focused. Don't kill who?"

"I am focused," Paradise said authoritatively. "And, stop trying to poke holes into everything I say. Just be quiet for moment and listen."

"*Alright, I'm listening,*" nodded Blurry.

"My parents had a physical fight that was extremely traumatizing. It was harrowing because I'd never heard them argue before. So, seeing them physically fight messed me up. I tried to separate them; but, I couldn't. I'd never felt anyone that strong before. My Aunt-*tee* didn't intervene, which messed me up too. I don't know … maybe she was traumatized too. Together, we witnessed my parents fighting, my grandmother disappearing, and an entity appearing in our kitchen."

"A WHAT?! Girl your story sure is ugly, but I like it," Taka said, in a southern drawn way that conjured Suge Avery from the movie, The Color Purple.

"Yeah, there was an otherworldly presence in our kitchen. Before, the fight started my grandmother vanished. She reappeared in her altar room. She retrieved and then released a supernatural force. Within seconds, she reappeared in the kitchen. She arrived just in time, because the entity was in the process of killing my father," recalled Paradise, who was visibly shaken.

"Oh, okay. So, that explains why your grandmom said, "Don't kill him," said Blurry consolingly.

"When my grandmother said, "Don't kill him", my parents stopped fighting and the entity froze." In a voice that rang with honesty, Paradise truthfully said, "My Mom-Mom used a banishment spell. Well, I won't say 'spell', because that sounds too witchy. So, I'll say she used an ancient mantra. And, when that otherworldly spirit heard the mantra, it fled and never returned to our home."

Taka was slightly unsettled, as she asked, "What kind of Sugar-Honey-Ice-Tea were y'all into?"

"Never mind all of that," said Blurry to Taka.

"Do you know how she disappeared?," he asked of Paradise.

"Yes, I know how she did it. But, I've never done it."

"My grandparents told me that your grandmother wore the prettiest head wraps," Lulu told Paradise.

"I don't know why she liked those turbans, 'cus she had a beautiful head of white hair. It was long and wavy. But, I digress," Paradise admitted. She went on to tell what she knew in a compelling way. "Mom-Mom removed a long herb from her lavender turban. Then, she wrapped it around her pinky and left ring finger. She inhaled deeply. It sounded like the air came from her toes. I watched her step back and she disappeared."

Blurry changed his demeanor and tone from skepticism to sincerity when he said, "No disrespect Paradise. But I've got to know … did your grandmother use the Jinn to teleport?"

Paradise was clear and firm in her response. "My family didn't do dark work. So, "NO", she didn't use the Jinn to teleport."

In the mythology of Muslims, the Jinn were an intelligent race of beings. They were ranked lower than angels, and higher than mankind. As spirit-beings, when the Jinn wore the cloak of flesh, they looked like humans and other familiar animals. Back in 2002, on CBS News, Sheik Mubarek Gilani reportedly said that he, "Can control those invisible Jinn." So, according to Sheik Gilani, he wasn't a threat to the United

States, as was suspected. In his opinion, he "Could have been the government's salvation."

"Everything ain't the devil Blurry," said Lulu, defending Paradise.

"Things are only called magic when people don't understand the technology," said Paradise to Taka.

"*Oh, I know. My father's a Sufi Muslim,*'" thought Taka.

"I know everything ain't the devil. I was just asking because the floating rumor around the DoD claims that Dr. Safwat used the Jinn to teleport," Blurry stated.

After having a flashback, Lulu said, "Before you answer that Paradise ... yo Blurry, don't you remember that cat out in Flatbush? He used to *put-in-dat* work?"

Blurry tilted his head as if to say, "*Who*?"

Lulu squinted his eyes as if doing so would help Blurry's recall. His narrowed eyes conveyed, "*Oh, you know who I'm talking about.*"

Seems Lulu's approach worked, because a second or two later, out comes, "Oh yeah, you talk'n about Baby Face from Brooklyn."

"Yes sir. Tell Taka and Paradise about him," said Lulu.

"According to multiple eye-witness accounts, 5-0 couldn't arrest Baby Face. Not that they didn't try. They would approach his vehicle; guns draw, and pointed right at him.

He would simply exhale, and then 'poof' - he'd disappear," Blurry recounted.

"He 'poofed' multiple times," Lulu clarified in support.

This caused Paradise to hit rewind. She wanted Blurry to explain his skepticism. So, she asked, "When I said my grandmother used that science, you felt some type of way - why?"

"Honestly, I don't know," Blurry admitted.

Taka wanted to know more. "What did you mean when you said, Dr. Safwat used the Jinn," she asked Blurry.

"According to the story, ancient mystics who knew the science of teleporting used the Jinn. Some unnamed people at the DoD believed that the 2008 movie, Jumper, was loosely based on Dr. Safwat's life," said Blurry to Taka.

Taka pushed further. "But, that doesn't explain his alleged connection to the Jinn."

"It's alleged Dr. Safwat could walk across the room, vanish, and reappear within seconds. He demonstrated his magical ability in a New York city hotel room, in the presence of several people whose names have been redacted. According to their testimonies, the doctor had nothing in his hand. In a low tone, he mumbled some undecipherable words in Arabic. He took a deep breath, stepped forward, and then disappeared. A few seconds later, he returned walking in from behind them. Everyone in the room was shocked and amazed. They got shook up because he returned with that day's daily newspaper from Cairo, Egypt," said Blurry.

"And you didn't want to learn how to do that?," Taka asked in wonderment.

In a voice heavy with remorse, Paradise confided that, "At the time, I wasn't into spiritual work like that. Plus, a few minutes before my mother's first suicide attempt, she made me promise not to use magic to solve my problems."

"Damn. That's F'd up. I'm sorry to hear that," said Taka quietly.

Paradise was curious. "You're sorry about what? … to hear about my mom? … or, about me not learning how to jump?"

"Both," Taka and Blurry said sincerely … and, again, in unison.

Paradise told the two that, "As far as my mom goes, she had a white savior complex. According to my grandmother, my mom joined the religion of our enemy. My mom's Caucasian pastor told her, "Suffer not a witch to live." Crazy or not, my mother knew not to cross my grandmother. Plus, deep down, she knew my grandmother wasn't a witch."

Even though Taka was joking when she told Paradise - "Well, Blurry called Bo. So, I guess he's got a white savior complex too ..."

Taka's comment got Blurry heated real fast. You could hear it when he snapped, "That shit ain't funny. We got out of Minnesota didn't we,"

"My mom-mom used to say, "Is-ah-Bell-La, Je ai été formé par le Prophéte." That's French for, "Isabella, I was trained by the Prophet." And I'm a Prophetess, who was trained by the Prophet. The Prophet was my great-grandfather, Cicero Montoyier." She would go on to say, "From thee GOD, to the little gods; from the little gods, to the ancestors; from the ancestors, to the elders; from the elder's mouth, to your ear Is-ah-Bell-Lah. That's one way the Great Spirit speaks to you," said Paradise to an intrigued Taka, Lulu, and Blurry.

"Whoa, that's deep," said Blurry to Paradise.

"Who's Isabella," asked Taka.

"Isabella Rosemarie Montoyier is my birth name. I share the same name as my grandmother. But, as long as I can remember, my parents, and Aunt-*tee* Ida always called me Paradise."

"During my teenage years, I was torn between my mother and my Mom-Mom. I promised my mentally ill mother that I wouldn't use magic. But, my grandmother taught me magic anyway. I didn't want to learn magic because I wanted to honor my mom's wishes.

Around the age of 14, or 15, Mom-Mom and I started to bump heads. She used to get so mad. She would say,

"Is-ah-Bell-Lah, stop being so unruly." At 16, I went my way and she went her way. Oh, I still had my magic lessons, but, when I was really ready to learn she died unexpectedly, taking the knowledge on how to teleport back to the grave," Paradise said sadly, and with great regret.

"That's an odd statement," said Blurry.

"What's so odd about it?," asked Taka.

Lulu interrupted long enough to announce, "We're thirty minutes outside of St. Louis."

Speaking to Taka, Blurry's intention was to direct her focus on something significant. "She said that her grandmother took the knowledge "back" to the grave."

Paradise reminded them. "Hello ... I'm right here."

"What did you mean by that statement?," Taka asked Paradise.

"My Mom-Mom was raised in the graveyard."

Taka was nervous when she questioned Paradise. "What do you mean she was raised in the graveyard?"

"She took sacrifices to the graves of our beloved ancestor," said Paradise instructively.

Alarmed, Taka blurted, "What-chu-talk'n-bout Willis?! Sacrifices as in cat bones? … and chicken blood sacrifices?"

"NO! My family didn't do dark work. Our family ritual, or ceremony, didn't involve human blood, or animal blood. Mom-Mom used to say, "Never give spirits blood! Because they become unruly! When they become unruly, they become uncontrollable! And, when they become uncontrollable, they become violent!"

"Next time, say 'OFFERINGS', not sacrifices. 'Cus the word 'sacrifice' makes me think of cat bones, cowry shells, and witchcraft," Taka suggested.

As his fingers gestured air quotes, Blurry used Taka's suggestion to pose the question, "So, what type OFFERINGS did she give your ancestors?"

"Most of the time, it was cigar smoke, lots of liquor - lots of good liquor, some occasional flowers, and candy. If she really needed an answer to a problem, she cooked Papa Cicero's favorite meal and left it in front of his mausoleum. She'd talk to his spirit; tell him to go to God, and to bring back the merciful answer. Papa Cicero responded to Mom-Mom by sending a butterfly, or a dragonfly. Those two insects were used to acknowledge Mom-Mom's presence and request. And whatever answer she needed, it would appear in her dreams. Or, it would arrive through an old book, or a kind stranger," said Paradise proudly.

"But, I caution you, don't go in the graveyard after midnight," warned Paradise.

"Don't worry, ain't no-body fool'n with you like that," said Taka scarily.

"Why not?," inquired Blurry.

"Because that's the time the spirits come out to play. Good spirits, as well as bad spirits. That's why you need a tool to work within the graveyard," Paradise said informatively.

"What's a tool?," said Taka inquisitively.

Having reached their destination, Lulu announced in an automated tone much like that of the GPS, "We're here."

8

GOT SAVED

St. Louis, Missouri

Lulu parked near the storefront church in St. Louis, Missouri. Blurry and Taka celebrated their release from the close quarters of the tiny car with three deep knee bends, two neck rolls, and one deep breath. Paradise scanned the area, looked at Lulu and Taka, and said, "Are you sure we're at the right place?"

"He said the Spiritualist Church of God," Lulu said, recalling the instructions he'd been given.

"I know that's not a spiritualist church," said Paradise.

"How do you know that?," a curious Blurry questioned.

Taka attempted to answer the question. "Because the music wouldn't be bump'n like that."

"What do you know about the spiritualist church?," asked Paradise in return.

"Nothing. But, I know my mother is holy and sanctified. And, their church-be-party'n just like this one," said Taka.

Blurry's reaction was one of confusion. "I thought you were Muslim."

Apparently, Taka was confused too. Slightly embarrassed, she explained, "I don't know what I am. I was raised Moslem in the Moorish Science Temple of America. My father was a self-proclaimed Moor, who later converted to Sufi Islam. And, my mother? She's a straight up Praise-His-Sweet-Name Christian."

Lulu remained 'on point', scanning the street for blue light cameras, cops, and nosy neighbors. His look signified, "*All is clear, it's safe to go in.*"

Blurry stepped inside the tiny church first. The Holiness Church rented the space from the owner(s) of the Spiritualist Church of God. The Holiness Church's usherette held the door for Taka, and Paradise. She directed Lulu, and Blurry, to the right side of the church. The other usherette, who was dressed in all white, directed Paradise, and Taka, to the left side of the sanctuary: The church rules were clear: women sat on the left, and the men sat on the right. The tiny church was packed, and the four were forced to sit apart, on their respective sides in the rear of the church.

Remember when Taka said her father was a Moor? That meant he did not consider himself to be colored, negro, or black. He chose - for nationality reasons - to self-identify as a Moor. In the face of that fact, Taka's mom continuously pounded her father with, "You can call yourself whatever you want. But, I know these bills need to be paid. And Thomas, you're darker than I am. So, in my eyes you're black …"

Whispering, Taka commented, "I told you this was a holiness church."

"What gave it away?," muttered Paradise humorously.

They smiled because the woman in front of them caught the Holy Ghost. The woman stood, shouted, and in an altered state, fervently spoke in that foreign, celestial language … in what is commonly referred to as 'speaking in tongues. Both the music and the choir's singing kept her in the sway of her holiness dance.

As they sang, Glory! Glory! Hallelujah!, one could hear, if not see the bass player and the drummer competing with the organist for the pastor's attention. The Spirit of the Lord filled the tiny church. The well-fed minister wore a two-toned blue suit. He wiped the sweat from the back of his bald head, winked at the organist, and shouted, "Praise Him! Praise Him! Praise His Holy Name!"

His cadence caused the parishioners to scream and shout even more. To Lulu's and Blurry's surprise, they found themselves nodding their heads too. They rocked and rolled with the rhythm of the bass drum. Taka tapped Paradise on the arm lightly and they smiled, watching Blurry enthusiastically snap his fingers. When Blurry started to fidget, Lulu swayed and whispered, "Yo man, you alright?"

No, he wasn't. Blurry's disposition changed. He went from swaying in the flow, to being agitated. His voice was barely audible when he said, "Hey Lu, we need to go."

"Go? Go where?," asked Lulu in annoyed confusion.

With urgency in his voice, Blurry told Lulu, "Yo man! We need to go NOW!!!"

"What about Taka and Paradise?"

"Will you come on," insisted Blurry.

Lulu and Blurry stood, walked out of the church, and ran without stopping for two city blocks. Slightly winded Lulu demanded an explanation.

"What the hell Blurry ... what's wrong with you?!"

"We had to leave Lu,"

"We had to leave for what?"

"We just had to."

"But Blurry! Why'd we have to leave like that?"

"Man, don't you know?"

"Don't I know what?"

"All come on Lu? Don't you know, we almost got 'Saved'!"

Lulu listened to the words his long-time friend and partner said. He saw the seriousness in his straight face and, felt the sincerity in his eyes. Yet, none of that kept Lulu from shaking his head, buckling over, and laughing hysterically.

Being 'saved' meant several things: a person confessed that he was a sinner; that he repented of his sins; that he accepted Jesus Christ as his Lord and Savior; that he believed the blood of Jesus Christ 'saved' him from eternal damnation in hell; and that his place in heaven was guaranteed.

When they saw Blurry and Lulu leaving the church, Paradise and Taka automatically followed suit, though they had no idea they'd be running for two blocks. By the time they caught up, Paradise was struggling to slow her breathing rate, and Taka, who was hyperventilating, had to sit on the street curb and take deep, steady breaths. And, after the pounding their soles took from all that running, their feet were swollen, and throbbing. Not knowing what happened, they were both nervous, and concerned.

Taka was shaken. "What's wrong?"

And, Paradise paced herself as she inquired,

"Is everything alright?"

Although Lulu finally regained his composure, he took a deep breath, wiped the tears from his eyes, and said, "Blurry said we needed to leave because he almost got saved."

As he began to recount the conversation that started the whole thing, Lulu could feel the absurdity and he started to laugh again. It was so infectious, Paradise and Taka laughed too.

They laughed, in part, because Blurry had been affiliated with the Canadian Brotherhood of Light. Their esoteric society followed the teachings of Sanat Kumara. Legend stated Sanat Kumara lived millions of lifetimes, throughout the universe. Sanat Kumara, the 'Ever Young', had three brothers. The Kumara brothers appeared on Earth as little boys, endowed with supernatural powers. Their father was the creator-god, Brahma. When Sanat Kumara lived in Atlantis, as an adult, he established the 'Path of Initiation'.

"All jokes aside. You know we've got to go back," said Taka sincerely.

"Why? I'm not going back to that church!," Blurry said staunchly.

"Did you forget? We came here to meet June Spade at the church," Paradise reminded Blurry.

"Who's looking for June Spade?," asked a bystander, who'd overheard that part of the group's conversation as she was passing by.

"Do you know her?," asked Taka.

The passerby was an elderly, African-American woman. She had silver hair, and spoke in a soft, yet, reserved manner. "That depends on who you are."

"Would you happen to know today's date?," asked Lulu.

Members of the 21st of June used that question, as a way of identifying unknown members within their secret order.

In a muted tone, the elder responded, "It's the 21st."

As usual, Taka was confused.

Attempting to respectfully correct her, Blurry kindly said, "Pardon me ma'am, I believe you're mistaken."

Being from a different era, the elder with her worn and spotted face that belied both her wisdom and, her tact withheld any response. However, her placid facial expression soberly conveyed, "*I am not at all confused.*"

"Every day is the 21st," said Lulu.

"That's what I thought," the frail elder confidently confirmed, revealing a gold-capped tooth as she spoke.

Looking at Lulu, Taka pondered then rebutted. "I'm pretty sure today's the 18th."

The agitated bystanding elder ignored Taka and Blurry. She turned her attention to Paradise, creepily telling her, "I know you."

"I don't think so. It's possible you've mistaking me for someone else," said Paradise slowly and respectfully.

"What! ... are Y'ALL slow?!," the elder wondered aloud. Then, she snapped a sarcastic shot directly at Lulu. "Where'd you park the short bus?" Somehow, Blurry, Taka, Paradise, and Lulu instinctively knew not to respond.

The elder proceeded to set the record straight. "I may be old," she told Paradise, "but, I'm in my right mind." And, to drive her point home, she restated the comment contemporizing it with a simple, "Don't get it twisted!

"I'm far from slow ma'am. And, this is my first time in St. Louis," said Paradise, herself now agitated.

"That may be. But, I knew your momma, your grand-momma, and your great grand-daddy. They called him The Prophet. His daughter took over where he left off. We called her Madame Montoyier. So, I figured you must be Nina's daughter. 'Cus you look just like her," said the bystander with a straight face.

Paradise, along with Lulu, Taka, and Blurry stood in shock.

"You sure y'all ain't slow?," expressed the stranger frustratingly.

In a polite, yet serious tone, Lulu reiterated what Paradise said, "No ma'am ... we're far from slow."

"Then stop acting like it! You were instructed to meet me at the church!," the elder aid boldly.

"That's on me ma'am," admitted Blurry.

"Don't tell me you're all muscles and no brains."

"No ma'am," said Blurry.

"Navy, or Air force."

"U.S. Army Ranger ma'am."

"My deceased husband, along with his two brothers, fought the Nazis in World War II. Their segregated unit helped liberate Dachau, the first concentration camp built in Germany by the Nazis.

"That sounds like the Devil's Punch Bowl," said Blurry.

"The what?!," uttered a confused Taka.

"Natchez, Mississippi - 1865 to 1866 - the Negro American Holocaust," said the informative elder.

Attempting to educate Taka, Blurry said, "20,000 freed slaves were killed after being forced into a post-slavery concentration camp." Her unspoken reaction was "Get the 'F' out of here!" However, the look on Lulu's, and Paradise's face suggested that they too had been oblivious.

Without warning, the elder woman grabbed Blurry's hand, and playfully teased Taka with, "Don't worry honey. Your soldier is safe with me."

"That's not funny," quipped Taka with a straight face.

"It wasn't meant to be. Now, help me carry these bags," commanded the feisty stranger with the thick southern accent.

Taka grabbed the shopping bags reluctantly, flared her nostrils, huffed, and thought to herself, "*What kind of Jedi mind trick is this?*"

The embolden shopping bag director informatively said, "I received a call. The man on the other end said to expect four guests. He also told me that they'd need safe passage for the night."

"I don't like the way you spoke to me," Taka told the brash shopping bag director in the diabetic shoes, and compression socks.

Little did Taka know, she'd engaged the queen of off-handed remarks. The elder cavalierly responded, "You need thicker skin."

The elderly woman's boldness, dismissive attitude, combined with her frank delivery rubbed Taka the wrong way. But, Taka was hungry, so she followed behind them ladened with grocery bags.

The elderly woman grimaced a bit, as she worked her knees climbing her porch steps. She was recently widowed, her husband having died in his sleep only three and a half weeks earlier. They lived around the corner from the Spiritualist Church of God. The spotted-faced stranger appeared to be in her early 90s. Her wrinkled brown skin showed signs of a chronic condition called, vitiligo, which produced white splotches on her brown hands, arms, and face.

"Come in the kitchen. I'm not going to bite … but, then again … well, who knows? … I just might bite me a piece of this fine cho-co-latte," she said yummily, as she slowly licked he lips at Blurry.

"Lady, I wish you would," flashed across Taka's contorted face. She wasn't feeling the elder's sense of humor at all.

"Lighten up sugar. I'm just yanking your chain. I would tell you to give him some ..."

"Ut! I know she didn't ..." appeared on Paradise's face.

Blurry blushed, Lulu covered his eyes, and the elder said, "Calm down cowboy, 'cus ain't-nothing happening tonight."

Quietly, Blurry was feeling some-kind-of way. The rise in his pants was having its own hopeful dialogue. It asked that throbbing question, *"Why not?"*

"She's on her cycle," the elder intuitively informed Blurry, before turning and asking Taka caringly, "Heavy or light?"

Completely embarrassed, Taka mumbled, "Heavy."

"Are you able to eat?," the elder asked with sensitivity.

"Can you cook?," questioned Taka.

"Oh. Now, you're insulting me. I'm from Louisiana honey, so, of course I can cook. But, I ordered Chinese food," she said humorously.

The elderly women opened her front door, and crossed the threshold on her left foot. Then, she scanned her home, sighed, and sweetly said, "Make yourselves at home. If you need to use the bathroom, go upstairs. It's on your right."

After they freshened up, Taka discretely whispered to Paradise, "Why does she have black curtains covering her mirrors?"

"I'll tell you later," mumbled Paradise.

"What's your name?," Lulu politely asked the elderly woman.

"No names. But, you can call me Ms. Mattie."

"Okay Ms. Mattie, I'm Lu…".

"I distinctly said "NO NAMES"," she reiterated abruptly. Though with Paradise it was different. "I can't help but know your name," Ms. Mattie respectfully told Paradise.

"*My name isn't Nina, if that's what you're thinking,*" said the look on Paradise's face.

"Your name is Isabella. But, your family called you Paradise. Well, your grandmother never called you that. If, I'm not mistaken you and her share the same name," said Ms. Mattie.

"Yeah, she used to say, "Très bon mon petit"."

"That's right. She hated speaking English. She spoke that French. I remember the founder's wife had to translate," said Ms. Mattie intriguingly. Enthusiastically, she went on. "She spoke German and that Haitian Creole too. She learned that from your auntie's people. By the way, how is that fast aunt of yours? Eee-Dee. No, no, that ain't right. Give me a minute. Let me think. It's uh, Eye-Dah ... Eye-Dah May Boo-Shay … that's it. Her name Ida May. How's she doing?"

"After my parents broke up, things fell apart. We haven't been close since."

"Say no more child. I understand," said Ms. Mattie compassionately. The matron shut down what apparently was an uneasy subject for Paradise, by beckoning everyone to the table. "Y'all come on in here and eat."

When they gathered around the kitchen table, they discovered a feast. Ms. Mattie had ordered caramelized Peking duck, steamed vegetables, chinese sweet noodles, vegetarian spring rolls, asian greens, and fortune cookies. They held hands around the table, Ms. Mattie said the prayer, and they ate.

Taka and Blurry shared the same thought. If, she said, "*Call me Ms. Mattie, than who's June Spade?*" Unbeknownst to them, the name 'June Spade', was code for the 21st of June. The German last name 'Spade', had a dual meaning. In the German language, the word meant 'late', or 'tardy'. And, then there was the card playing game known as '21' ... only some people call it 'spades'.

Ms. Mattie owned her home, the Spiritualist church, and a few other properties on the street. She also served as the church's minister decades ago. But, she resigned when she unintentionally levitated during a church service. When the attendees realized she was hovering above the floor, they screamed and ran out of the church. After that traumatic experience, she discontinued her practice of mediumship. For most spiritual churches, their order of service began with a prayer to God, followed by a hymn, some public announcements, and pure mediumship. A medium usually conducted the spiritual service, because they served as the 'intermediary' between our world and the spirit world.

9
MS. MATTIE
Cane River, Louisiana

In addition to serving fortune cookies for dessert, Ms. Mattie made beignets (pronounced: *ben-yea's*), a glorified French donut covered in powdered sugar. Beignets are a New Orleans staple, and are served up as a favorite during Mardi Gras. The fact that Blurry, Taka, and Lulu continuously licked their fingers and smacked their lips was testament enough to their goodness.

"Ms. Mattie, these donuts make you want to smack your momma," Blurry said soulfully.

Now, to Blurry's defense, he didn't know his statement would offend Ms. Mattie. Being 'ol school, she found NOTHING cute, humorous, or comical about mothers - any mother, ever being slapped for anything. Blurry had barely put the period at the end of his sentence before Ms. Mattie sternly snapped, "I never liked that expression." After letting the dust settle on that comment, Ms. Mattie followed up with a softer remark, "But, I assume that means you're enjoying them."

"Yes, they're very good," chimed Lulu, Taka, and Blurry at the same time.

"I figured their taste would remind you of home," Ms. Mattie affectionately told Paradise.

"It does … and, thank you for the meal."

"No. I thank you, Paradise."

"Why are you thanking me?"

"I'm thanking you for blessing my home with your presences. If, I had more time, I would have made you a King Cake," Ms. Mattie said sincerely.

"The beignets are wonderful. But, I'm glad you didn't make the King Cake," Paradise said seriously.

King Cakes are another edible Mardi Gras tradition. It is said that the cake represents the three kings of Bible days, the festival of Epiphany, and the pre-Lenten celebration of Carnival, Mardi Gras as its called in New Orleans. The actual King Cake is a braided ring of danish dough. The person braiding the dough would insert a tiny baby doll into the dough before the cake was baked. When the case was done and cool, the cake was decorated with a delicious green, purple, and gold sugar topping. As good as it is, Paradise had no desire for King Cake. In her former life, she had been married to an abusive man called, 'Mr. King Cake'.

"Do y'all have money?," asked Ms. Mattie curiously.

"Don't look at me, because I'm in overdraft," said Taka.

Ms. Mattie was becoming agitated. "I'm not asking you to give me any money."

Wanting to understand, Lulu said, "Yes, ma'am … why do you ask?"

"They'll be tracking your debit card transactions …"

Blurry's thoughts were so in sync with those of Ms.Mattie, that before she could finish her sentence, he unconsciously cut her off and completed her statement. "Armed with that information they can predict our next move."

Not one to be caught off-guard, Ms. Mattie rebounded quickly, snapping, "Stand down soldier. I'm steering this ship."

"Yes, ma'am. We're aware of that ma'am. We're bounty hunters," Lulu proclaimed.

Ms. Mattie was unimpressed, and a little disturbed with what she was hearing. "And, what does that have to do with the cotton fields in Mississippi? And, will y'all please stop volunteering information. I'm not the cops! Nevertheless, your situation must be serious. If it wasn't, you would not be in my home."

"We're innocent Ms. Mattie," Blurry said defensively.

"There you go again, all muscle and no brain. If it involves white folks - you're guilty! I don't care how many alibis you have," said Ms. Mattie with a straight face.

"Under normal circumstances, we would have paid our corporate lawyers …" said Lulu before he was interrupted.

Dismissing Lulu's unfinished comment, Ms. Mattie sought to have the group understand the gravity of their circumstance. Her voice reflected the sober outlook that governed her mindset. "Money can't make this go away."

"What do you mean by that?," Lulu asked in earnest.

"I thought Money Answers Everything?!," said Paradise.

"Ecclesiastes - the tenth chapter, nineteenth verse - I'm aware of that Bible scripture," Ms. Mattie confirmed.

Paradise was more than aware, she thad that phrase tattooed on her left ass cheek.

"Money can buy y'all 'tools'; but, it won't stop them from pursuing you," Ms. Mattie informed Paradise.

"I figured that much," acknowledged Paradise remorsefully.

"Do you know who's after us?," inquired Blurry.

"You said it was white folks. Remember, I'm from Louisiana, so, you know I know …"

Taka was nervous. So much so, that she stammered, "These aren't ordinary white folks. The gov … ern … the government is involved."

"If you got Him, and some powerful 'tools', they-can't-do- you-nuth'n," assured Ms. Mattie, she pointed to heaven in reference to God.

Having listened intently, Taka asked, "What's a 'tool'?"

Ms. Mattie looked at Paradise, and Lulu, shook her head and sadly said, "Y'all in trouble."

"I have my 'tools'," Lulu advised.

"And, I know that yours are on the way," an enthused Ms. Mattie said to Paradise.

Paradise was shocked. "They are? Wait, how do you know that?"

Taka was bursting at the seams. "Wait ... before you answer that, what's a 'tool'? … and, how can I get one?," she asked impatiently. As usual, Taka's question would have to dangle a while.

Looking sharply at Blurry, in an almost interrogative style, Ms. Mattie inquired, "What about you Big Fella? Do you have your 'tools'?"

"Wait! … wait!! … WAIT!!!," yelled Paradise, making it perfectly clear that no other issue, or concern, was going to be discussed until a fundamental one was addressed. "Nobody is getting their questions answered! 'Cus we don't

KNOW this woman! But, she knows my name! And, she said she met my momma, my grand-momma, my aunt-*tee,* and my great pop-pop too!" Taking command, she demanded an answer to her question, "Who are you Ms. Mattie?"

Unaffected by Paradise's irritation, the elder happily eased up. With a slight smile, and in a voice of regard and respect, she went on, "It's about time you asserted yourself."

Everyone seemed to be in a pensive mood. Ms. Mattie broke through their brooding. "You four elements sit tight, while I'll make us some sweet tea."

The residue of Paradise's frustration could still be heard in her voice as she let the hostess know, "I'm not thirsty Ms. Mattie."

Ms. Mattie took note of the group's bismal response to her courteous offer, and shifted back into 'position'. "Well, I'm thirsty. So, you're going to have to wait. Exercise some patience. You'll get the answer to your questions after I make my drink. In the meantime, y'all need to meditate," she said authoritatively.

Paradise flared her nostrils; Taka sucked her teeth, while Lulu and Blurry did as they were instructed. They had black belts in Wing Chun Kung Fu, and were accustomed to meditating. Paradise twirled her thumb around the tip of her index finger to help pass the time. Taka sat back, closed her eyes, and quietly wondered, "*Why am I broke? I bet Lulu buries his money.*"

When Ms. Mattie called them the four elements, she literally meant what she had said. Paradise, the Pisces - a water sign - represented the fishes, and the master magician. Lulu, the Taurean - an earth sign - represented Taurus the Bull, and the master of money. Taka, the Sagittarius - a fire sign - represented the archer, the master of adventure, and the higher mind. Blurry's zodiac sign, the twins - an air sign - represented Gemini, the masters of words and communication.

Prior to becoming an international bounty hunter, Lulu worked as a forensic accountant in midtown Manhattan, New York.

Forensic accountants combined their accounting knowledge with investigative skills. Their findings were used to support, or to destroy various litigants in very important court cases. In other words, Lulu had been tasked by his firm to uncover, what, or who caused the 2008 U.S. Banking and Mortgage scandal. Over the course of three months, he discovered that predatory lenders deliberately sold bad mortgages to the middle, to low-income segment of home buyers. Those adjustable notes of bad debt were designed to double, or triple in price. That meant those homeowners' mortgage payments rose two, or three times the original mortgage amount in 2008. In turn, the homeowners were unable to remit the amount due. The result is that the housing market bubbled, and the economy crashed because those unsuspecting homeowners couldn't afford to pay their mortgage.

Lulu started burying his money after he read the book, Confession of an Economic Hit Man, by John Perkins. In that book, Mr. Perkins alleged that 'corporate leaders' paid a three-lettered agency to kill heads of state, and other leaders, who attempted to break free from the petrodollar. Lulu discovered under the Bretton Woods Conference of 1944, that the U.S. dollar had been firmly established as the global reserve currency. That word 'petrodollar' meant a national unit of currency earned by a country from the export of petroleum.

When Lulu became an adult, he started Fortune Hunters, an international bounty hunting business, with the help of his best friend, Blurry. Shortly afterwards, the home Lulu's grandparents owned went 'underwater', causing them to lose their property. An 'underwater' mortgage meant his grandparents owed more on the mortgage than their house was worth. Their home had been worth $175,000; but, they owed the crooked bank $225,000. Lulu took that - as he should have - personally. So, he spoke to one of his connects and he said, "You CAN'T prey on a community who owns their homes, business, and schools."

Lulu sought the help of the Neighborhood Assistance Corporation of America (NACA). Those friendly people helped Lulu's grandparents secure a 15-year mortgage at a fixed rate of less three percent. Full disclosure: Lola and Jose Rafael Correa had to fill out a LOT of paperwork, with Lulu's help of course.

As Paradise impatiently waited for Ms. Mattie to make her award winning sweet tea, she thought about her last conversation with her grandmother, Madame Montoyier. They talked about the 21st of June, avoiding unsavory people, and finding the Fixer. The Fixer was a group of mystical men, and women, who made magical talismans called, 'tools'. A talisman was an object, a stone, or jewelry, infused with supernatural powers for good luck.

When Lulu said, "Under normal circumstances, we would've have paid our corporate lawyers.", he meant that he would have paid the prosecutor to drop the case against Blurry and Taka. In those instances, wherein the prosecutor wasn't into bribes, someone from Lulu's team got paid to incentivize the court clerk. In most cases, money paid for 'services' such as lost transcripts, deleted trial dates, and documents stamped with the notification: You failed to file on time.

In the event, a jealous judge wanted to play, he retrieved his monetary gift from a hallowed law book. But, no Judge in their right mind would have helped Lulu, Blurry, or Taka. They wouldn't, or couldn't, help because of the National Director of Intelligence's having personal involvement, with Paradise's case.

"Ms. Mattie, the suspense is killing me ... are you almost done?," Taka asked softly, and in a non-threatening tone.

"Here you go, baby," she said as she began handing out the tall, cool glasses. "It's time y'all tasted Ms. Mattie's award winning sweet tea."

"Hey, Paradise!!!," said Taka.

"Um, this tastes real good. Now, can we move forward?," Paradise asked anxiously.

Ms. Mattie found herself correcting Paradise. "That was borderline rude baby. You didn't have to snatch that child's drink." .

"I apologize Taka."

"It's alright," Taka replied.

"I said NO NAMES. But, Taka - that's a pretty name. What does it mean?," inquired Ms. Mattie.

"It means eagle or hawk in Japanese."

Lulu added another perspective. He informed them that, "In the Bangladesh monetary system, a taka is equal to 100 poisha."

"That man is smart! He's a 'keeper' Paradise," said Ms. Mattie.

Paradise inhaled deeply, and held back her blush.

Then, without warning, or seeming reason, Ms. Mattie started rambling on and teasing Taka. "100 poisha? … what's that - 100 pennies? … 100 pennies is equal to one American dollar ... so, are you the eagle, or the hawk? … or, do you prefer to clap your butt checks for that almighty dollar?"

Feeling she had been unnecessarily taunted, and not having any inkling on how she should respond, Taka - though frustrated, chose to remain quiet. However, her reaction was not lost on Ms. Mattie, who paid close attention to Taka, taking careful note of how her disposition shifted from normal to upset.

Unable to control all her internal combustion, Taka pointedly asked Ms. Mattie, "Why you keep picking on me?!"

"Eagle, or dollar?"

"Huh?"

"E-GAUL, or DOLL-R?!"

"I AM AN EAGLE, Ms. Mattie!," bellowed Taka.

"Then, that explains why you're in overdraft," said Ms. Mattie insultingly.

"I'm not taking any more insults," protested Taka to Blurry.

"Relax baby. I'm attempting to toughen y'all up. 'Cus when they come, they're coming hard. And, they're coming for your jugular. So, y'all got to protect-ya-neck," said Ms. Mattie caringly.

Eyebrow raised, Blurry whispered to Lulu, "Man, did she just quote Wu-Tang?"

Not waiting, or needing Lulu to respond, Ms. Mattie mouthed, "All 36 chambers." And, to demonstrate she could mentally multitask, in rapid succession, she said, "Sit tight Paradise, I didn't forget you."

The Wu-Tang Clan was a revolutionary rap group from Staten Island, New York. Around 1993, the song Ms. Mattie quoted from appeared on the group's certified platinum album entitled, Enter the Wu-Tang: 36 Chambers.

"Taka and Chocolate Soldier, I want y'all to look me in the eye," said Ms. Mattie. Blurry and Taka followed her instructions. They stared at her intently.

"I see the blue ring around your brown eyes," Taka commented.

"I'm not talking about the high cholesterol circling my eyes. What I'm about to say isn't meant to be repeated. But, I'm going to tell y'all anyway. Are y'all listening?," Ms. Mattie asked.

"We're listening," answered Taka and Blurry in unison.

"Y'all know them garden gnomes?" Ms. Mattie asked, with a straight face.

"What?," Blurry asked of Taka.

"He's that travel agency's mascot."

"I know what it is Taka. But, why is she talking about garden gnomes?"

"Now, you Four Elements, listen closely. In the lore of the gnomes, their hats were originally white. They turned red when they were used for cups. The gnomes filled their cone hats with the menstrual blood of virgins. Legend says they drank the blood for its magical properties."

Confused and curious, Taka asked Ms. Mattie, "Why would you tell that story?"

"You know that's disgusting," said Paradise to Ms. Mattie.

"Oh, I agree," Ms. Mattie told Taka and Paradise.

"Who told you that fairy-tale?," asked Blurry.

"It's in one of those Disney books by Bosley … first name Walter. He worked counter-intelligence for one of those three-letter groups. Latitude 33, that's the name of the book," said Ms. Mattie.

Acknowledging her mental capacity, Lulu inquired, "How do you know so much?"

"I may be old baby, but, that doesn't stop me from going on the enter-nets."

"*Enter-nets, now that's funny*," thought Taka. Knowing she might never have another opportunity to correct Ms. Mattie - and in light of all that had been heaved upon her, she quickly seized the moment to be 'The One'. "The word is pronounced In-ter-net," she proudly assured the elder.

"I know what it's called! But, when I go online, I lose track of time and sometimes I get trapped. It's like I've voluntarily entered Anansi the Spider's magical web," said Ms. Mattie thoughtfully.

"Speaking of blood, the 'powers that be' have done it again."

"What do you mean Ms. Mattie?," Paradise asked in a strange and unusual way.

"For about eight thousand a-pop, the older elite are extending their lives by getting blood transfusions," Ms. Mattie advised.

"So, what's the big deal?," said Taka.

"What's the big deal? They're getting their blood from milk carton kids … the younger the better," said Ms. Mattie.

Unable to wrap her head around what she just heard, a stunned Taka turned with skepticism to Paradise. "Is that true?," she asked.

"You mean is that True Blood?," Paradise said jokingly.

"Alright Sookie Stackhouse," Ms. Mattie light-heartedly added.

Blurry chimed in to jokingly announce, "Vampire alert," to Lulu.

"Y'all didn't hear about that?," asked Ms. Mattie.

"No Ma'am," said Lulu.

"Who's that billionaire who invested in Facebook?," Ms. Mattie inquired.

"Zuckerberg," Taka shouted proudly.

"No, not him baby … the other boy."

"Who, Peter Thiel?," offered Lulu.

"Yeah, that's him," said Ms. Mattie.

"What about him?," Blurry asked in earnest.

"What about him? Wow … what are you young people doing with your time?," Ms. Mattie asked in dismay.

"We're avoiding vampires," Paradise remarked humorously.

"Vampires, now that's funny - NOT. You must have gotten your humor from your father, 'cus your mother and grandmother weren't the jokey-joke types. Well anyway, Peter Thiel, the billionaire, reportedly said that he's very interested in using young peoples' blood for life extension purposes. I was online, and read that on The Daily Beast back in August of 2016," said Ms. Mattie to a sober-minded Paradise.

"Yeah, those billionaire philanthropists have been funding anti-aging research for years. I read a similar article in

Life Extension Magazine, when I worked at the DoD library," Blurry stated.

"You and that library," teased Lulu.

"*Don't hate,*" said the light-hearted look on Blurry's face.

Craving to get into Ms. Mattie's head, and deeper into the mysteries, Taka appeared *thirsty* (for more knowledge). So, she respectfully asked, "What else you got Ms. Mattie?"

"Now, I need to give y'all the NOT-so-pleasant news. I have to tell y'all this, so y'all will NEVER FORGET what kind of force y'all are dealing with," said Ms. Mattie with the sincerest heart - and a stern face.

With an intense curiosity, Taka asked, "What do you mean?"

"There's an evil that is hell bent on destroying our people. I'll use Dr. Harry Bailey as my example," Ms. Mattie explained.

"Who?," Blurry asked.

"*Oh, so you don't know everything,*" said the expression on Paradise's face.

Blurry returned the look with one of his own. "*Oh, you got jokes.*"

"There's a book called Medical Apartheid, and in that book there's an infamous quote by Dr. Harry Bailey. Dr. Bailey was a psychiatrist from New Orleans, and he was NOT a friend of our people. With the help of the three lettered group, he received funding to create an evil vaccine. Years later, J. Edgar Hoover would admit that the government feared the rise of a black messiah. So, those G-Men used COINTELPRO to wage war against the minds of our people. With that policy in full effect, Dr. Bailey's mind control vaccine had become a preferred COINTELPRO weapon. The vaccine was invented as a control substance, designed to produce 'perfected' behaviors in those to whom it was administered. The controlling factor of the vaccine caused many of our precious black boys to lose their speech, as well as their WILL POWER, their ambition, and their ability to feel, or to be affected by pain … And don't get me started on the B-I-E," Ms. Mattie advised with great disgust.

"That sounds like autism," Taka commented to Blurry.

"That also sounds like MMR, the rumored autism-vaccine reported in the movie, Vaxxed," said Blurry to Ms. Mattie.

"Well, that may be. Now, listen to what Dr. Bailey said about his mind control experiments. In New Orleans, he reportedly said that it was cheaper to use niggers than cats, because they were everywhere. In his opinion, our people were cheap experimental animals. Many-a-hospital agreed with his assessment, and started using negroes and other patients in their behavior modification and other drug experiments," said Ms. Mattie sadly.

"Oh my God, that's depressing," Taka confided.

"It sure is baby. It sure is," Ms. Mattie lamented.

COINTELPRO stood for the Counter-Intelligence Program. It was a program operated by the FBI from 1956 to 1971. The agency used covert activities along with some illegal enterprises to discredit, dismantle, and destroy unwanted domestic and subversive groups. The Nation of Islam, along with its leader - Elijah Muhammad - had been a primary target for COINTELPRO. However, he was not alone. Other targets included, but were limited to members of the Civil Rights Movement; Reverend Dr. Martin Luther King's Southern Christian Leadership Conference; Malcolm X; the Black Panther Party, and other black power movements.

J. Edgar, who Ms. Mattie talked about, was a powerful figure, and was the Director of the Federal Bureau of Investigations (FBI). In an internal memo dated March 4, 1968, entitled, "COUNTERINTELLIGENCE PROGRAM BLACK NATIONALIST - HATE GROUPS RACIAL INTELLIGENCE," the programs number two goal reportedly stated: Prevent the RISE OF A 'MESSIAH' who could unify, and electrify, the militant Black Nationalist movement. Remember when Ms. Mattie said, "*Don't get me started on B-I-E...*" In 2017, the FBI coined the term Black Identity Extremist (BIE) - "*...critics say designation broadly targets* *black activists and first prosecution may have begun,*" reported AlJazeera.com (20 March 2018).

10
THE PROPHET
Cane River, Louisiana

Paradise had another sip of Ms. Mattie's sweet tea. Blurry and Lulu helped themselves to another serving of sweet noodles, asian greens, and caramelized Peking duck. Taka was still sulking, because she felt Ms. Mattie had been unnecessarily cruel. Ms. Mattie wasn't fazed by Taka's sullen demeanor. She chalked it up to a bad case of menstrual cramps. Ms. Mattie finally gave Paradise the information she sought regarding her family's history. Paradise listened intently.

"I was born near the Rivière aux Cannes," said Ms. Mattie.

Paradise was surprised. "The Cane River in Louisiana?"

"Natchitoches Parish, Louisiana to be exact," specified Ms. Mattie.

"C'est la maison de gens de couleur libre," said Paradise in French.

Ms. Mattie smiled, and happily respond, "Très bon Paradise."

"H-e-l-l-o." Taka said as though her voice was a reverberating echo. "Y'all got three other people in the room, and we don't speak French," she said light-heartedly.

"Welcome back baby," Ms. Mattie said to Taka, with warmth and sincerity.

"*Glad to be back,*" nodded Taka.

"Ms. Mattie said she was from the nack-a-tush parish. In the late 1800s, that was the home of the Gens de Couleur Libre, also known as the Free People of Color," said Paradise, educating Taka, Lulu, and Blurry.

Proving she could laugh at herself, Ms. Mattie teased, "I'm not that old!" They smiled and Ms. Mattie wiped the ring of sweet tea from her barely visible mustache.

"After I got married, I moved to Shreveport Louisiana. That's where I met Paradise's grandmother, Madame Montoyier. The year was 1963, the 21st of June to be exact. I served as her interpreter up until her death," said Ms. Mattie.

"What do you mean you served as her interpreter? Did y'all work for the U.N. or something?," questioned Taka.

"No baby. We didn't work for the United Nations. We worked for our nation, so to speak," Ms. Mattie explained.

Blurry didn't mean to, but found himself having to interrupt the conversation. Frustrated, he asked, "What's up with that dog?!"

"Don't be annoyed Soldier. He's been barking like that for the last three days."

Still very annoyed, Blurry suggested, "Can you call your neighbor and tell them to shut that dog up?"

"It won't do any good," Ms. Mattie said sincerely.

"Why wouldn't it? Blurry and I can go over there …"

"And, Lu and I will shut it down …"

"Real quick!," Lulu said confidently.

"It isn't anything y'all can do," sighed Ms. Mattie with the straight face of certainty.

She then turned to Taka and asked, "What time is it baby?"

Looking at Ms. Mattie's grandfather clock, Taka rubbed her eyes, and informatively but sleepily yawned, "It's 2:30 in the morning."

"Thank you, baby ... like I said, there isn't anything y'all can do."

"Why not?," Blurry still wanted to know.

Paradise injected, "It's a Cane River superstition."

"That may be. But, if a dog barks like this one has been barking, that means bad news is headed our way. The old folks used to say, if a dog barks between two and three in the morning, that means someone in the community is going to die," Ms. Mattie said to Lulu.

"Don't be scaring them, Ms. Mattie," urged Paradise.

"Well, it's a mute point anyway. The dog stopped barking," noted Taka.

"Please continue Ms. Mattie," said Lulu.

"Like I was saying, Paradise's grandmother taught us how to weaponize our spiritual gifts."

"She did what?!," asked Taka skeptically.

Instinctively, Lulu and Paradise looked at Ms. Mattie horrified. They looked horrified because they didn't want Taka and Blurry to know they were in the 21st of June.

"Why don't y'all two relax? I know what I'm doing," Ms. Mattie said to the two of them.

"Let me start over, because I'm getting ahead of myself. I first met your grandmother when she was 17 years old. The year was 1951, so I had to be 29, or 30. But, we didn't speak to one another at that particular time," said Ms. Mattie to Paradise comfortingly.

In awe of the opportunity Ms. Mattie represented, Paradise was naturally excited, and full of questions.

"Why didn't y'all speak? … what did she look like? … who was she with?"

"Those were some terrible, terrible times. We were surrounded by hateful toubabs, evil lynch mobs, and those horrible, horrible - and did I say - horrible, Ku Klux Klan rallies. That was the Jim Crow era in the Deep South. Let's see, by my count, we were nine, or ten years out of slavery …"

Toubab was a West African word used to describe people of european descent, a/k/a white folks.

"*Slavery, this woman's crazy*," thought Taka.

Having read the twisted look on Taka's face, Ms. Mattie sat back, inhaled slowly, sucked her teeth, and waited.

"That can't be right Ms. Mattie. Lincoln freed the slaves in 1865. With the exception of Juneteenth, everybody was free well before the period you're talking about," Taka stated smugly.

Juneteenth, also known as Freedom Day, and Emancipation Day is a celebration of the June 19, 1865, announcement regarding the abolition of slavery. The announcement was made some two and a half years after President Lincoln's Emancipation Proclamation, which became effective January 1, 1863. The June 19th holiday is observed predominantly by Southern black folk in recognition of the emancipation of the last remaining enslaved people from Texas.

"So, there wasn't any slavery in 1942," Taka continued.

Maybe it was the late hour, or the foursomes' apparent ignorance, or both … in any case, Ms. Mattie was growing very impatient. "You don't know shit!," she snarled. "In the South, they had a system called Peonage."

"What's Pee-Uh-Nij?," asked Lulu humbly.

"Peonage was a system of debt slavery, involuntary servitude, convict labor, and sharecropping all-day-long for no money," Ms. Mattie said instructively to Lulu. "That was the Southern system. That was toubabs' system. Peonage, or debt slavery, allegedly ended in 1942, under Circular 3591 of the FDR administration."

"Why'd you say "alleged"?," Paradise questioned.

"I said it, because the Feds received Peonage complaints well into the 1950s," Ms. Mattie told Paradise.

FDR stood for Franklin Delano Roosevelt, who was the 32nd President of the United States. The history of American Peonage, or involuntary servitude, had been documented by Blackmon, in the book, The Re-Enslavement of Black Americans from the Civil War to World War II. Additionally, PBS, an American public television network also broadcasted a documentary called, Slavery by Another Name.

It had been a long day for everyone. Tired and disgusted, Ms. Mattie told Paradise, "I don't have time for this shit! I'm going to bed."

"Hey … I mean, wait … what about my story?," Paradise pleaded.

"You tell her the story! Since you know every got-damn thing," Ms. Mattie barked to Taka.

More disappointed than pissed, Paradise mumbled, "Damn, Taka," under her breath.

Taka dropped her head in shame. Lulu shook his head, and Blurry casually said, "I'm exhausted. I'm turning in too."

Dispirited, Ms. Mattie told the group about their accommodations. "Gentlemen, y'all take the bedroom on the right. Taka, and Paradise, you all take the bedroom on the left. There are two single beds in each room. All of the sheets and pillowcases are clean."

Paradise looked at Taka and instructively mouthed, "Apologize."

"Uh, Ms. Mattie," Taka said remorsefully.

"Yeah," Ms. Mattie said with a distinct chill in her voice.

"I apologize."

Ms. Mattie didn't respond right away. She inhaled deeply, and exhaled the last of her angst, looked back, and light-heartedly told Taka, "Girl, bye."

"Huh? What does that mean?," asked Taka nervously.

"It means apology accepted. Now, y'all get some sleep. 'Cus we leave at day-break," said Ms. Mattie.

Taka and Paradise smiled.

Blurry mumbled to Lulu, "Whew, that's a relief."

As they started to walk toward their respective bedrooms, Ms. Mattie asked Paradise, "Can I speak to you for a minute?," She then caringly said, "Lu, Chocolate Soldier, and Taka, I'll see y'all in the morning."

"Good night Ms. Mattie," they said in unison.

Lulu and Blurry entered the bedroom on the right. Taka walked slowly into the bedroom on the left. Ms. Mattie hobbled to the refrigerator, opened the freezer door, and removed an unopened package. She handed Paradise the large envelope that had delivered by DHL, an international courier service. The envelope was clearly marked, 'URGENT LETTER - Open Immediately'.

Paradise's brown eyes grew wide. She leaned against the kitchen counter, and took a moment to catch her breath. She recovered quickly, wiped the sweat from her brow, and read the shipping label. The mysterious envelope had been shipped from the American Embassy at Plateau de Serpent, Djibouti (pronounced: *Ja-boot-tee*), East Africa. It had been addressed to MS. JUNE SPADE, c/o Spiritualist Church of God, St. Louis, Missouri, USA. In an unceremonious demonstration of pure excitement, Ms. Mattie told Paradise, "That envelop arrived yesterday!"

Eager to know, Paradise enthusiastically whispered,

"Is it what I think it is?"

Ms. Mattie gently assured her, "Now, you'll get the answers you seek."

"Thank you," mouthed Paradise.

When Paradise walked into the bedroom she flinched. She immediately discovered Taka had a bad case of sleep apnea. By the sound of things, it appeared Lulu and Blurry had a slight case of it too. Though quiet would have been the preferred companion for her solitude, Paradise didn't allow those lumberjacks sawing wood deter her from opening her mysterious gift.

The anonymous sender from the American Embassy failed to leave a handwritten note. Paradise understood the content inside the large envelope came from 'The Fixer'. The Fixer had sent her a 24 carat gold ankle bracelet. Upon seeing it, Paradise raised her head, looked toward heaven, and in deep, silent gratitude mouthed, "Thank you, Great Spirit, Mom-Mom, and Pop-Pop Cicero."

Paradise clasped the jewelry around her left ankle. She stripped to her undergarments, removed her bra, climbed into bed, and drifted to sleep.

What Paradise wore wasn't any ordinary piece of jewelry. Its craftsmen used paranormal forces to infuse and create her talisman. However, she needed one more piece of jewelry to serve as her super talisman - the one that would complete her supernatural experience. A ceremony was required that would render the faculties of invisibility, untold power, and fearlessness unto Paradise.

With regard to the faculty of invisibility, it didn't mean she'd have the ability to vanish. It simply meant that no ill-intentioned person could see her, unless sanctioned by the Great Spirit. If Paradise was ever in the presence of such an ill-intentioned, or unsanctioned person, they would - knowingly, or unknowingly - fall into a hypnotic trance. And, in that hypnotic state, that powerful illusion would transform Paradise into crystal. This would cause confusion for those of malicious intent, leaving them bewildered as to their purpose for seeking Paradise.

Paradise had been trained as an exorcist. Her instructor was her grandmother, who taught Paradise the science of exorcism. Under the authority of the Great Spirit, an exorcist was commissioned to cast out demons from people, places, and things. Madame Montoyier had given Paradise a very powerful exorcism ritual, which was proven effective. The exorcism ceremony had been passed down within the family with great care and regard from generation, to generation.

According to the Madame Montoyier's prophecy, Paradise incarnated during this present lifetime to resurrect a 'ghost army'. In order to lead an army of deceased ancestors, disembodied spirits, and ghosts, she needed her talismans for power, protection, and fearlessness.

The Fixer was a group of mystical men, and women, who made magical tools - an object, a stone, or jewelry - called, talismans. The purpose of the talisman could vary, as they were created and infused with supernatural powers for a variety of reasons: protection, wealth, good health, and good luck. The Fixer used little children to make Paradise's talismans. Why little children? Because they were virgins … untouched, chaste, and free of the sin and soiling. They've never seen violence, television, or the movies. The Fixer insured their world remained calm and safe.

A long time ago, when Paradise's mother was alive, she and her mother had a conversation about talismans. Paradise, out of childlike curiosity, took it upon herself to be present and a part of the discussion. For a point of clarity … they spoke to one another in French.

Nina shared an encounter she had concerning her tool. "Mamma, I spoke to pastor about my talisman and he said I needed to get rid of that pagan object."

Madame Montoyier responded, asking, "So, what did you tell him Nina?"

"I froze, I didn't know what to say," Nina replied.

"Why'd you freeze?," the then 12-year-old Paradise asked.

"I knew he'd refuse to understand," Nina explained.

"*So, why'd you tell him?,*" thought Paradise in English.

In order to provoke her naive daughter into a different way of thinking, Madame Montoyier thoughtfully posed her next comment. "Nina, when this subject comes up again … ask your pastor to explain to you why 'dem police need a bulletproof vest for protection."

"Oh, I see Mom-Mom," Paradise interrupted. "We have tools for protection, just like 'dem police have guns and bulletproof vests for protection."

"Tres bon mon petite, tres bon petite," Madame Montoyier said happily to her young protégé.

Prior to her death, Madame Montoyier instructed Paradise to contact The Fixer. The anonymous contactee lived in the Republic of Djibouti. It's alleged that the contactee had direct access to The Fixer. Paradise never believed Madame Montoyier's prophecy, because she never believed in 'contactees'. Contactees were people who claimed they were abducted, or contacted by alien beings. Since Paradise didn't believe aliens existed, all 'contactees' were liars. And, since all contactees were liars, The Fixer didn't exist. And lastly, since The Fixer didn't exist, Madame Montoyier's Djibouti contact didn't exist either.

Paradise's thought was, "*Since none of those things exist. There's no need for me to call Mom-Mom's fake telephone number.*"

Paradise underwent unnecessary hardship because she failed to adhere to Madame Montoyier's instructions regarding the 'contact'. The instructions were simple: Paradise was to dial the Djibouti telephone number, let it ring three times, and then hang-up. Eventually, Paradise made the necessary call, but well after Madame Montoyier's passing, and only after the safety of her own life had taken a turn for the worse. When Paradise finally called the Djibouti telephone number, she wasn't able to hang up as instructed, because someone answered on the second ring and politely said, "Hello, you have reached the American Embassy at Plateau de Serpent, Djibouti."

Paradise panicked. She hadn't been told what to do if someone answered the line. Without thinking, she dropped the telephone, caught a cab, and attempted to close her bank account. She was stunned when the bank manager claimed she never had an account with their institution. Frantic, Paradise started to wig-out. Naturally, the teller was not prepared for Paradise's moment of madness, and threatened to have her arrested. Paradise fled the scene.

A few months later Paradise encountered a woman named, Dixie May Johnson. She worked in Langley, Virginia, for one of the three-letter agencies. At the time, Paradise was under the influence of a strong narcotic. It was not self-induced. Nevertheless, she erroneously believed Dixie May, served as Madame Montoyier's case officer. Paradise trusted Dixie May because she produced photographs of Madame Montoyier, Nina, and Paradise at various stages of their lives. Dixie May allowed Paradise to believe she knew The Fixer. So, Paradise wrote her name on a linen handkerchief with a gold gel pen. Dixie May handed Paradise a straight pin. Paradise pricked her index finger, dripped a drop of blood onto the linen, and placed it inside a ziploc bag.

"I'll get this to The Fixer right away," said Dixie May.

Paradise then exited the Washington, D.C. hotel room. Paradise was unaware that three members from the 21st of June encountered Dixie-May and her bodyguard, JC, in the elevator. Dixie May escaped harm, but, JC wasn't so lucky. He was tasered, carried to a waiting car, and shot in the back of the head. His assailant used a nail gun to do the job. One of the perpetrators removed the ziploc bag Paradise had given Dixie May, from JC's suit jacket. Also removed from the dead man's front pants pocket was an envelope filled with Paradise's money. Those three members insured that Paradise's blood-stained linen arrived to The Fixer safely.

The authorities ruled the bodyguard's death a suicide, even though, they discovered his hands and feet were bound behind his back. Unbeknownst to Paradise, an elderly black couple along with Lulu killed Dixie May's bodyguard. The killing had been a justified act because he planned to destroy Paradise's life.

Paradise woke briefly when she heard Ms. Mattie yell out, "Lu and Chocolate Soldier turn on your side." Forced to get up, she grumbled as she closed their bedroom door. Must have been magic because they stopped snoring - As Ms. Mattie started drifting off again, she mumbled to herself, "Lu, don't let Lex kill you."

11

BACK STORY

Peru, South America

As they slept, Lulu began talking in his sleep. Not loudly, but, in a nearly inaudible tone. When Ms. Mattie began to close their bedroom door, she heard Lulu mumbling and thought he may have been softly speaking to her. So, she briefly stood in the doorway to try and understand what he was saying. Lulu murmured, "Lex, I'm going to kill you."

"*Whoever Lex is? That man will be the death of you*," thought Ms. Mattie.

Lex is Lulu's half-brother. Lulu had been obsessed with killing him for more than twenty-five years. Why? Lex attempted to murder Lulu when he was nine years old, by plunging a screwdriver into his right ear. Although Lex was unsuccessful in accomplishing the gruesome task, he did do permanent damage to Lulu's ear and naturally, his hearing.

Lex was unable to complete his undertaking because of the intervention of a third party, who shot him, forcing him to flee the scene for his own safety.

Lulu's life was saved by his mother's lover, brother God-Body 3X, a member of the Five-Percent Nation. The Five-Percent Nation, or Nation of Gods and Earths, as its also known, was founded by Clarence 13X, in 1964. Previously, brother Clarence 13X had been a member of the Nation of Islam.

The commotion Lex created when he attacked Lulu interrupted the intense 'ABR' session God-Body 3X was having with Lulu's mother. ABR means Adult Breastfeeding Relationship. When the twins, Josefina and God-Body 3X heard Lulu scream, God-Body 3X raced into his room and redirected his pent-up energy with a flurry of hallow points. Lex' bulletproof vest was riddled with bullets. With the exception of one, Lex's vest stopped God-Body's lethal projectiles. Lex escaped the tiny Bronx apartment through a window, with only a ruptured spleen.

The military unit to which Lex was assigned required him to provide a human sacrifice. Lulu was the unsuspecting 'Chosen One'. Thanks to God-Body 3X' temper, Lulu survived, and Lex failed that specific mission. Lex's unit had him extracted, repaired, and shipped to Hawaii. Now, check this out… Lulu's 40 years younger than his half-brother Lex and they never had any contact after that tragic event.

At the time of the attempted murder, Lex appeared to be extremely muscular. He had a bald head, a clean shaven face, and coco skin. Lex had a tattoo on the right side of his neck that read, 'SAMA'EL'. In Jewish or Hebrew lore, Sama'el serves as Satan's helper, and is known as the Angel of Death.

How could Lulu know then that if it wasn't for Lex, he would have never met Blurry, Paradise, or become involved with the 21st of June?

Following his emergency ear surgery, the court awarded Lulu's maternal grandparents custody. Lulu had great difficulty standing because the surgeons removed his right ear drum. In addition to being dizzy most of the time, he rarely spoke and when he did, he tended to stutter. The speech therapist associated his stuttering with Post Traumatic Stress Disorder.

As part of his healing and development, Lulu's grandparents placed him in a martial arts school, located in Harlem, New York, for Kung Fu training. Those classes helped restore his balance and confidence. While there, Lulu met Blurry. Although Blurry was three years older that Lulu, that didn't stop them from becoming instant best friends.

And, being in a martial arts program didn't stop the boys from being bullied. The local boys called Blurry and Lulu 'the retarded twins', harassing Lulu because of his deformed right ear, and Blurry because he had extremely poor eyesight. The bullying didn't stop until they earned their green belts, after which all that 'rah-rah' they experienced got shut down! Having met, and overcome being bullied, they looked forward to earning the coveted black belt.

Blurry received his nickname because he had extremely poor eyesight. He wore super thick eyeglasses as a teenager because his foster mother, Wanda Jackson, couldn't afford his corrective eye surgery. Truth-Be-Told: Blurry wasn't identified as 'legally blind' because Mom-Jackson, threatned the Ophthalmologist with bodly harm. Over the course of time, Blurry and Wanda, along with Lulu and his grandparents, raised the money to help restore Blurry's sight. It goes without saying, "Blurry's controversial double eyed stem cell research procedure was extremely successful."

Lulu received his nickname as result of his childhood stutter. At the time he had great difficulty saying his name, Luis. Whenever he attempted to say it, it came out in a stammered fashion - Lu-Lu, Lu-Lui, Luis, Luis Taylor Fortune. Lulu identified himself as Luis Taylor Fortune. Even though, his birth certificate says, 'Luis Taylor Tapia'. For the record: Lulu didn't use 'Tapia', to spite his mother, or grandparents. He used his father's surname, Fortune, as a means of forcing his father to acknowledge his existence.

But, his effort failed because his father, Rygial Fortune, NEVER acknowledged his existence. For reasons unknown, Lulu stopped stuttering after he received his green belt in Wing Chun Kung Fu.

When Lulu was ten, or eleven, years old his grandparents feared for his life. They believed Lex would return with a vengeance and again attempt to take young Lulu's life. So, Lola Tapia, his maternal grandmother, sought the advice of the Babalaô, the 'Father of Mysteries', in the Yoruba religion. For whatever reason, Lola didn't like the Babalaô's prognostication. So, she went with what she knew: praying the Catholic Rosary for a better answer. A few days later, Lola won their Catholic church's 50-50 raffle to New Orleans.

Lola traveled with her beloved husband, Jose Rafael Correa, to Louisiana, and stayed at the Pontchartrain Hotel, in New Orleans. Their hotel housekeeper at the time was Paradise's Aunt Ida. Ida saw Lola crying, and asked - in English - what was wrong. Because Lola didn't speak English, Ida got a Spanish speaking housekeeper to translate. When Ida heard what happened to young Lulu, she took Lola and Jose Rafael Correa to see Madame Montoyier. On the couple's behalf, Ida explained the circumstance that caused their concern to Madame Montoyier, who agreed to help. In French, Madame Montoyier informed Nina, "Tell them I knew they were coming."

Jose Rafael Correa translated Nina's message from English into Spanish for his wife. Lola conveyed her understanding and appreciation with a nod, followed by a smile, and tears of joy. Lola and Jose Rafael Correa were happy because Madame Montoyier made ten year old Lulu a talisman … a 'tool' for his protection. In Spanish, Lola asked Madame Montoyier, "How much …"

"No charge. This is one is free," Madame Montoyier said, as she waved goodbye to Lola and Jose Rafael Correa.

In English, Nina told Jose Rafael Correa, "One day my mother may call upon you for a favor." He translated her mafia-styled message in Spanish for his wife. And, without question, or hesitation, they simultaneously said, "Yes, we understand."

After their visit with Madame Montoyier, Lola and Jose Rafael Correa returned to New York. In their possession were two supernaturally infused dimes. In Spanish, Lola told young Lulu not to worry about Lex, or anyone else. She continued to say, "These mystical objects were prepared by The Prophetess for your protection."

"You mean these little dimes will keep evil Lex from trying to kill me?," Lulu asked his grand-dad in Spanish.

"*Yes*," nodded Jose Rafael Correa to his grandson.

Madame Montoyier transformed those dimes into talismans, by 'fixing' them. In doing so, those coins would prevent and/or stop Lulu from dying pre-maturely.

The Prophetess' instructions for using the tools were simple, and were given in French. Whatever shoe, or sneaker, Lulu chose to wear, she said, "Tell the boy to put one dime in each shoe and to place them under each shoe insert."

The focus of the military unit Lex worked for was sorcery, and stealing ancient relics, and rituals. It was classified as a special operatives unit for the United States Department of Occult Acquisition (OAU). Their designating shoulder patch was a logo of a skull, with the numbers 666 written across its forehead.

JC, the so-called 'suicided' bodyguard that Lulu left on the bike trail in Washington, DC's Georgetown Waterfront Park, worked for the OAU. His death wasn't investigated for two reasons: 1) his unit never liked him, and didn't feel the need to expend the resources necessary to pursue identifying the perpetrator; and 2) Dixie May ordered the unit to 'stand down'. Those directives meant do NOT investigate the circumstances surrounding the bodyguard's death. Perhaps the real reason her orders went unquestioned, and were followed without question, had to do with the fact that Dixie May, had been responsible for paying for some of the unit's off-the-book expeditions.

Dixie May commissioned the OAU's last theater of operation with unvouchered funds. The theater of operations was an undisclosed location in the South Pacific Ocean, below the equator, off the coast of Peru, in South America. Dixie May, had plugged into the rumored system of hidden finance. The OAUs secret source of unlimited funds had been illegal drug money, and counterfeit bearer bonds. In the world of black-ops, off-the-book monies were called, 'unvouchered funds'.

The OAUs Peruvian mission was listed as 'Above Cosmic Top Secret'. According to those tin-foil-hat-wearing conspiracy theorists, that particular classification was 38 levels above 'Top Secret' clearance. Whatever the classification, the Peruvian government had no idea the OAU was within their coastal waters. The OAU searched those waters for the 'Dark Lord'.

According to the ancient South American legends, he lived under the sea. The ancient Mayan, Egyptian, and Tibetan Priests called the Dark Lord, the 'Nameless One'. But, rest assured, the Nameless One had many names.

Depending on the culture, the Nameless One went by Oannes, Nommo, Triton, and Dagon. As in Dagon - the fish-god - in the Christian Bible, Dagon, or Oannes, had been the ancient Babylonian god who created the merfolk. Human cartoons like 'Aquaman' and 'Ariel' a/k/a 'My Little

Mermaid', helped popularize merfolk culture. Mermaids and mermen are half-human/half-fish Sea dwelling creatures. In Greek mythology, Triton, a merman, lived in the sea and had human-looking gods for parents. His father is Poseidon, and his mother is Amphitrite.

According to the Dogon people of Mali, West Africa, the Nommo were described as amphibious, hermaphroditic, fish-like creatures. In biology, a hermaphrodite is a being, creature, or human, which has both male and female reproductive organs.

Lex' unit traveled the earth in search of ancient artifacts, lost cities, and powerful magic rituals. His crew searched the Peruvian sea for the rumored location of Oannes' progeny.

The overlords, or military overseers, for whom Lex and his team worked, wanted them to retrieve a magical flute. That mystical instrument when played in the correct sequence allegedly opened 'Heaven's Gate'. Heaven's Gate was also called, the 'Silver Gate' and 'Golden Gate', were access points leading 'in and out' of our realm and dimension. The constellation tones between Scorpio and Sagittarius served as the frequency, or key, to opening the Silver Gate. Supposedly, Lex' unit recovered that celestial knowledge from an inscription found on a pyramid rumored to be submerged, in an area alleged to be located ten miles off the coast of the Bimini in the Bahamas.

Lex never believed that so-called magical flute, existed. But, like most soldiers, he did what he was told. He never believed that Oannes story either. He didn't believe those stories because the magical flute needed to come from a mermaid. And, according to the rumored inscription on that sunken pyramid: The key that opens the Silver Gate comes from a bone flute. A flute carved from the rib of a pregnant mermaid provided the best pitch.

From Lex' understanding, mermaids never existed. So, from his perspective, the period spent in Peru had been a total waste of time. But, what he thought had no bearing on the OAU's decision to send a second unit into the Brazilian jungle at the same time unannounced.

The second unit returned to the ancient city of Artificial Lights. Its exact location was hidden from Google's satellite view. The ancient builders constructed a large tarp made from an indestructible material. From the sky, that ancient tarp had been photographed as normal jungle foliage. The artificial lights were giant green glowing stones. The glow varied from a ripe lime to emerald (green).

In The Book of Mormon, it states: God gave Jared some glowing stones - Ether 2:16-18. Jared used those stones at night as a source of light. Those glowing stones allegedly helped him navigate his barge to the New World, in what is now known as North America.

The OAU, or Americans, appeared to be two, to three steps behind the English, French, and Germans. In the late 1800's, British intelligence allegedly sent Sir Richard Burton to the Brazilian jungle to study the Lost City of Artificial Lights. In the 1800s, another English professor returned to England with a glowing stone. He allegedly stole a glowing stone from a warrior tribe in Papua New Guinea.

According to the legend of Adi Buya, that specific glowing stone had mystical properties. The island's warriors rubbed that unnamed stone with sacred oil which caused it to glow. When the sacred stone glowed, those fearless Papua New Guinea warriors touched the tips of their spears and arrows to the surface of the oiled, glowing stone. That ritual, or mystical ceremony, provided those warriors with good luck. Whenever they were in battle, they were impervious to enemy fire, seemed to become invisible, and were blessed with supernatural abilities. After the English professor absconded the glowing stone, those warriors lost their paranormal advantage that sacred stone provided.

Back in the oceans of Peru, Lex lamented over the loss of his OAU compadre and close personal friend, Preston M. Sinclair, whom he, his unit, and their associates simply called, 'Sin'.

Sin had been in an arranged, loveless marriage, with an unhappy wife. No pun intended - the two shared a paranormal 'Nomance'. In addition to going through the motions, passing time (six months), waiting for something better to come along, their marriage at best could only be described as horrific … especially for Mrs. Sinclair. She called him, without affection, 'Mr. King Cake'. And, he called her Paradise. Yes, the same Paradise now resting in Ms. Mattie's home; the same Paradise who's the descendant of Nina, Madame Montoyier, and The Prophet, Cicero …

As stated, the relationship between Sin and Paradise was tempestuous. Their last physical fight resulted in Paradise slipping and Sin prevailing. Sin's assault caused Paradise to be put into a medically induced coma. Paradise spent several weeks in the hospital under the name Jane Doe.

But, when she was discharged from the hospital, the attending staff referred to her as 'Angelina Ferrari Bridgewater', a name Paradise was completely unfamiliar with. The staff was unaware they had been misinformed, because Sin failed to present the facility with accurate patient information. Instead, he presented Angelina's U.S. Passport. Since Paradise and Angelina looked exactly alike, Sin was able to get away with the misrepresentation. Angelina had worked as an American spy in Bogota, Columbia, until her death … murdered by members of a ruthless Columbian drug cartel. Her case officer had been Dixie May Johnson. Paradise had no knowledge of the set-up, and was unaware that she, in fact, had been handpicked to replace the deceased Angelina.

These were the events that led up to Paradise's marriage to Sin: On Paradise's 19th birthday, Madame Montoyier died in her apartment. After the Coroner's Office removed Madame Montoyier's body, Paradise consumed so much liquor, she became intoxicated, and in drunken haze, she ventured out into the streets during the Mardi Gras in New Orleans. Sin, Lex, and the bodyguard, JC, followed Paradise's every move that night. Sin met Paradise on the corner near the Pontchartrain hotel.

With his heavy West Indian accent, and smoldering good looks, Sin would have been hard to resist under normal circumstances. He had an inescapable, naturally mesmerizing, sensual presence. This, combined with Paradise's inebriated vulnerability, made the idea of them hooking up a sure shot. Still, as arousing as that thought might have been for some, Sin had a different objective with Paradise. To ensure his success, he placed several accursed strings of colorful Mardi Gras beads around her neck. Doing so helped him capture and control Paradise's mind, body and soul.

Paradise was ripe for victimization … In her drunken trance, she willingly followed Sin into the hotel. What was done to her in that room could only be described as debauchery. Not only did she have sex with Sin, two unknown women joined in, and unbeknownst to Paradise, they recorded the X-Rated event. Much of what happened that night occurred without Paradise's knowledge, much less her consent. Unconscious throughout the entire ordeal, Paradise had no clue that Mr. King Cake stole her innocence, he stole her identification, and he stole part of her life. The final exploitation came once she awoke to her realization: Sin had done his 'do', leaving naked Paradise 'discarded' under a sheet of newspaper, on a foul and soiled mattress.

Years later, Sin would re-enter Paradise's life. This time, he brought a different kind of magical weapon. This time, he would not use cursed jewelry (Mardi Gras beads) to manipulate her. This time, his weapon of choice was called 'blackmail'. And, with that recorded sex tape in his possession, he had enough dirt on Paradise to force her to marry him under the name of Angelina Ferrari Bridgewater.

A month after Paradise recovered from her injuries; she discovered Sin's physiology included a third strand of DNA. The government and its genetic scientists knew of the extra strand, and its significance. The unique makeup of Sin's biology made him invaluable to their covert operations. Unfortunately, the geneticists associated with his case were not so crucial. Once they completed their research and development, they were systematically silenced. It was made to appear that each had taken their own life … when, in fact, each had been 'suicided'. Suicided means murdered. But, the coroner is encouraged to describe the death as suicide.

The irony is that, in reality, Sin's third strand wasn't DNA at all. It happened to be a sentient being composed of silica, that attached itself to Sin's DNA. It had tiny claws, webbed feet, and a protein coating. That otherworldly creature came through his father's line by the way of Melchiresha, the King of Evil. According to the Qumran text, also known as the Testament of Amram, Melchiresha lived on earth as a giant, snake-faced deity. Sin inherited his evil nature from that serpentine parasite.

Paradise had a nightmare that involved Melchiresha. He wanted her allegiance. She refused. Paradise struggled to wake. When she finally opened her eyes, she gasped. Paradise had that nightmare inside Dixie May's hotel suite. She found her way to Dixie May's hotel thanks to a crooked judge. He's The Honorable Matthew T. Peterson, a federal judge, which had a predilection for cross-dressing. Unaware of the back-story, Judge Peterson thought Paradise was the real Angelina. He received some incriminating documents from 'Angelina' in Denver, Colorado. Matthew T. poisoned 'Angelina' after he took those implicating papers, but then panicked. He called Dixie May for direction, and was instructed to fly 'Angelina' back to Washington, DC.

Dixie May knew Paradise wasn't 'Angelina'. But, she'd made Paradise an offer she couldn't refuse. Dixie May agreed to help Paradise escape Sin. While Paradise agreed to help the government, she had no intentions of sharing her magical secret. Dixie May paid the air-fare to fly Paradise back to Las Vegas, Nevada. At the time, Paradise lived in Sin City (Las Vegas) on Paradise Road. The motel was formerly known as the Mardi Gras Inn.

Dixie May had given Paradise some poison to incapacitate Sin. But, to Paradise's and Dixie May's surprise, Sin - along with his sister, Enchantment, had been targeted for assassination by someone else … a multi-lingual Kabbalist.

12

FEEFOO LE'SPIRIT

New Orleans, Louisiana

Ms. Mattie allowed Taka, Lulu, Blurry, and Paradise to sleep longer than planned. They had scheduled to leave her home at day-break. According to Ms. Mattie's grandfather clock, the time was now 7:15 AM. Their escort out of St. Louis, Missouri had been rescheduled for 1:00 PM.

As Paradise slept, she dreamt about Enchantment and Sin. They were killed along with a few cops inside of Paradise's Las Vegas motel room. The Qliphoth - the evil or impure spiritual forces in Jewish mysticism - had been engaged as the weapon of choice for their demise.

The person who orchestrated that demonic hit used Qabbalistic magic. Qabbalah, or Kabbalah, magic had been the historic branch of Jewish mystical traditions. Those traditions employed the use of spells, amulets, talismans,

Psalm enchantments, and supernatural invocation by way of magical bowls.

The Qliphoth has been mentioned on the shadow side of the Kabbalistic Tree of Life. These dark forces hailed from Sitra Char, which in Aramaic refers to the realm of evil, also known as the 'other side', and is the opposite of holiness in the Kabbalah. When summoned, those merciless Qliphoth welcomed the opportunity to join the Kabbalist's war party. Avi Weinberg was that multi-lingual Kabbalist.

When Madame Montoyier was alive, Avi was her Attorney. Following her death, he continued in his legal role as the manager of Paradise's trust fund.

Madame Montoyier never gave Paradise, Cicero's message, because at the time of her death she and Paradise were bumping heads. As a result of their estranged relationship, Paradise NEVER discovered Avi's treachery until she received that Flintstones lunch box. That nostalgic, metal container contained her divorce papers from Sin, lighter fluid, a book of matches, two mini video cassette tapes, and instructions. The two mini cassette tapes were destroyed immediately in an unsanctioned fire Paradise started in a remote location of the Las Vegas McCarran International Airport. There, in a vacant area of the airport parking garage, the recorded pornographic images of her first encounter with Sin and the two women, she gleefully burned.

Those burnt instructions also included a message with strong implications made by an anonymous author. The message revealed information that strongly suggested Avi had set Paradise up. The innuendo was that Avi did so to steal the money from her trust fund, which was valued at 1.2 million dollars.

The total reported value of her family's fortune was 10.5 million dollars. Madame Montoyier made the family's fortune from various investments. The money she earned from her spiritual work paid for real estate, stocks and bonds, and a silent partnership in a black hair care company. Her partnership in the hair care company was 'silent' because she was unable to buy those assets directly. So, she hired Avi Weinberg, whom she met in New Orleans, on February 21, 1965, to broker her deals.

Avi had recruited Sin to blackmail Paradise. In addition to her general degradation, part of the plan included video-taping the orgy, as potential evidence that Paradise had engaged in actions contrary to a key stipulation in her trust fund. Therein was a clause, which roughly stated: Scandalous behavior would not be tolerated. If, any credible evidence is presented to the Court, the Judge had the legal right to take Paradise's money and family fortune.

The betrayal was engineered by Avi, with the intention of presenting the sex tape to the Probate Court, knowing two things: that he had justifiable cause; and, that upon its review, the court's decision would have been to split Paradise's fortune with him.

As alternative plans go, Avi was prepared to overlook Paradise's indiscretion, and ignore her sex tape, if he could exchange them for one of her family's rituals: A sacred family ceremony that had been coveted by the intelligence community for years. Avi told the Israeli government he had an American client who knew the secret to resurrecting the dead, and that he could acquire that information in exchange for an undisclosed amount of money. The Israelis' understood resurrecting the dead meant resurrecting a ghost army. So, they had agreed to the terms of Avi Weinberg's proposal. They agreed because they knew all-too-well what Simeon Toko did to the Belgian Colonial Army.

According to several eyewitness accounts, on January 4, 1959, the African Avatar, Simeon Toko, invoked a celestial army. A small number of people called those beings, 'cherubim' and 'seraphim'. But, the majority of the Angolan citizens from Leopoldville - the capital of the Belgian colony of Congo - witnessed an army of one thousand non-terrestrial, human-like beings. A few brave Angolans reportedly told journalists that the ghost army Simeon Toko raised resembled the Twa people.

The Twa were the so-called Pygmies who lived in the rainforest of the Democratic Republic of Congo (DRC). Simeon's ghost army was imposing, extremely muscular, and supernaturally strong. One witness account described a 'soldier' on the road whisking a five-ton truck away with one hand! Another reported that the Belgian Colonial Army fired bullets at the swift moving ghost army, only to find that their bullets had no effect on the resurrected army of supernatural beings. The horrified Belgian soldiers became disoriented. They panicked and fled the battlefield. Only then, did Simeon's African ghost army disappear as suddenly as it had appeared.

One year later, the Belgians were forced to leave Angola. The spiritual intervention Simeon received helped end slavery in the Belgian Congo. The regime of Belgium's King Leopold II, no longer had slaves to steal Angola's rich, natural resources of diamonds, ivory, and/or rubber. Avi told his Israeli handlers, "On January 4th, Kinshasa celebrates Simeon Toko Day." Kinshasa served as the Capital and largest city in the DRC.

Neither, Avi Weinberg, nor his Israeli handlers got what they wanted. Sin not only pimped Paradise, he double-crossed Avi, and got the OAU involved. The OAU had been Dixie May's playground, and she never liked Sin. When she discovered that Avi killed Sin, she wasn't upset one bit. Avi attempted to kill Paradise along with Sin and his sister, Enchantment. Avi wanted Paradise dead because their situation had gotten out of hand. Plus, with Paradise removed from the scene, he and the Probate Court planned to split her uncontested inheritance. However, Paradise used her mystical abilities to escape death.

After Paradise escaped Avi's clutches in Sin City, she went to the city's airport, to speak with an airline receptionist and, to retrieve Dixie May's one-way ticket to New York's JFK Airport. But, the 21st of June had Paradise's flight rerouted to Devils Lake, North Dakota. They rerouted her flight because of the oath they pledged to Madame Montoyier, vowing to protect Paradise with their lives. Certainly, Paradise had the free-will to do whatever she wanted. The 21st of June, however, was tasked with doing whatever was necessary behind the scenes to ensure her safety. An example of this is when, unbeknownst to Paradise, the society's Council of Elders were forced to intervene after she'd given Dixie May her blood-stained handkerchief. In response, they dispatched Lulu and the elderly African-American couple to retrieve it.

Paradise, along with her family, had been under government surveillance and investigation for years. The unwanted scrutiny resulted from Madame Montoyier's connection to Dixie May's husband. While Madame

Montoyier's spiritual work had helped her husband become the senator for the State of Georgia, she later regretted taking on his case. At the time, she needed the money. So, Avi Weinberg, who'd met the senatorial candidate at a $500 per plate fundraiser, introduced the two. During their chat, Avi said many things, one of which implied that Madame Montoyier had the ability to raise the dead. The comment triggered the senator's curiosity.

Madame Montoyier fulfilled her part. Thanks to her spiritual work, the candidate's dream of becoming Georgia's senator became his reality. Yet, a portion of his focus was always drawn back to Avi's comment about Madame Montoyier's ability to raise the dead. Periodically, the senator would discuss this with his wife, Dixie May, who also pondered the notion. One day, as they talked about it, she said, "Maybe she can weaponize them too."

The senator sought to further engage Madame Montoyier's spiritual services, but when she refused, he threatened to harm her daughter and granddaughter. Not a good move. In addition to learning he'd pushed the wrong button, he quickly discovered that Madame Montoyier had become his adversary. In French, she forcefully told Avi to tell the senator, "I'll send an army of ghost to kill him, and the entire United States Senate."

Dixie May's husband didn't care what happened to his colleagues. He only cared about himself. So, he immediately withdrew his threat and stopped his pursuit. But, Dixie May never did. Although she would ultimately redirect her attention to Paradise, after Madame Montoyier's untimely death, Dixie May assumed it only natural to pursue Nina as the next-in-line. But, due to Nina's suicide attempts, that too proved to be a poor choice. The repeated attempts rendered Nina unreliable. She was considered 'damaged goods'.

Eventually, Nina got her wish. She died inside of the Louisiana State Mental Hospital. At the time of her death, the coroner ruled on her cause of death. Dryly, he announced, "The cause of death is a broken heart." Nina's Hollywood handsome husband had broken her heart. And, mentally, after she found out he'd left her for her best sister-friend, she abandoned her mood stabilizing charm (tool), its power abandoned her and she never recovered.

Madame Montoyier passed from a broken heart too. Whether their actions were direct, or indirect, intentional or not, both Nina and Paradise contributed to her demise. Nina, because she refused her mother's help: This left Madame Montoyier feeling she had failed in her ability to save her daughter. Oh, without question, she possessed the spiritual knowledge, the political connections, and the money to help Nina recover. She was simply powerless to overcome what was to be Nina's own self-fulfilling prophecy. On more than one occasion, Nina told her mother in French, "Mamma, you can't save a person who doesn't want to be saved." Her statement, combined with her lack of fight, left Madame Montoyier physically, spiritually, and emotionally depleted. Nina's statement enraged Paradise.

If, Paradise had had a better relationship with her grandmother, her grandmother would have stayed on this side of life [a lot longer]. Madame Montoyier surrendered her life to the 'Angel of Death', because she believed; she could do more for Nina and Paradise from the World of Spirits. Speaking of the Spirit World, the 'Spirit of Hopelessness' ruined Nina: That means no magic, no prayer and no ritual could free a person, who didn't want to be free.

When Paradise finally accepted Nina's refusal to accept Madame Montoyier's help, Paradise sought to reconcile her relationship with Madame Montoyier. Paradise was hopeful that her grandmother would join her in celebrating her nineteenth birthday. So, she extended an invitation to Madame Montoyier to come to her tiny apartment in the Lower 9th Ward. Paradise intended to use the occasion to apologize for the indifference she'd shown her grandmother. It's needless to say, "Madame Montoyier happily accepted Paradise's birthday invitation."

Three days before Madame Montoyier's unexpected death, Paradise met her on the banks of the Lake Pontchartrain, in New Orleans. By that time, the two had been estranged for a little more than a year, and Madame Montoyier wanted to rekindle their relationship too. So, she asked Paradise to meet her at Lake Pontchartrain to perform the egg ritual. As a little girl, Paradise always enjoyed that ancient ceremony. When Paradise arrived on time, Madame Montoyier smiled, and was encouraged. Each was genuinely happy to see the other.

Then, without warning, the Spirit of Sadness came upon Madame Montoyier. In an instant, the dam that had held the past year's trauma in-check broke, and there seemed no relief for what was uncontrollably welling inside Madam Montoyier. Fortunately or unfortunately, the Spirit of Stoicism stopped her from crying. Being the lady she was, Madame Montoyier decided to end their family outing (without providing an explanation). The Spirit of Stoicism remained until she was able to collect her thoughts. Madame Montoyier stood a little straighter; she raised her head and pulled her shoulders back. Then she tucked her basket of fresh duck eggs firmly under her arm, released a deep exhale, and began to slowly turn away.

Before Madame Montoyier waddled away, Paradise looked deep into her dimming chestnut eyes, and caught sight of what her grandmother had been feeling. Now, having seen - and felt - the depth of Madame Montoyier's grief herself, Paradise tried to lighten the moment. She offered a loving smile, and in French, playfully said, "You're not going anywhere Mom-Mom. We both know you're going to live forever." Madame Montoyier returned the smile, inhaled slowly, and proceeded to hobble away.

In German, Paradise yelled, "Hey, where are you going? What did I say?" Although Madame Montoyier continued on, never looking back, a telepathic response had been given. *"I'm too distraught to talk right now. It appears I'm walking the green mile,"* said Madame Montoyier's back as her bowed legs slowly shuffled from Paradise. The green mile is a figure-of-speech that referred to the pathway to death.

At the time, Paradise didn't realize Madame Montoyier was in the transitional phase. She really was dying. Much to her own surprise, Madame Montoyier wasn't prepared to die. Long before Nina lost her mind, Madame Montoyier use to tease her and Paradise in French, by saying, "When death comes, I'll kiss it in the mouth." Unable to digest the comment, Nina responded in French saying, "Don't talk like that Mamma. And 'yes', I know it's a figure-of- speech. But, I don't like that kind of talk."

Madame Montoyier honored Paradise's wish by visiting her tiny apartment on her nineteenth birthday. After, they exchanged pleasantries, Madame Montoyier told Paradise to avoid unsavory people and to seek the protection of the 21st of June. Paradise, noticed her grandmother was getting tired, so, she helped her sit. Madame Montoyier plopped onto Paradise's wooden folding chair. Paradise figured Madame Montoyier needed some water to drink, as she turned to retrieve the revitalizing liquid, Madame Montoyier mummbled, "Je peux les aider plus de l'autre cote." In French, that meant, "I can help them more from the other side."

When Madame Montoyier refused to wake, Paradise called 9-11 and the first policeman on the scene couldn't revive her. Both Madame Montoyier and Paradise were startled when the coroner remorsefully said, "Young lady, it appears your grandmother died of a broken heart."

Even though she'd just entered into the realm of spirits, Madame Montoyier also heard what the coroner said. But, she was unable to respond in the customary human way. So, she re-appeared inside of Paradise's apartment as the FeeFoo Le'Spirit. The fee-foo-lay spirit of Madame Montoyier appeared as a tiny white light. She darted across the room into Paradise's kitchen as if she was an excited lightning bug. Two, of the three paramedics present rubbed their eyes. They became skittish, and nervously thought to themselves, "*Am I seeing things?*"

Paradise missed Madame Montoyier's mystical manifestation because the Spirit of Stoicism had her attention. That spirit now stood in service to Paradise, fortifying her with strength. Encouraged, she did not shed a tear. But, the coroner along with the paramedics, and the police only felt the Spirit of Sadness enter the room. When they left Paradise's apartment, the Spirit of Intoxication came upon her, enticing her to drink. She submitted, and in one gulp drank close to a quarter bottle of Remy Red Cognac.

"Paradise, wake up," coaxed Lulu tenderly.

Startled, Paradise asked, "What? What's wrong Lulu?"

"You were having a nightmare," he said consolingly.

"Yeah girl, you woke everybody up," chirped Taka nervously.

Defensively, Ms. Mattie clarified, "I wasn't asleep."

"Was I screaming?," asked Paradise worriedly.

"Nah," blushed Blurry.

"But, you punched a hole in Ms. Mattie's wall," Taka said fearfully.

"Look at your knuckles," Blurry said to a surprised Paradise.

Agitated, Lulu directed Blurry to, "Turn around."

Paradise had gone to sleep wearing a black thong and no bra.

As Ms. Mattie handed Paradise a red robe, she said, "Here baby, put this on."

Blurry turned around slowly.

Embarrassed, Paradise took the robe and covered herself. Afterwards, she humbly said, "Thank you Ms. Mattie." She then said, "Thanks for telling me Lulu," as she softly punched him in arm.

"No names," Ms. Mattie told Paradise.

Paradise acknowledged the reminder, as well as the damage she'd done. "Sorry. And, I'm sorry about your wall too," she said apologetically.

"*Don't worry about it. I'll get it fixed,*" nodded Ms. Mattie in acceptance.

"I dreamt my Mom-Mom was in my apartment and she appeared as the Fee-foo-lay …"

"What's that Paradise?," said Taka inquisitively.

"Fefoo Le'Spirit is the flickering white light of the recently departed. That person's spirit goes from one room to another room and then it disappears," Ms. Mattie told Taka instructively.

Paradise sniffled, "My Mom-Mom rarely appears in my dreams."

"Don't tell me someone's about to die," said Taka nervously.

"We're all going to die Taka," said Paradise in a nonchalant tone.

"You know what I mean," Taka quipped.

Worriedly, Lulu nodded, "*I know what you mean,*" to Taka.

Concerned about her nightmare, Lulu shared his observation with Paradise. "It sounded like you were arguing with the grim reaper."

"And, you hit him with a two-piece," said Blurry humorously.

"Ha, ha, NOT funny Blurry," snapped Paradise anxiously.

"Well. Whatever you were fighting, hopefully it's gone," Taka told Paradise to comfort her.

In an effort to regroup, Ms. Mattie rallied everyone to, "Get cleaned up. After we eat, we'll be on our way."

13
RUNNING BRANCH
Amite, Louisiana

Despite getting washed up, Blurry, Taka, Paradise, and Lulu had to put yesterday's clothes back on. Still, it was good to freshen up. Ms. Mattie wore a powder blue sweat suit and flip-flop sandals.

Ms. Mattie made her guests a high fat, anti-seizure breakfast to eat. The meal was comprised of a lot of scrambled eggs drenched in butter, along with the fattest strips of beef bacon. No wheat products were served. Ms. Mattie's vegetable of choice was sliced avocados, sprinkled with celtic sea salt and cayenne pepper. To drink, the group had their choice of alkaline water (pH 8.5) or Young Coconut milk to drink. Paradise opted for the coconut milk, while Blurry, Taka, and Lulu drank the alkaline water. It's rumored healthy human blood has a pH balance of 7.4 and; unhealthy humans with a blood pH of 7 or less, may be cancerous.

Ms. Mattie also gave Paradise, Taka, Blurry, and Lulu two forbidden items. She placed before them a small vial of white powder and sandwich bags that contained an illegal South African plant. The foursome looked at each other with skepticism. Blurry furrowed his brow trying to figure it out. Taka bravely blurted out, "I don't do coke!"

Disappointed with their reaction, Ms. Mattie yelled, "Why would I give y'all cocaine?"

"It looks like coke," said Paradise.

"This is what your great granddaddy fed us at sunrise service," said Ms. Mattie to Paradise. Turning to Taka's comment, she answered, "And it's NOT COKE! Its white powdered gold."

Taka remained doubtful. "Same thing to me."

"White powdered gold as in monoatomic gold?" inquired Blurry.

Though he didn't mean to sound like a smart-ass, Blurry spoke to Lulu and vociferously injected, "I read about that in the DoD Library."

"You and that library," said Taka to Blurry, humorously.

"What is it?," Lulu asked with great curiosity.

"Harvard scientists used nano gold particles to successfully reverse the age of mice. And, the black pharaohs of ancient Egypt made cone shaped cakes of white powdered gold. The pharaohs ate those gold powdered cakes for vitality, mystical prowess, and spiritual enlightenment," Blurry informed Lulu and Taka.

Ms. Mattie added, "The ancient Israelites continued the tradition."

Unaware and curious, Paradise pressed for clarity. "What do you mean?" she asked.

"Moses burnt the Children of Israel's golden calf. The ash from the golden calf had been turned into white powdered gold. That white powdered gold was put into their water and they drank it," Ms. Mattie told Paradise and Lulu.

"My mother bees-all-up in her Bible, but, she ain't NEVER told me no story like that," Taka said to Ms. Mattie.

"It's in there. Exodus: 32nd Chapter, 20th verse. It states: And he took the gold calf, the people had made and burned it in the fire; then he ground it to powder, scattered it on the water and made the Israelites drink it. Read The New International Version," said Ms. Mattie informatively. "You know who taught me that?," she asked turning to Paradise.

Unsure if she was correct, Paradise answered the question with a question, "My great granddaddy, Cicero?"

"No, it wasn't him. But, I had the privilege of meeting him. The year if I remember correctly was 1950? No, no, it was 1951," said Ms. Mattie in sweet remembrance. Looking to Lulu, she provided the answer, "No, it was Paradise's grandmother, Madame Montoyier, who explained that story to me in private." Now turning to Blurry, Ms. Mattie said, "Chocolate Soldier, you may like this ... Paradise's great granddaddy, Cicero - the man we called The Prophet - he knew the secret to making monoatomic gold."

"Mon-No-Ah-Who?," said Taka humorously.

"What are you a Sagittarius?," whipped back Ms. Mattie.

Intrigued, Taka asked, "How'd you know?"

"You're always joking around," Paradise chimed in light-heartedly.

"That too, but y'all Sagittarius' fear life not having any meaning beyond this physical world," Ms. Mattie said to Taka.

"I don't know what that means. But, I know there has to be more to this life than this physical world."

Ms. Mattie's suggestion to Taka was simple. "Reduce the judgment, stop exaggerating, and you'll discover the answers to what you seek."

"Like I was saying, The Prophet gave us cone-shaped, white powdered gold. Tiny little things, we ate them at sun rise, along with a thimble of Mississippi Moonshine. Your grandmother explained that The Prophet used a 24 carat gold coin to make our white powdered gold. We had to use moonshine to wash it down because wine was hard to come by back then," Ms. Mattie told Paradise with a straight face.

"You said sun rise service … was it Easter Ms. Mattie?," said Blurry engagingly.

"No, it wasn't Easter. I remember it was summertime, late August to be exact. The Prophet said, "Welcome brave souls. Never forget this is the first day of Thoth," said Ms. Mattie to Blurry.

"The first of who?," said Taka questioningly.

"Thoth, or Tehuti as he is also known, was the ancient Egyptian god of the moon, magic, and writing. His daughter Auset, is better known as Isis. And, I'm NOT talking about those Nazi influenced Arabs either. But, I digress. The first of Thoth meant the New Year. But, I didn't know how that could be since, the Roman calendar observes the New Year on the first of January. But, I digress again. No offense Paradise, but, your great granddaddy was the oddest man," said Ms. Mattie respectfully.

"What do you mean?," Paradise asked.

Ms. Mattie reflected, and then humorously said, "We were living under Jim Crow. Black folk in the fields could barely read, or write. And, The Prophet - your great granddaddy - had us in the graveyard at sunrise talking about ancient Egypt."

"Who died?," Lulu inquired.

"Nobody died. We were there for a baptism."

Taka, Blurry, and Lulu were shocked. "A BAPTISM!"

"Didn't I say her great granddaddy was odd?," said Ms. Mattie to Taka, Lulu and Blurry.

"Again, no offense Paradise," Ms. Mattie said.

"None taken," said Paradise dryly.

"Who got baptized in the graveyard? And why would anybody subject themselves to that?," Taka asked squeamishly.

"What's inside this sandwich bag?," asked Paradise abruptly.

"Hoodia Gordonii," Ms. Mattie replied.

"The appetite suppressant," Taka informed the group.

"It's the real thing," Ms. Mattie said confidently.

"So, what do we do with this white powdered gold?," said Taka.

Ms. Mattie was exasperated. "If, you've got to ask …"

"I'm going to hold onto it," Taka commented with some trepidation.

Ms. Mattie had a South African associate smuggle the Hoodia Gordonii into the United States. The San Bushmen, of Southern Africa, used the herb on their three-day hunts. A few bites of that leafless plant sustained and nourished them for the entire hunt.

With a facial expression filled with curiosity, Blurry asked, "Why do we need this?"

"It may help with treating indigestion, small infections, and it may serve as an appetite suppressant. But, be careful with it. Don't eat too much," Ms. Mattie recommended to Blurry.

As Ms. Mattie entertained their questions about Hoodia Gordonii, Paradise reflected on her mother, grandmother, and great granddaddy.

When Paradise was young, Nina told her that Madame Montoyier had been baptized in the graveyard. She wasn't a willing participant; but, her papa, Cicero, insisted. He claimed that Jesus performed miracles in the graveyard ... that Jesus healed the sick in the graveyard ... that Jesus would cast demons out of people in the graveyard ... that Jesus prayed in the Garden of Gethsemane - and that the Garden of Gethsemane was a graveyard ... and, that Jesus talked to two dead men in the graveyard. They were his ancient ancestors. They talked about future events. Their names were Moses and Elijah and they had been dead for hundreds of years. Madame Montoyier had some difficulty accepting her father's last statement, so, in chata (choctaw) he said, "The story of Jesus talking to two dead men was called the Transfiguration. Jesus also said, "Greater things will you do," Isabella. The Good Book also says when Jesus rose from the dead; the bodies of many holy people who had died were raised to life too. So, I wonder where they are now. What do you think Isabella?"

"Where does it say that Papa?," asked the then seventeen year old Madame Montoyier, in choctaw, of her ninety-eight year old father, Cicero.

"Matthews: chapter 27, verse 52," he informed her.

Cicero chose to speak the Native American language, Choctaw, to Isabella in honor of her deceased mother. She had been murdered by the night riders when Cicero wasn't home. Isabella and her twin brother were two years old at the time. The locals said Madame Montoyier's choctaw mother was extremely attractive. What some folks may have called, 'Miss America Pretty'. Nevertheless, it appeared her beauty also served as her curse.

On the night of her tragic death, Running Branch - Isabella's mother - had been extremely tired. In choctaw, Cicero told her, "I'm going to New Orleans on business. I'll be back in two days. Keep the children close and sprinkle those herbs around their bassinet, as well as our bed."

"I will husband, come back soon," said Running Branch.

"*I will,*" nodded Cicero.

Cicero walked out of their tiny home in Amite, Louisiana. From Running Branch's perspective, Cicero appeared to vanish. As she had been instructed, Running Branch began to sprinkle the powdered flowers and herbs around the twin's bassinet. That magical mixture had been 'fixed' to ward off any and all evil. However, being exhausted from her chores of the day, Running Branch's energy waned when it came to sprinkling those ward-away herbs around the bed she and Cicero shared. The call to sleep dominated any reasoning, or instruction she'd been given.

In his gut, Cicero had a bad feeling. Unable to dismiss the strong, unsettling signals, or to shake off the dread that accompanied them, he cancelled his trip. In less than three hours, he returned home. When Cicero entered the tiny house, he noticed his twin's crying. As he looked about his home, he wept too. He cried out because of the horrific crime scene he'd walked into. Running Branch had been brutally raped and murdered by three Night Riders.

Cicero lamented uncontrollably. So inconsolable was he that a neighboring sharecropper and his wife could hear him wailing. The brave couple quickly ran to his aid. Those two hardened negros offered to help Cicero avenge Running Branch's death. Cicero abruptly ended his sobbing, and wiped his light brown eyes. His brief display of agony was gone, transformed into resolve. With flared nostrils, he vowed revenge. Before he sent his brave neighbors away, he thoughtfully spoke to them in a combination of broken English and French. Cicero told them, "Y'all have seven children who need you. So, please, take your shotguns and shells home with you. What I need to do, I can do alone. By day break, the death of Running Branch will be avenged. And, after tonight y'all will never see me or our children again."

No words were necessary. The husband and wife, in support and regard, simply nodded, "*We understand.*" But, they didn't leave right away.

The sharecropper's stocky, brown-skinned wife took the twins, Isabella and Charlie-Boy, to her tiny shack. The couple's oldest daughter watched the children, so that they could help Cicero clean up Running Branche's blood. Their assistance also allowed Cicero to care for his wife's body respectfully, and to tend to laying her to rest properly. After washing her body thoroughly, Cicero 'dressed' his wife by wrapping her body in a clean bed sheet.

Under the cover of darkness, the large, dark-skinned sharecropper helped dig a deep pit, in a secluded area well chosen by Cicero. The two carefully lifted and placed Running Branch's shrouded body into the grave. In gratitude, Cicero rewarded their kindness by telling them to include something of value along with a hand-written note during the burial. He said, "Drop what you have into her grave gently."

They followed his instructions. The stocky woman wrote, "Running Branch, kill 'dem mans dead." On behalf of her illiterate husband, she wrote, "Tell d'Lord help us keep our land." And, though they were extremely poor, the sharecropper and his wife were generous in spirit. They gently dropped their only silver dollar along with their notes into Running Branch's grave. Afterward, the men covered her body with a mound of dirt. Cicero thanked the couple, and announced, "I'll pick my children up in one hour." When he spoke, Cicero sounded like the deceased orator Paul Robeson.

The year of Running Branch's murder was 1937. Going to the sheriff for help solving crimes against negroes was not an option. More importantly, the Amite Sheriff and his two deputies were the Night Riders who brutally raped and killed Cicero's wife. Cicero knew it had been them because earlier that day, the sheriff said, "Hey uncle, you know yous one uppity nigger." Cicero remained silent, but anger burned through his light brown eyes.

"Don't you be eye-balling me BOY!," said the younger deputy.

The red-neck sheriff quickly added, "You so dumb, you married a Choctaw. 'Dem Choctaw, along with four other tribes, enslaved your people."

"Nobody likes your kind boy," stated the older, muscular deputy.

The three continued bandying about.

"But, I sho' like his pretty wife," said the younger deputy.

The sheriff jested, "Hey boy, if you're not careful, we might just pay that pretty gal of yours a visit."

"She's more like his granddaughter," chuckled the muscular deputy.

The sheriff and his deputies laughed hysterically. Cicero contained and concealed his anger well. The only indication he was fuming were his flared his nostrils. The three lawmen were so busy howling at their own ignorance, they were unaware that Cicero had walked away completely unnoticed.

The Cherokee, Chickasaw, Choctaw, Creek (Muscogee), and Seminole were the 'Five Civilized Tribes' of Native Americans who had enslaved black folk. Cicero knew the U.S. Government owed black folk billions of dollars for their Indian/Native American enslavement. While, Cicero wasn't in the position to enforce the Black Freemen Indian Treaty of 1866, he was certainly in the position to avenge his wife's brutal death.

Fifteen minutes after the large sharecropper and his stocky wife returned to their tiny shack, Cicero searched the field for the spiritual herbs his revenge required. He located what he needed, braided the long herbs together, and went to retrieve his children. The sharecropper's stocky wife bundled each of Cicero's children in colorful swaddling cloth. Her husband then helped her swathe the twins in yards of fabric to the front and back of Cicero's body, to facilitate his ease of movement while traveling. Cicero fled Amite, Louisiana, for New Orleans on foot, and on horseback.

At daybreak, the heat of the sun evaporated whatever water was within the braided herbs, causing the intertwined strands to snap. Rumors spread quickly. The Amite town folk said the Angel of Death killed the sheriff and his two deputies. Each of the local coroners' records reported the same notation: cause of death is unknown. Their best guess was that each of the men died of a heart attack.

The sharecropper received the wish his wife had written on his behalf. Their three acres of land remained with their family long after his, and his wife's death. Prior to their death, they would occasionally bury a silver coin at Running Branch's unmarked grave.

When Madame Montoyier turned seventeen, Cicero baptized her in a rubber-lined grave. The baptism took place in a negro graveyard. They found a town outside of New Orleans, where negroes were buried in the ground. Madame Montoyier's baptism was witnessed by a few brave colored folk and their children. The attendees were sworn to secrecy under the pain of death. To date, those anonymous families never shared Madame Montoyier's baptism story with anyone.

Cicero stood five feet and eleven inches, and because of his smooth, bronze skin, looked as though he was bi-racial. Cicero had a strong set of ivory colored teeth, which Madame Montoyier contributed to his sugarless lifestyle. Cicero refused to wear a beard and mustache. He shaved himself up until the day of his death. His hair was naturally curly and thick. It resembled white lamb's wool.

Decades later, Madame Montoyier had a conversation with Nina about her father. As was their custom, they spoke to one another completely in French. She said, "I would never do you like Papa did me. But, now I understand why he did it. He never got over mamma's death. And when Charlie-Boy died at the age of five, I thought Papa was going to kill every toubab in New Orleans. As you know, Papa never remarried. Plus, he was old when he had me and Charlie-Boy. So, I guess marriage was out of the question anyway. I lived with Papa for twenty-one years…"

"How old was Papa Cicero when he died Mamma?," questioned young Nina.

"Let's see … you were born in 1963, Papa died in '55 … so, he had to be 101 years old," answered Madame Montoyier.

Intrigued, Nina inquired, "Why do you think Papa baptized you in the graveyard Mamma?"

Madame Montoyier was forlorn when she responded, "He figured the good spirits needed to be more acquainted with me. I must admit that following the baptism, my spiritual gifts did increase. But, honestly Nina, I truly believe Papa thought that was the only way he could protect me."

Years later, when Paradise was ten years old, she asked Madame Montoyier in English, "Mom-Mom, where did Papa Cicero come from?"

Patient, yet terse, Madame Montoyier snipped in French, "Why are you speaking English to me Is-ah-Bell-Ah?!" She went on to explain, in French, "Papa said he was born on a breeding farm. He never knew his African mother. But, over time, he discovered his father was French. Papa's father owned a thriving tobacco plantation around Baton Rouge."

Because slaves were viewed as a commodity, or asset, breeding farms, and plantations, served as a financial tool designed primarily to increase the wealth of slave owners, by developing a system of forced sex among breeding-aged African and/or enslaved teens. Males served as 'studs', forced to procreate under duress - and the female slaves were repeatedly subjected to rape - intercourse solely for the purpose of impregnation and producing offspring. The ultimate goal was an endless stock of future slaves for sale, or labor. However, with certainty, other sexual abuses were rampant on breeding farms as well … all occurring under extreme duress for those affected men, women, and children.

14

BAD ROOSTER

Harlem, New York

Paradise sat silently at Ms. Mattie's table in a deep daze. She didn't know Lulu and Blurry had left the house. They returned with Lulu's two suitcases. When Blurry sat next to Taka, Lulu worriedly said, "Ms. Mattie, is she still out?"

"Baby, will you do me a favor."

"Sure Ms. Mattie," Taka said willingly.

"Go upstairs. Go into my bathroom and bring down my box of smelling salts," Ms. Mattie requested.

Honestly confused, Taka asked, "What are smelling salts?"

Honestly perplexed, Ms. Mattie answered Taka's question with one of her own, "Are you kidding me?"

"I'm not joking Ms. Mattie, I've never heard of smelling salts," said Taka sincerely.

"It's respiratory stimulant. An ammonia inhalant, there should be three, or four ampoules left," said Ms. Mattie kindly.

"Why do you have them Ms. Mattie?," said Blurry.

In a scooting fashion, Ms. Mattie told Taka, "Hurry up baby."

Taka stood quickly, and ran up the stairs.

Ms. Mattie sincerely said, "My nephew, by marriage, had bad seizures. He came to live with us after World War II. One evening, he had a seizure in bed. My husband revived him with some smelling salt. He looked at me and said, "The boy can't live like this." So, we took some 'shrooms in search of an answer …"

"Shrooms?," said Lulu and Blurry in unison.

"Yes, we took some magic mushrooms. That's how my husband and his two brothers discovered Paradise's grandmother, Madame Montoyier. But, I digress. The spirit of that fungi, told my husband to give our nephew a healthy high fat diet, no wheat products, and no sugar."

"Did it help?," inquired Lulu.

Ms. Mattie's response oozed with confident confirmation. "Sure it did. He went from five seizures a day, to one every five, or six, months, and that seemed to happen when he replaced the sugar with high fat meals."

"Where's he at now?," asked Blurry.

"The last I heard, he died in a nursing home somewhere in the Bronx," Ms. Mattie recollected.

"I was born in the Bronx, and Blur…"

Ms. Mattie interrupting Lulu mid-sentence, and abruptly told him, "Don't tell me where you're from." After which, she softened her tone, "Please don't take it the wrong way. But, the less I know the better."

In an unspoken understanding, Lulu and Blurry nodded, "*Okay,*"

"What is Taka doing?," demanded Ms. Mattie to Lulu, who could only shrug his shoulders.

"Do you mind?," Blurry asked respectfully. "I'm going to go help Taka."

"No, I don't mind … but, hurry, we need to wake Paradise up. It's not good for a person to be outside of their body for too long," Ms. Mattie nervously advised.

Blurry quickly stood, and walked out of the kitchen.

Ms. Mattie redirected her attention, "Lu, don't worry, Paradise will be fine."

With real concern, Lulu asked, "How can you be so sure?"

"She's got her 'tool', and it was made to keep her safe." .

"*Okay,*" nodded Lulu.

"Now, it's your friends I'm worried about," said Ms. Mattie.

"I've got a bad feeling. I felt it last night," Lulu commented.

"It was the neighbor's dog, wasn't it?"

"*Yes,*" nodded Lulu.

"When he stopped barking, I hoped that death had passed us by. Yet, I can't shake this feeling something is terribly wrong. Lu, you will need to brace yourself," said Ms. Mattie. She was obviously disturbed.

Stressed, Lulu asked, "What do you mean?"

"You're friends won't be coming to New Orleans with us," said Ms. Mattie soberly.

"Why not?," whispered Lulu nervously.

"Spirit didn't tell me why. But, something inside of me is saying it's time for us to pivot ..."

"What does that mean?," Lulu asked anxiously.

Between her coughing and gasping, Paradise was woozy when she quickly said, "There's something wrong with Blurry's mom."

Suddenly, and without warning, Paradise, Lulu, and Ms. Mattie heard Taka scream. The shrill of it was as though she'd witnessed a murder. Instinctively, Lulu thought something happened to his best friend. So, Lulu ran out of the kitchen first, Paradise was a close second, and Ms. Mattie limped behind them.

"Yo, Blurry you alright?," asked Lulu protectively.

"Hey Taka, what's going on?," Paradise yelled.

"*Damn! What's my curtain doing on the floor?,*" thought Ms. Mattie.

Trying to nudge an answer from Blurry, Ms. Mattie, in a low diffused tone, gently inquired, "Chocolate Soldier, are you okay?" No response. She tried a different approach, "Taka baby, please tell me what happened," she asked caringly.

Taka and Blurry were visibly shaken. Blurry attempted to speak but his words sounded like a faint mumble.

"Paradise, I can't stay here any longer. I need to go home," said Taka as she trembled in place.

"What happened?," Paradise asked Taka.

"Who's banging on the door like that?!," Lulu said aggressively.

They clearly heard three distinct and very loud knocks

"I thought I was the only one who heard that," said Paradise.

"I'm going down to check it out," said Lulu protectively.

"Don't go baby," Ms. Mattie said cautiously.

Paradise was becoming anxious. "Why not?," she asked.

Ms. Mattie told the group, "That's death knocking on my door."

Courageously, Lulu exclaimed, "I'm not scared to die."

"Paradise, I've got to get out of here," repeated Taka.

"Lulu, don't go! Come back," screamed Paradise.

Paradise yelled a few seconds too late. Lulu had removed his nine millimeter (gun) from his waistband, and was already on his way. Everyone heard Lulu scream. Something about it bolted Blurry into action. He snapped to attention and ran to Lulu's aid. As quickly as they ran down the steps, they returned to the bathroom with greater speed.

"What happened? What did you see?," asked Taka hysterically.

"The front door was opened," Blurry stated.

"What do you mean it was opened?," questioned Ms. Mattie.

Lulu nervously reiterated, "It was open."

"Well, did you close it?," inquired Paradise.

"Nah, we just ran back up here," said Blurry.

"Well, what did you see?!," screamed Taka.

"There was a rooster on Ms. Mattie's porch … it kept flapping its wings."

"It's like it wanted us to notice it. After, it was satisfied it walked backwards," said a stunned Lulu.

"And, then what?," asked Paradise.

"I don't know!"

"What do you mean you don't know?," said Paradise drilling into Lulu.

In his confused state, Blurry injected, "When Lu turned away, I saw it disappear."

Panicky, and seeking some kind of assurance, Taka pleaded, "What's going on?"

Ms. Mattie wanted to comfort Taka, but needed answers. So, she attempted to gently coax her. "When you came upstairs, you saw something … someone. Who did you see in the mirror baby? Was it my deceased husband?"

What Taka experienced was so unexpected; it left her confused and hazy. She tried to explain what she saw, "No ... I don't know. It wasn't a man ... it was a woman."

"I don't know who that could be," Ms. Mattie remarked.

Taka's description was sketchy, Lulu pushed her a little. "What do you mean you saw a woman?"

"Hey Chocolate Soldier, that rooster y'all saw wasn't real," said Paradise to Blurry light-heartedly.

"The HELL it wasn't," said Blurry defensively.

"So, what are you trying to say Paradise? That what I saw in the mirror wasn't real either?," remarked Taka in a clearly annoyed tone. "Don't get it twisted - you can trust and believe, I'm not play'n mirror, mirror, on the wall ..."

"No, I believe y'all saw what y'all say y'all saw. I'm just saying …"

"WHAT ARE YOU SAYING PARADISE?," Blurry fired off aggressively.

"YO, YOU BETTER FALL BACK BLURRY!"

"Will EVERYBODY CALM DOWN," shouted Ms. Mattie.

"Can you describe who, or what, you saw?," Lulu calmly asked Taka.

"Of course I can! What do you think, I'm an idiot? I graduated top of my class," Taka said in defense of her ability to recall.

"Whoa … don't bite my head off. I'm not coming at you," assured Lulu.

After Taka calmed herself, she provided some additional detail. "I know you're not come'n at me Lu. I'm just nervous. So, I apologize. I saw a short black woman in her late 60s, or early 70s. She had a short auburn afro, brown eye, and a birthmark above her lip ... left side."

"Don't tell me anymore," Lulu said sadly to Taka.

Uneasy about asking, yet eager to know, Paradise questioned Lulu. "Why? What's going on … do you know that woman?"

"Is anybody else hot?," Ms. Mattie asked stressfully.

Suddenly, some other worldly thing occurred. It happened so quickly, Taka wasn't certain if it was real or her over active imagination. Perplexed, she asked, "Whoa, did y'all feel that?"

"Yeah, I felt it too. Look at my arm, I've got goose-bumps," said Paradise to Taka.

In a trance-like state, Ms. Mattie soberly stated, "There's a woman here."

"What does she look like?," asked Paradise.

"Taka described her accurately."

"What does she want?," Taka asked nervously.

"I don't know yet. She has me smelling some type of fragrance. It smells like sandalwood mixed with patchouli."

"I don't know who that can be," reflected Taka to Paradise.

Paradise looked at Lulu and Blurry, but they were unable to speak. Their eyes were filled with water though they refused to cry. Ms. Mattie was welling up too. She fanned herself, wiped her cheek and continued on. "She's showing me an image of New York … she's showing me her bedroom …. there's some - someone else in the room. Oh, NO!," screamed Ms. Mattie before she collapsed.

"Taka hand me those smelling salts!," Lulu commanded. "And, Paradise pour Ms. Mattie a cup of water."

Paradise quickly rose and removed a small paper cup from the dispenser. She turned the faucet handle, filled the cup with cold water and hastily drank it. Paradise then pulled another cup down and filled it with water. Though nervous, Lulu had the presence of mind to control his angst. Rather than jolt Ms. Mattie back into consciousness, he - in his wisdom - let his hand slowly glide the capsule just below her nose. Doing so, allowed the scent of the smelling salts to waft into her nostrils in a more natural manner. After a few inhales, Ms. Mattie came through gasping and coughing. She then reached for the cup of water, and poured it onto her head.

Stunned, Lulu and Paradise asked, "What'd you do that for?"

"It's hot. Pour me another drink Paradise."

"What did you see?," inquired Taka.

"You described her accurately," Ms. Mattie told Taka.

"Thank you baby," Ms. Mattie said to Paradise, as she took the cup. She drank the water slowly, inhaled deeply, and said, "Lu, will you please get Bernard a chair."

In an agitated tone, Blurry aggressively asserted himself. "Yo, I'm good Son! I DON'T NEED NO DAMN CHAIR."

"*I'm-a-eat that 'cus you're grieving,*" nodded Lulu to Blurry.

Checking his overreaction, Blurry apologized, "My bad Lu."

"What did my mom say Ms. Mattie? I can take it," Blurry asked calmly.

Paradise and Taka were shocked at what they were hearing. Lulu was caught off-guard. He felt Blurry's pain. Mom-Jackson had been a mother to him too. And, Ms.

Mattie who had been the unsolicited messenger was not done.

Ms. Mattie exhaled slowly, wiped her mouth deliberately, and cautiously proceeded, "Before I collapsed, she said, "Agent Bruno did it"."

"Who's Agent Bruno?," Lulu asked Blurry.

"I don't know. But, whoever he is, he's a dead man," Blurry assured Ms. Mattie and Lulu.

"Did she say anything else Ms. Mattie?," asked Paradise.

"Stay out of New York. It's a trap…"

Blurry was going deep in the zone. Gearing up to handle his business, he was straight-laced, and straight-faced.

"Yo Lu, I'm-a-need you to run them keys."

In support and respect, Lulu nodded, "*I understand.*" He reached into his pocket, removed his car keys and tossed them to Blurry.

Paradise was disturbed. She flared her nostrils, took a deep breath, and in a caring, but gingered tone, said, "Didn't you hear what your mom said? She said STAY OUT OF NEW YORK! … and she also said IT'S A TRAP!! And, what about your warrant?"

Blurry was too hot to handle. Like most people when they see 'red', he was running on emotions and completely ignored the real point Paradise was making. He shouted, "Fuck-a-Warrant! I AIN'T going back to Minnesota."

In an almost mother-like manner, Ms. Mattie pleaded, "Don't go son. They're trying to smoke you out."

"I'm going with you Bernard," Taka announced. Her use of his formal name subconsciously signaled that there would be no discussion, and no argument on the issue.

Lulu and Blurry removed their guns from their waistbands, and immediately turned toward the opened bathroom door. What drew their attention was someone saying, "Ain't nobody go'n nowhere!"

Startled, Paradise screamed.

"Y'all put those guns away," said Ms. Mattie authoritatively.

"You alright Aunt Mattie?," asked O.G.

"I'm fine Junior."

Talking to Lulu, O.G. said, "Put it down partner." The looks on Lulu's and Blurry's face said, "*LOWER YOUR GUN!*" Being out-manned, and therefore out-gunned, O.G. wisely complied with their unspoken words and holstered his gun. When Blurry and Lulu felt comfortable, they also holstered their guns. As discretely as she'd taken it out, Taka quietly retracted the blade of her razor sharp box cutter, which she instinctively pulled out in readiness. Paradise forcefully exhaled, releasing a good bit of tension.

Ms. Mattie was her usual cool-as-a-cucumber self. She matter-of-factly stated, "Junior, you're late." Followed by the nonchalant introduction, "Paradise, meet your cousin."

15
FAMILY
Harlem, New York

Lulu gave Blurry two unopened burner phones from his suitcase. Then, Ms. Mattie forced O.G. to give Blurry his smartphone number. O.G. complied, when Lulu gave him one hundred dollars. Lulu also removed a stack of small bills from his suitcase. Taka estimated Blurry received a little over fifteen hundred dollars.

"Do you need more?," Lulu asked Blurry.

"Nah, I'm good."

"Be careful Brother …"

"Yeah, you too," Lulu said with unmistakable sadness to Blurry.

O.G.'s facial expression couldn't hide the question he was itching to ask. It was twisted with curiosity and confusion.

Unable to contain himself, he blurted out, "What ... are y'all GAY?"

Ignorance was the one thing nobody needed to deal with … especially Blurry, given recent circumstances. That's why everyone was surprised the only response O.G. got from Blurry were his flared nostrils. Even Lulu didn't feed into it, choosing instead to turn a deaf ear to the comment. It was important that they stay focused, and in the zone.

The ladies, however, were a different story. They didn't have to go deep, like Lulu and Blurry. They were free to run interference.

Not knowing what would make him ask such a thing, Taka - between anger and disgust - questioned O.G. "What's wrong with you?"

Paradise wasn't so nice. She tore into O.G. "They ain't gay! He just lost his mother, STUPID!"

"Oh my bad, I just lost my grandpop, and my uncle within the same week," O.G. informed his uncaring listeners.

"Be careful Paradise,"

"You too," said Paradise thoughtfully to Taka.

Paradise's hope for Taka centered on her safety and protection, she made her instruction to Blurry simple,

"You take care of her."

Blurry responded to Paradise with a nod of mutual regard, "*You take care of my dude.*"

Paradise smiled a quiet smile, and nodded, "*We'll take care of each other.*"

"*Thank you again Ms. Mattie,*" nodded Blurry.

"Bye Ms. Mattie," said Taka sadly.

Ms. Mattie wished Taka farewell, her voice resonated with the sincerity her heart held for them. "Bye baby, I'll be praying for y'all. Y'all take care, you hear?"

Blurry and Taka walked out.

Despite the commotion he created, in the midst of all the well wishes being given, O.G. genuinely felt slighted. Not wanting to be left out, he inquired, "A brother don't get no love?"

"You came in crooked," snarled Paradise.

O.G. compounded his poor standing by hurling out another off-handed comment. With a wiley smirk, O.G. said, "Aunt Mattie, you sure she's my cousin? 'Cus she's fine as Hell!"

"*If, you say another word, I'm a shoot you in your mother-F'n face,*" said the murderous look in Lulu's eyes.

O.G. was a reformed gangbanger. So, he wasn't afraid of gun play. But, he wasn't ready to die that day either. He was very familiar with Lulu's look, what it meant, and how viable the threat was. He acknowledged his understanding, and adjusted himself accordingly.

The initials 'O.G.' stood for 'original gangster'. Ms. Mattie's great nephew lived in the Soundview section of the Bronx, in New York. He had come to St. Louis to attend his uncle's memorial service. O.G. had multiple tattoos on his light-skinned body, he appeared to be in his early 50s - but, looked sixty - and, he had a salt and pepper beard that complemented his curly gray hair. He stood five feet, ten inches tall, and with the exception of his beer belly, appeared fit.

"Hey, Aunt Mattie, I rented an eight seater minivan. After, I drop y'all off in New Orleans, my wife and I are flying back to New York."

"Why's the back door open?," Ms. Mattie asked O.G.

"I don't know. When I arrived, I couldn't open the front door. The harder I tried, the harder it was to open. So, Maria leaned out the window and hollered to go around to the back," O.G. explained.

"Where's Maria now?," asked Ms. Mattie with concern.

"She's in the van with the baby."

"Is that my gun?," questioned Ms. Mattie.

"When I saw the back door open, I went in your freezer and found it under the frozen peas,"

Ms. Mattie was relieved. She told Paradise, "I thought that was my gun."

"Where's the clip?,"

"I got frustrated … I couldn't find it!"

"The bullets are in the box of rice,"

O.G. acknowledged, "That's right."

Ms. Mattie confessed, "It's a good thing you didn't find that clip. 'Cus this could have gone the wrong way."

"*I agree,*" nodded O.G.

Looking toward Paradise, O.G. commented, "So, you're my cousin."

The tone of Paradise's voice was far more expressive than the four words she spoke. "I don't know you," she curtly retorted, evidently unimpressed with the possibility that she and O.G. could have a familial bond.

"I don't know you either," O.G. confirmed. "But, my aunt says we're kin," he said to Paradise happily.

"As far as I know, I ain't got no family! … I'm the last of my kind," said Paradise with a straight face, and stern voice.

O.G. was becoming confused. "I don't know what that means. Aunt Mattie said you and I are cousins."

"You ain't my DAMN cousin!," Paradise said forcefully, as though using considerable vocal vigor would change their bloodline connection.

"Enough Paradise!," Ms. Mattie said. "Daniel is your cousin … and, he's my great nephew." Baffled at Paradise's reaction, Ms. Mattie went on to say, "And, honestly, I'm surprise you haven't figured it out."

"Let me touch your hand," suggested Paradise.

"That's alright. There's no need for all of that. Your cousin is Tubbee Jones' grandson," Ms. Mattie informed Paradise.

Paradise was confused and frazzled. "Who?," she asked. "I don't know any Too-Bee Jones."

O.G. joined in. "I'm Michael's oldest son," he told Paradise enthusiastically.

"Who? I don't know no damn Michael! Weren't you listening? Didn't you hear me say, I am the last of my kind?"

"What are you - a werewolf?," asked O.G. seriously.

"I ain't NO DAMN Werewolf! I'm a human being just like you," Paradise stated angrily.

"Why are you cursing so much?," O.G. asked. "All I know is our grandfather - Tubbee Jones - had four children. He had two girls, Donna and Karen … she was the youngest. And, my Pop - Michael - he's the middle child, Grand Pop fathered them with my grandmother, Betty Jones. Now, according to my Pops, our Grand Pop Tubbee had another daughter, named Nina. She lived with her mother, Isabella Montoyier, in New Orleans. Apparently, you're my Aunt Nina's only child, and your first name is also Isabella."

"Well, they call me 'Paradise'! And, my mother and grandmother are dead …"

"I'm sorry to hear that. From what my Pops said, you're grandmother was a palm reader…"

"She wasn't NO DAMN palm reader," emoted Paradise angrily.

O.G. was completely bewildered. He expected some confusion and alarm. However, he was unable to fathom where Paradise's negativity, resistance, and hostility was coming from. Her responses and reactions were beyond any ignorant, and/or off-handed comment he made earlier. Something wasn't right.

Being a reformed gangbanger had its perks. For instance, O.G. knew when to take things personally … If, he had taken everything to heart, he'd be dead. So, he let Paradise get what she was feeling off her chest, without letting it bother him (too much). As gentle as possible, O.G. softly asked,

"Why are you so upset?"

Paradise barked back, "WHAT?!"

"You know you got anger issues?," O.G. said light-heartedly.

Paradise was rattled. Perhaps it had been too much, too soon. At any rate, she had become belligerent. "I AIN'T GOT NO DAMN ANGER ISSUES," Paradise stated explosively. There was no more talking to be done on that subject.

Having had all she was going to tolerate, Ms. Mattie did some barking of her own. You could tell she was 'done', and that she meant business, because she referred to O.G. by his birth name. "Daniel Emory Jones, it's time to go."

Paradise became angry because she never knew her maternal grandfather. Nina and Madame Montoyier rarely spoke of him. He was rarely mentioned because he abandoned them. So, the historic rundown her cousin Daniel provided caught Paradise by surprise.

For all of the grandness that rightfully became associated with Madame Montoyier, in 1963, things were simpler. That's the year Paradise's paternal grandfather, Tubbee Jones, met Isabella Montoyier in New Orleans. She worked as a part-time barmaid in one of the area's local, but popular juke joints. Tubbee, was a veteran, having been honorably discharged after serving in the Korean War. He enjoyed the atmosphere and the variety the juke joint provided. That smoky, rowdy hang out offered patrons a bar, gambling, live Blues music, and an ample area for dancing. It offered Tubbee one thing more: Isabella. He spent many nights there, enjoying her company, drinking moonshine, laughing, and singing the blues. Over time, what Tubbee and Isabella shared deepened into a romantic relationship. And, as 'Fate' would have it, one thing led to another and Isabella became pregnant. Four weeks into her pregnancy, Tubbee took her to meet his favorite aunt (Mattie) and uncle. They lived in Shreveport, Louisiana.

Tubbee and Isabella drove from New Orleans to Shreveport, in less than five hours. After making the proper introductions to his relatives, Tubbee kissed Isabella on her forehead and walked out. Before abandoning her in Shreveport, Tubbee truthfully sniffled, "Don't get me wrong uncle, I loves Isabella. But, I'm going back to New York, because my wife and kids need me."

Inside Ms. Mattie's St. Louis home, her great nephew, Daniel, grabbed her suitcase. Lulu grabbed his suitcases too, and stepped onto the front porch first. Paradise followed behind him. Ms. Mattie locked the front and back doors, and set the house alarm. After helping Daniel load the luggage into the silver minivan, Lulu opened the door so that Ms. Mattie and Paradise could enter the vehicle and get themselves situated. Before Lulu had a chance to step into the minivan, Daniel caught his attention with a quietly spoken request, "Yo, can I holler at you for a minute?"

"*Yeah, what?*." nodded Lulu.

"You and I aren't going to have any problems are we?," questioned Daniel sincerely.

Lulu considered answering Daniel, but the Spirit of Unforgiveness was present. It intervened, acting completely outside of Lulu's original intention, reminding him of the offenses and trespasses Daniel committed earlier that day. The spirit said, "*Fuck him Lu! You're not obligated to respond. Plus, he tried to play you and Blurry with that Gay joke. So, fuck him… And you need to check him for talking to Paradise like that.*"

From the minivan, Ms. Mattie was calling out, "Daniel, are y'all coming?"

"*Okay, I see what this is,*" nodded Daniel to Lulu.

Lulu got in the van, closed the door, and never acknowledged Daniel. Daniel got behind the steering wheel, closed his door, and poked his bottom lip out.

"You okay babe?," said Daniel's Puerto Rican wife, Maria.

"'*Yes'and 'No' … but, I'll be alright,*" nodded Daniel to Maria.

"The GPS said we should take I-55 South to New Orleans …"

Without realizing it, Daniel uncharacteristically snapped at Maria. "How long will that take?!" Thinking it was something she'd done, Maria's eyes filled with water. When she started crying, Daniel paused and sincerely said, "Honey, I apologize. I didn't mean that."

"Okay," Maria said. "If, there isn't any traffic, the GPS said we should be there in 9 ½ hours. And, you know I'm extra sensitive right now. You heard what the doctor said before we left …"

"Yes, I know Maria. I was there. He said your hormones were out of whack and …"

"Are you calling me 'whack'? … or, are you calling me 'fat'? … which is it Daniel? Why are you being so mean to me?," Maria asked tearfully.

Daniel rubbed his temples, started the van, and drove slowly. He remained quiet because he didn't want to make matters worse. His wife had a hormone imbalance caused by her pregnancy. As they traveled toward New Orleans, she transitioned from 35 to 36 weeks gestation. Maria and Daniel had flown into St. Louis against the airline's policy regarding air travel for pregnant women. Maria was so close to the 40 week term, it looked like her baby might arrive at any time.

For visual comparison only: Maria looked like a busted version of Sofía Vergara, the Colombian-American actress from the popular American TV Show, Modern Family.

In a voice meant to console, Lulu said, "Yo, Daniel."

"*Oh, you're talking to me now?,*" thought Daniel.

"Yeah," Daniel responded cautiously.

"If you need any help driving, let me know."

Daniel appreciated the gesture, and replied, "Okay, thanks."

As men, Daniel and Lulu understood that 'okay, thanks' was code, and it meant, 'Yo brother, you see what I'm dealing with … thanks for your support and understanding.'

"Su nombre es María derecha?," Lulu said to Maria in Spanish.

"Sí, ¿cuál es tu nombre?," Maria replied.

"Mi nombre es Luis y este Paraíso," said Lulu to Maria.

"Yes, Paradise and I have met. And you know I speak English right?," Maria told Lulu.

"Si ... I mean yes," said Lulu.

"Hey," said Lulu to Paradise, as she punched him in the arm. Paradise jealously whispered, "Paraiso? Since, when you been introducing yourself as Luis?"

Ms. Mattie shook her head.

Playfully, Lulu silently mouthed, "Well, that is my name," to Paradise.

"You know what I mean?!," mouthed Paradise right back to Lulu. Only, she was serious.

"I see we're not the only couple with problems," said Maria to Paradise.

"Oh, we're not a couple," Lulu and Paradise said in unison.

Maria and Daniel simultaneously chuckled and remarked, "Who are you kidding?"

Paradise and Lulu smiled. Ms. Mattie looked at them and mouthed, "Don't forget rule Number Three."

Rule Number Three, or Spiritualist Rule No. 3, stated: Never have sex with your clients. Violators of that cosmic rule encountered a supernatural 'spanking', sanctioned by God. Paradise and Lulu grimaced, nodded in agreement, and shared the same singular thought: "*I can't wait until this is over.*"

"Daniel said we were driving his aunt and four of her friends to New Orleans for a knitting, or cupcake convention," Maria said questioning Paradise.

Daniel attempted to correct her. "I said, "quilting"."

"Cupcakes, knitting, or quilting … it's all the same. I thought your aunt's friends were going to be old."

"So did I," whispered Daniel to Maria.

"I beg your pardon," Ms. Mattie told Daniel and Maria.

Daniel and Maria flinched.

Ms. Mattie turned to Paradise, inhaled deeply and softly said, "I have to tell you something."

"What is it?," asked Paradise curiously.

"I'm worried about your friend," Ms. Mattie advised.

Seeking clarity, Paradise started at the top of her list. "Who, Lu?," she nervously asked.

"What's going on?," Lulu mouthed to Paradise.

"I don't know," she mouthed back.

"Are you paying attention Paradise?," whispered Ms. Mattie.

Bracing herself, Paradise muttered, "Bad news first."

"Okay, if anything happens to me, remember this - you've got a soldier for life. I'll be on the other side waiting for your instructions."

"I don't like that kind of talk Ms. Mattie," Paradise said in a hushed tone.

"Now, here's the bad news - Bernard's mother ..."

Maria was beginning to panic. Her voice bespoke her stress and her concern, "Da-Da-Daniel ... oh, god ... som-something's wrong."

With a fear and apprehension unlike anything he'd experienced even during the worst of his gangbanging days, Daniel cautiously asked, "What's wrong?"

16
ACTIVE SHOOTER
Big Prairie Township, Missouri

With no major traffic issues to impede his driving, Daniel was able to maintain his speed, and to make good of the time. They were in Big Prairie Township, Missouri. That 98% Caucasian town was near the New Madrid fault line, a seismic region that sits between St. Louis, Missouri, and Memphis, Tennessee.

Good thing too. Maria's water broke. That meant their baby entered the birth canal, and revealed her hairy crown. O.G. wondered if his unborn child was psychic, or just a considerate soul. Thanks to Spirit of Serendipity along with Ms. Mattie's help, their newborn daughter had taken her first breath, a half mile from the nearest medical center.

Naturally, Daniel panicked - though the situation required that he remain composed. As he pulled up to the facility's emergency room, Lulu instinctively jumped out to provide assistance and support. He and Paradise retrieved the medical staff. Two emergency room attendants came to the vehicle to aid Maria. When they arrived, they found the newborn baby coddled in Daniel's hands. Both he and his newborn baby girl were covered in her afterbirth.

Ms. Mattie, Paradise, and Lulu were - in equal parts - happy, and sad. They were happy because Maria and Daniel were celebrating the birth of their first child. They were sad because the birth had caused a delay in their timeline they could not avoid.

They needed to be in New Orleans for a variety of extremely important reasons. In Paradise's case, she needed to find Avi Weinberg. She wanted paybacks for his contribution in ruining her life. Lulu's purpose was to keep Paradise safe. If Paradise sincerely suggested that they go to the moon, Lulu would gladly find a way to get her there.

Neither Lulu, nor Paradise had any idea what Ms. Mattie and the Council of Elders for the 21st of June had planned. Their intentions were to coronate Paradise as the new leader of their mystical order. However, they understood otherworldly forces were in play, and they were determined to prevent that ceremony from happening.

As the medical staff helped Maria onto the gurney, Ms. Mattie approached the couple and caringly said, "Daniel and Maria, congratulations. Have you all thought of a name?"

"We sure did, and thank you," Daniel told his great aunt.

Speaking directly to Ms. Mattie, the paramedics gave the following instruction for her safety, "Ma'am will you please step back." Ms. Mattie complied. Paradise followed suit.

Lulu said, "Yo, O.G."

"*What-up*?," nodded Daniel in acknowledgement.

"Congratulations," said Lulu sincerely and with a smile.

"Thanks man!," Daniel said beaming.

As they spoke, the two shook hands, and did that half-hug thing (that men do).

Meanwhile, Ms. Mattie asked, "Paradise, can you walk me to the lady's room?"

"Sure I can," said Paradise helpfully.

Before tending to his newest patients, the emergency room doctor made an announcement. "You folks can wait in the visiting area until we get the baby and this hispanic woman settled in."

Sensing the intent of the physician's offensive slight, Daniel responded immediately, and proudly. "This woman is my wife. Her name is Maria Lopez-Jones, and that's our beautiful baby girl."

The attendant interrupted with indifference, to coldly question, "Do you have health insurance, or Obamacare?"

Daniel's nostrils flared. "I have insurance!," he answered angrily. "I work for Con-Ed … I mean Consolidated Edison … an energy company out of New York."

"Very well," the doctor said dryly. "Go to the nurses' station to fill out the appropriate paperwork." Meanwhile, the medical team wheeled Maria into the hospital slowly.

Lulu was in his mode. In short order, he surveilled the parking lot … quickly studied the hospital's layout for all of the exits … and, made note of the facility's hidden cameras, as well as identified its blind spots. When Lulu entered the waiting area, he sat with his back against the wall. As he waited for Paradise and Ms. Mattie to return, he thought,

"*I hope Blurry and Taka are okay.*"

As Paradise accompanied Ms. Mattie to the bathroom, Daniel approached Lulu and said, "Yo, my man, security told me to move the van. Would you mind moving it for me?"

"*Sure, I'll move it,*" nodded Lulu to Daniel.

"Thanks man, I left the keys in the ignition."

"*No problem,*" Lulu gestured.

Daniel returned to the nurses' station, while Lulu returned to the van.

In a curious tone, Ms. Mattie asked, "Does this mean anything to you?" Paradise was curious too. "Does what mean anything to me?," questioned Paradise.

At the time, they were the only women in the ladies' room. Paradise thought she had escorted Ms. Mattie there because she needed to wash her hands. So, she was understandably confused when Ms. Mattie activated the automatic hand dryer. In actuality, Ms. Mattie needed to talk to Paradise in private, and figured - under the circumstances - the bathroom had been their only option. The sound the hand dryer generated offered another layer to ensure their conversation would not be overheard.

Ms. Mattie whispered, "Bernard's mother showed me some confusing items."

"Like what?," whispered Paradise.

"She showed me a Dixie flag, a desk calendar turned to May 4th, and the initials 'JC' circled in red. Do any of those items mean anything to you?"

"Honestly, at the moment, they don't."

"She was murdered ... and, it was a revenge killing," Ms. Mattie mouthed stressfully.

"A revenge killing …," Paradise murmured.

"I saw her body and it was contorted. I also saw the hangman …"

Worried, Paradise asked, "Strange fruit hangman, or Tarot card hangman?"

"Tarot," Ms. Mattie said sadly.

"Either way, Blurry and Lulu are going to lose it," said Paradise nervously.

"Well, don't tell him until we get to New Orleans," Ms. Mattie suggested protectively.

"*Okay,*" nodded Paradise reluctantly.

Strange fruit referred to black people who had nooses tied around their necks. They were lynched, castrated, and left hanging from trees by proud white folks.

The Hanged Man was the twelfth trump, or major arcana card in the traditional deck of tarot cards. In the traditional deck, the tarot is represented by 78 playing cards. The cards are used for divination purposes, by fortune tellers seeking knowledge of either the future, or of unknown events, by supernatural means. The upside down Hanged Man represents a sacrifice, a shameful traitor, or martyrdom. It also means that the person seeking answers is at a crossroads in life. The Italians call the Hanged Man, "Pittura Infamante," (pronounced: *pit-tu-ra im-fa-mon-te*).

"Shhhhhhhh," said Ms. Mattie protectively.

"*I didn't say anything,*" squinted, Paradise.

Silently, Ms. Mattie motioned to Paradise. She touched her ear with her dried blood stained finger tip, signalling that

Paradise needed to attune her hearing, and listen. When she did, Paradise heard what Ms. Mattie heard. Ms. Mattie quietly leaned against the bathroom door, and then promptly turned to Paradise. Her mind was focused, but her heart was racing. Under the force of urgency, she aggressively attempted to convey her grave message. "No matter what happens, go to New Orleans. Don't stop for me, or anyone else! DO YOU HEAR ME?!," Ms. Mattie mouthed. Paradise heard her and clearly understood that there was an immediate danger to be dealt with, though she didn't comprehend the exact nature of the danger. What she failed to grasp was just how dire their situation had become, and what the ramifications would be if she failed to adhere to Ms. Mattie's directive.

"I'm not trying to hear that! 'Cus you're coming to New Orleans with me and Lulu," mouthed Paradise reassuringly.

"Take your belt off," mouthed Ms. Mattie commandingly.

"What? Why?"

"Just do it! Hurry up!"

Paradise complied.

"Wrap your belt around the door hinge. Stick the tip of the belt through the buckle and tighten it," whispered Ms. Mattie forcefully.

Paradise had no idea what she was referring to. Perplexed, she mouthed, "What hinge?"

"Damn! Nevermind … the hinge is on the outside of the door." Ms. Mattie realized her initial plan was not going to work, because the door opened outwardly into the corridor. Therefore, its hinges were on the outside of the door. Ms. Mattie never stalled. "Okay, kick that wooden wedge over here," she whispered authoritatively.

"What?," Paradise mouthed.

"Just Do It!," grimaced Ms. Mattie.

Paradise kicked the wooden door wedge to Ms. Mattie, who used her foot to jam it solidly under the bottom of the bathroom door. Paradise put her leather belt back on. Then, they heard commotion inside the hospital. The sounds of people running, crying, and screaming hysterically: They also heard the rapid fire of an automatic weapon. Ms. Mattie and Paradise flinched. They knew there was an active shooter inside the building, and that he was shooting people as he walked through the halls.

Paradise vehemently flagged her hands motioning to Ms. Mattie. "Get away from the door … get away from the door!!," she aggressively mouthed.

Before Ms. Mattie could respond, the shooter had unloaded a round of ammunition through the bathroom door. The first bullet severed Ms. Mattie's spine, the second punctured her lung, and the third bullet caused Paradise to scream. When the shooter heard Paradise scream, he attempted to kick down the bathroom door. She ran into the last stall, locked the door, stood on the toilet, and crouched. Unable to gain access after kicking the door several times, the shooter got frustrated and walked away.

Ms. Mattie's wooden wedge prevented the bathroom door from opening. The shooter directed his frustration at two unarmed security guards, hiding under the Patient Advocate's desk. After he shot them, he exited the room and randomly shot another person. Paradise searched the bathroom for a window, so she could escape. But, that bathroom didn't have any windows.

"Why are you doing this?," wailed a victim in the hallway.

"BECAUSE I CAN!!!," screamed the shooter.

Paradise cringed when she heard that specific gun shot.

The active shooter appeared to be in his mid-30s. He had blonde hair, blue eyes, and a chipped front tooth. He wore army boots, camouflage pants, and a black T-Shirt with white letters that said, 'Build the Wall!' The shirt's statement was the rumored brain-child of an infamous president. The country of Mexico had been told to build an unrealistic wall along the border of its country and the United States. The wall was supposed to stop Mexican citizens from entering the United States illegally.

Lulu had planned to park near the front entrance of the hospital, but, the parking lot was nearly full. So, he reluctantly parked in the last space at the back of the lot. He ran toward the hospital when he saw large numbers of horrified people running out of the facility.

"What's happening?!," yelled Lulu to an unknown white man.

The young stranger along with his chubby cougar wife yelled, "There's an active shooter inside the hospital!"

Lulu considered running back to the van to get his gun. But, his higher mind told him to run inside the building. He complied with the command, located a fire extinguisher and removed it from the wall. Lulu held that fire extinguisher like a machine gun, and ran toward the gunfire. He paused momentarily, when he realized he was surrounded by blood, several dead bodies, and numerous wounded.

When Lulu reached the ladies' room, he peered through the bullet holes and nervously whispered, "June Spade. June Spade."

"Lulu, is that you?," murmured Paradise.

"Yes, it's me … are you okay? It's safe for now. You and Ms. Mattie can come out," he assured her.

"I can't," said Paradise sadly.

"Why not? And, why's the door stuck?," questioned Lulu.

Lulu looked through the other bullet hole again, and asked, "What the hell? Paradise, are you alright?"

"I'm fine. But, I think Ms. Mattie's dead."

"I can see that," Lulu confirmed, as he then instructed Paradise to, "Pull Ms. Mattie away from the door."

"Why?," Paradise asked stressfully.

"We can't stay here. Hurry before he comes back," said Lulu authoritatively.

Paradise wanted to panic. But, she wasn't allowed. "*No matter what happens never panic,*" echoed Madame Montoyier's voice inside her head.

Paradise dragged Ms. Mattie's bloodied and lifeless body away from the door. She removed the wooden wedge with her foot, took a deep breath, and walked out. Paradise and Lulu listened, and timed the gun shots before they ran. Lulu looked at Paradise. She was barely audible as she whispered, "Ut oh, I think he's coming back."

"That's an AR-15," mouthed Lulu to Paradise.

"What?"

In a hushed tone, Lulu informed Paradise, "There's more than one shooter. Listen. That's the sound of a glock, and that other sound is an AK-47."

Fear seized Paradise, who was grappling to understand and deal with her current reality. "Are you telling me there's more than one shooter?," she questioned.

"Keep your voice down. There's at least three."

"We need to find Daniel and Maria," whispered Paradise.

"What, are you crazy? We need to find another way out of here!," Lulu mouthed to Paradise.

As they cautiously walked through the dead and wounded, Paradise stopped abruptly.

Lulu squinted his eyes at her inquiring, "*What are you stopping for? Will you please come on?*"

"*I'm coming … just hold up a second,*" Paradise squinted back.

Paradise studied the hospital map on the wall. She made a mental note of the nearest exit, the baby floor, and closest stairwell. Lulu inhaled deeply, shook his head, and stepped in front of Paradise to enter the stairwell first.

When Lulu opened the stairwell door, he was greeted by one of the active shooters, who stepped out yelling, "Go back to Africa!" Paradise screamed. Lulu removed the safety pin from the fire extinguisher, and squeezed the trigger. The shooter fired a shot. And, Paradise screamed again. The fire retardant disoriented the shooter, allowing Lulu to move in for the kill. Following the chemical discharge, Lulu continued to use the extinguisher as a weapon. With it, he broke the shooter's wrist. The shooter screamed. Lulu tossed the fire extinguisher to Paradise. She caught it like a seasoned catcher in an egg toss championship. Lulu grabbed the gunman's AR-15 assault rifle before it hit the floor. The shooter was resourceful enough to remove the Rambo knife from his belt clip. Lulu stiffened his lips, flared his nostrils, and smoothly squeezed the trigger. With three shots to his chest, the active shooter was rendered 'inactive'. He was a thirty-four year old white male, with dark hair, pale skin, and an acne-scared face.

Paradise read the words on his blood stained hoodie before she stepped around him. It read, 'Build the Wall! OTM'.

"What's OTM?," mouthed Paradise.

"Stay close … it means 'Other Than Mexican'," mouthed Lulu.

Paradise followed Lulu up the stairs. When they reached the baby floor, Lulu peaked through the door and protectively said, "Stay back."

"Why?," whispered Paradise.

Lulu's eyes filled with water. But, he refused to cry. Paradise felt how he looked and she boldly said, "Move, let me see."

Paradise wasn't prepared for what she had requested. Daniel and Maria were among the dead. They, along with the nursing staff, had been shot in the back. The attendant that escorted Maria to the maternity ward had taken Maria's newborn to a place of safety. Their baby, along with the other infants had been wheeled to a more secured room.

Paradise sobbed, but without whimpering any sound. Lulu knelt beside Daniel and Maria to check for a pulse.

He touched their carotid arteries, shook his head, and sadly confirmed, "Their dead."

"You make another move and you're dead!," screamed the Big Prairie Township's squad leader.

The Big Prairie Township SWAT Team entered the hospital first. Paradise held her hands high, Lulu didn't move, and the squad leader yelled, "Drop the weapon!"

"Don't shoot. I'm dropping the weapon," said Lulu calmly.

"SLOWLY!," shouted the Squad Leader.

The red lights of several tactical laser were pointed at Lulu's chest. Wisely, he did exactly as he was told, laying the gun slowly, and slowly putting up his opened hands. The squad leader ordered, "Take him!"

17
THREE LETTERS
Nashville, Tennessee

Lulu was taken into custody by the Big Prairie Township SWAT Team. The local Federal Bureau of Investigation (FBI) focused their attention on him, and a few other witnesses. The Department of Homeland Security (DHS) was involved too. DHS had been notified because the captured shooter claimed he was part of the Islamic State of Iraq and Syria (ISIS). That rumored terrorist organization received their infamous claim-to-fame from their gruesome beheading videos. Those two three-lettered groups quickly discovered the 36 year old Caucasian shooter wasn't affiliated with ISIS at all. He, along with his deceased buddies, had been unemployed 'gamers'. Gamers are individuals who participate in role playing computerized zombie shooting games.

The FBI became involved because a mass shooting had occurred at the Missouri Medical Center, which fell into its scope of accountability. The FBI classifies a mass shooting as a single event wherein four or more murders occur.

The Big Prairie Township SWAT Team killed the active shooter responsible for the death of Ms. Mattie. Although Lulu had originally been the suspected third shooter, the security camera in the medical center's stairwell proved he was not. Additionally, it clearly showed that Lulu acted in self-defense when he killed the third shooter. Still, DHS refused to let Lulu go because his name appeared on the government's Federal Detain List.

Virginia Gregory, the National Director of Intelligence had outstanding federal warrants issued for Lulu, Taka, Blurry, and Paradise. They were wanted in connection to those five dead Germans in New Ulm, Minnesota's Flandrau State Park. DHS acquired knowledge of Lulu after the FBI ran a trace on his International Bounty Hunters license. The agency's computer screen stated: Federal Warrant, detain immediately.

The federal agents immediately removed Lulu from the other federal witnesses. Lulu didn't resist when they aggressively tightened the plastic cable tie around his wrist.

He quickly realized that he had been the 'most wanted' movie star in a real life who-done-it drama.

Agents were dispatched to collect Lulu. Though the damage done to Lulu's ear compromised his hearing, he had a keen sense of smell. He smelled the fear or stress sweat of an approaching SWAT team member, before they breached the baby ward.

Two agents from DHS placed a black hood over Lulu's head, before chaining him to the metal bench inside their windowless van. Pursuant to the USA Freedom Act of 2015, Lulu was transported from Big Prairie Township, Missouri, to an off-shore black site, located in some unknown locale.

The USA Freedom Act of June 2015, helped restore an expired provision of the USA Patriot Act. That act allowed the United States Government to detain its citizens without a warrant. The signers of that particular bill said, "This bill will keep Americans safe by providing the government with the necessary tools for intercepting and obstructing terrorism."

Lulu wasn't a terrorist. Neither was Paradise, Taka, or Blurry. But, the government needed them for questioning, and National Director Gregory wanted Paradise's supernatural help.

Rather than give in to fear, or panic, Lulu utilized the time to focus on mentally preparing himself to face unknown challenges, make split-second decisions, and to exploit any available opportunity. His fine-tuned skills of observation, judgment, timing, and experience were the resources he drew from. The result is that he identified a means to help Paradise escape. She did NOT want to leave Lulu, but he demanded she leave, shouting, "GO!"

"What, are you high?!," inquired the squad leader of Lulu.

"No sir," said Lulu to the squad leader.

"Then, who the hell you talking too?," said the angry squad leader to Lulu, who remained calm.

When he said, "Who the hell you talking too?," Paradise realized that while Lulu could see her, the SWAT Team could not. That's when they realized her 'tool' had kicked in. The supernatural forces of that talisman caused Paradise to become invisible. Using his eyes, Lulu motioned for Paradise to look under Daniel's dead body. He lied on top of his wife's lifeless body. Lulu hid the keys to the van beneath their dead bodies. Without Paradise's knowledge, Lulu stuck the van keys under Maria's neck. He made the conscious decision to do so when he checked for her and Daniel's pulse.

Lulu figured Ms. Mattie had given Paradise her talisman, and that her 'supernatural good luck charm' had been divinely infused for her protection.

Paradise also figured that her talisman allowed her to remain unnoticed. But, she hid behind Maria's gurney anyway … she hid just in case the illusion of her invisibility wore off.

In fact, she quickly realized her talisman performed better than Madame Montoyier reported. As Paradise watched Lulu being carted away, she remembered what Dixie May said, "When your Grandmother was alive, you, and Nina were untouchable. We sent countless agents to recruit you. But, they were always side-tracked, confused, or lost. You and Nina were invisible. It was like God himself ordained your divine hedge of protection…"

Paradise, along with the other horrified hostages, walked out of the medical center with their hands held high. They adhered to that police policy to prevent getting shot. During the exodus, a hysterical man attracted unwanted police and grief counseling attention. As the paramedics attended to the wounded, Paradise also attracted unwanted police attention as she searched the parking lot.

"Are you okay ma'am?," questioned a helpful Big Prairie Township policeman.

"Huh? Oh yes, I'm fine. No, I'm a little shaken …"

"Well, the grief counseling tent is the other way," suggested the helpful officer.

"Yes, I know. I just left there. But, I'm trying to find my co-worker. We got separated in all of the confusion," lied Paradise with a straight face.

"What's his name ma'am?," asked the probing policeman.

With her quick wit, Paradise said, "Oh, I see her."

"Debra!," yelled Paradise to a stranger in the parking lot.

Pointing to a cluster of people moving through the parking lot, Paradise said, "There she goes … thank you officer."

"I'm glad you found your co-worker. Would you like me to walk over with you," offered the unrelenting policeman.

"I can make it. But thanks for asking."

The officer's partner called out, "Yo Jim, can I get a little help over here?," Jim and Paradise parted ways.

An unknown woman emerged from the cluster of people Paradise had pointed to during her charade with the police officer. The woman approached Paradise and frantically said, "You found my husband?!"

Paradise had no idea why she had been approached. Perplexed, she communicated her confusion with, "Huh."

"You called my name. You yelled, "Debra"."

Pulled back into the masquerade she'd created, Paradise acted as though she was surprised. "Oh whoa, isn't that a coincidence? You and my co-worker have the same name."

"I didn't see anyone behind me," said Debra the skeptic.

"Your back was turned. We were passing through Big Prairie. I had a bad case of diarrhea, so, we stopped here. Then, we got caught up in all this craziness and …"

Debra's skepticism gave way to her stress. "And, you haven't seen my husband? His name is Daniel," she said to Paradise.

"*No, I haven't,*" nodded Paradise compassionately.

"Then, what good are you?," huffed Debra rudely. She walked away and approached another group of strangers in search of her husband. Paradise held back her urge to flinch when Debra said, "His name is Daniel." Flinching was her body's natural inclination, because Maria's husband shared the same name. Both men, Ms. Mattie, and Maria were four of the twenty murdered that day. When Jim, the policeman, had been called away from Paradise his partner quietly informed him, "It started in the cafeteria. At present, we've counted sixty maimed and wounded. But, we haven't checked all of the floors."

Paradise searched the parking lot for the silver van Daniel rented. She clicked the remote control door lock, followed the chirp, and walked to the back of the lot. Paradise located the vehicle, but found that she was unable to leave. Because of the shootings, the security team was instructed to guard the exits, which caused everyone to wait. Paradise, along with the other drivers, had to wait to receive an 'all clear' sign before exiting the parking lot. After a few moments, the command center radioed the security team and someone announced, "All clear, you can let the cars go."

Paradise, and the other drivers, drove away with mixed emotions. They were happy to leave; yet, were distraught over the shootings and the carnage left behind. There was anger too. They were angry with the police response, because law enforcement didn't enter the medical center right away. As Paradise followed the road signs to Interstate 55 South, she thought, "*I can't believe her name was Debra.*"

Paradise was prompted by her higher mind to pray. Traffic was heavy, so she used the time effectively. Paradise thoughtfully prayed, "Great Spirit, please send your holy angels to protect Lulu, Taka, and Blurry … Great Spirit thank you for protecting me … Papa Cicero, and Mom-Mom walk with Ms. Mattie, Daniel, and Maria, as they journey toward the light … Great Spirit, bless Maria and Daniel's newborn baby … and, send The Comforter, to heal all of those sick and wounded people. Lastly, regarding the senseless murders, please aide their families as they mourn their loss. Thank you Great Spirit. So must it be. Amen."

Paradise merged onto I-55 South headed toward Nashville, Tennessee. She inhaled deeply, and exhaled slowly to help calm her nerves. Inwardly, Paradise reflected on Ms. Mattie. Paradise was unable to comprehend why she'd chosen to die.

"*If, I got a 'tool', I know Ms. Mattie got a 'tool'. So, why did she die? Even if she knew she was dying, I'm pretty sure, she didn't want to go out like that,*" thought Paradise. Her hypothesis had been correct. Ms. Mattie had a 'tool' as well; yet, she deliberately left it home. She certainly didn't plan on being killed by a deranged gunman. However, Ms. Mattie knew she was dying. In her mind, she thought, "*After Paradise's ceremony, I'll drift off to sleep.*"

To her testament, Ms. Mattie lived a rich and full life. After her husband died, she didn't want to live alone. When she recognized the resemblance of Nina in Paradise's face she had a new hope. It had been her husband's desire that Paradise lead the 21st of June. So, Ms. Mattie decided to persevere, and continue to live, in order to see her husband's wishes fulfilled. But, the active shooter's bullet prevented Ms. Mattie's wish from coming true.

Ms. Mattie served as Madame Montoyier's interpreter for the 21st of June, translating her French into English. Of course, Madame Montoyier understood English. She simply refused to speak it. Rightly, or wrongly, that's how she honored her mother's death. She refused to speak the language of the men who murdered her mother.

"*Oh, NOW I know who Ms. Mattie is!,*" thought Paradise. "*Her husband was one of the original founders. His nephew was my grandfather Tubbee Jones. And Mom-Mom taught the Order how to weaponize their spiritual gifts. But, she didn't teach them how to resurrect the dead, or how to raise a ghost army.*"

Three brothers out of Shreveport, Louisiana, held the title of Founder of the 21st of June. Collectively, they were also known as the 'Three Wise Men'. During World War II, their segregated colored unit helped liberate Dachau, Germany, home of the first concentration camp built by the Nazis.

The Founders, or Three Wise Men, believed the Nazis would rise again. They also feared those Nazis would convince a few American politicians in Washington, DC, to build extermination camps. Over the years, they adjusted their initial prognostication, verbally concluding that, "Those American death camps are legalized abortion clinics."

Being from the South, they clearly understood there was white folk business and black folk business … and, that black folk stayed out of white folk's business. The Three Wise Men were tired of peonage, segregation, and Jim Crow. Yet, they knew their low level magic couldn't compete with war planes, biological weapons, economic isolation, police brutality, and/or the hangman's noose.

The founders needed a realistic solution to the conditions that plagued black folk. To access the deeper realms of knowledge their pursuit required, they ingested some magic mushrooms. The mystical properties of those hallucinogenic etheogens spoke to the Wise Men in 1946. But, patience would be required. For, although the magical mushrooms released their enlightening insights to the brothers, they had to wait 17 earth years, before engaging their answer. The answer to their request was Madame Montoyier. She was the solution. On June 21, 1963, after a lengthy conversation with the Three Wise Men, Madame Montoyier agreed to join their mystical order. An etheogen is the rumored gateway to the realm of the gods. Their world becomes accessible after the god-seeker consumes the genes of the sacred fungi.

"*Okay, that's how they found Lulu,*" thought Paradise.

As is customary, the DHS investigators in New Ulm, Minnesota, ran Lulu's name through their federal database. They discovered Luis T. Tapia a/k/a Luis T. Fortune … a/k/a Lulu Fortune, rented the vandalized Chrysler 300. The identification number on his bounty hunters license appeared on their computer screen. DHS had a field agent retrieve Lulu's business license from the State of Nevada. They also discovered Bernard H. Jackson was Lulu's business partner. Using facial recognition technology, they were able to positively identify Blurry, matching his driver's license photo with the image on the smartphone belonging to Hanna, the New Ulm jogger.

National Director Gregory, along with DHS, took special interest in Blurry. He became their primary focus of attention when they discovered he worked for the Department of Defense. The fact that once-upon-a-time Blurry held a high level of security clearance didn't help either. DHS figured out

Taka's identity in a manner of minutes. They pulled her photo ID from the Bounty Hunters Convention that had been held in Minneapolis, Minnesota. She too was seen on Hanna's smartphone video, with the big black bounty hunter - Blurry. DHS had knowledge of the Minneapolis Bounty Hunters Convention, so they had a field agent run a trace.

When the Minnesota State Troopers ran a trace on Lulu's license plate, the records listed the vehicle's owner as Uptown Press. The Uptown Press published infrequent community newsletters in Harlem, New York. The company's up-to-date Delaware Corporation had been owned by Sabrina Tapia. Sabrina's Uptown Press was registered as a foreign company operating in the State of New York. DHS conducted a soft background check on Sabrina Tapia, and quickly discovered that Lulu was her half-brother.

DHS moved expeditiously to put the pieces together. Two DHS agents were immediately dispatched from the Virginia office because Sabrina lived within their jurisdiction, in Norfolk. After an hour of questioning, the agents were convinced she had no knowledge of Lulu's whereabouts.

Two and a half hours into her trip, Paradise - who was now in Nashville, Tennessee - ingested the white powdered gold Ms. Mattie had given her. Within a few minutes, the magical substance triggered the question, "*Have you considered who killed Wanda Jackson?*"

18
BLOOD TEST
Bordeaux, Tennessee

Paradise was forced to leave Lulu in Big Prairie Township, Missouri. He got snatched by the three letter group. Per National Director Gregory's instruction, he had been flown to a black site. It was her desire to discover Paradise's whereabouts. The white powdered gold (WPG) helped the function of Paradise's synapses to perform better. The powder triggered stronger electrical signals between her brain cells. This, in turn, meant that she had improved connections and activity, clarity of thought, and a better grasp of her emotions. Her brain cells were in a 'happy place', because they were functioning optimally.

However, the power of the powder would be challenged. The Spirit of Negativity presented itself and tested the theory of WPG when it said, "You know they're water-boarding your boyfriend as we speak."

Immediately, the science of the WPG effect kicked into gear. The synaptic activity in Paradise's brain fired off electrical impulses like powerful, mini lightning strikes. In milliseconds, her higher consciousness downloaded all her logical mind needed to know. "*Acknowledge the thought and take command by sitting up. Slow your mind, control your breath, give into happiness, and realize Lulu's situation will work itself out. Start listing everything you're grateful for and this will repel the Spirit of Negativity.*"

Paradise did as her internal dialogue instructed: she gave thanks for her life, for the air she breathed, and for the vehicle in her possession. She refused to think about Lulu, Blurry, Taka, Ms. Mattie, Daniel, and/or Maria, as she had already offered prayers on their behalf. Paradise quickly realized she had driven through a Tennessee town called Self Preservation, wherein, all passengers are instructed to put their oxygen masks on first. That airline reference meant Paradise needed to save herself first, and help her family and friends second.

Speaking of family, Paradise needed to locate her estranged godmother, Ida May Bouché. She lived in New Orleans, which happened to be Paradise's final destination. Even though they had been estranged, Paradise needed her help. When Paradise lived in Las Vegas, she received a letter from Aunt-*tee* Ida. Her aunt's poorly scribbled letter said, "Paradise, we had to pay a lot of souls for you." That comment invited the Spirit of Delusion into Paradise's fragile mind. That unwanted spirit spoke through subtle suggestion - *"Wherever those souls came from, ask your Aunt-tee to get you some more"* - tempting and encouraging her to think of things that didn't need to be thought.

"*I'm NOT built to play on that side of the table. Plus, my Aunt-tee doesn't know how to capture souls,*" thought Paradise.

"*Well, that may be. But, how else will you get your precious Lulu free?,*" taunted the dark, negative spirit.

"Spirit of Delusion, leave me be! I rebuke you in the name of Tout ce qui est Saint," yelled Paradise as she sped down the road. '*Tout ce qui est Saint*' means 'All That is Holy', in French. Paradise had no intention of following the Spirit of Delusion's command. Like Paradise acknowledged, she wasn't built to play on that side of the table. In other words, she didn't want to participate in a supernatural poker game that used human souls as bargaining chips.

Driving the van alone proved to be priceless. It afforded Paradise the solitude to process things through mental and verbal self-talk. "*There had to be another way to save Lulu's life,*" Paradise thought. Aloud, she said, "I know … I know … I said I wouldn't think about Lulu right now. But, that thought just ran across my mind," as though she was speaking to the WPG regarding its counsel.

"Let me see, the question was asked, who killed Blurry's mother, Wanda Jackson? Ms. Mattie said she had been shown a Dixie flag; the date - May, 4th; the letters 'JC' circled in red; and the Hanged Man Tarot card," Paradise commented out loud.

According to the road sign Paradise just passed, Nashville is 15 miles ahead.

In another flurry of synaptic activity, the download occurred instantaneously. Paradise shocked herself when she blurted the revelation, "Oh damn! ... Dixie May killed Blurry's mother in retaliation for the Lulu and that old couple killing JC!!"

Dixie May's bodyguard, at the time, was JC. In actuality, Dixie May didn't care about JC; but, she did care about Paradise not meeting her at Waldorf Astoria Hotel in Manhattan, New York. She also cared that Paradise's blood-stained handkerchief had been removed from JC's suit jacket. Dixie May remembered Lulu from an incident that took place in an elevator in the Capitol Suites Hotel, located in Washington, DC. It was in that elevator that the elderly black couple attacked and tasered JC. Dixie May was in the elevator when the attack took place and she escaped unharmed.

The white powdered gold helped Paradise decipher the clues Ms. Mattie had relayed to her. The Dixie flag represented Dixie. The day calendar pointed to the month of May. So, Paradise interpreted that to mean Dixie May orchestrated Mom-Jackson's death. She then discerned that breaking down the date - May 4th - and the letters - JC - was slightly more involved, as they had to be viewed and worked out in tandem. The letters JC circled in red on the 4th day of May meant 4JC … Mom-Jackson had been murdered for JC. The Hanged Man tarot card indicated revenge, a martyr, and a dead traitor. When viewed from Dixie May's perspective, Paradise was the traitor, as she had promised to help the government, via Dixie May, in exchange for her freedom from Sin.

Virginia Gregory, who was the National Director of Intelligence, had Lulu moved to a black site, for his safety. She also wanted to locate Paradise before Dixie May did, because she knew if Dixie May killed Lulu all bets were off. Paradise would not help the National Director, or the government acquire Anglo-American dominance without the Nazi influence. Plus, the National Director hated the Tall Whites' rumored presence in American politics. If true, it meant that individuals like Dixie May, who weren't human in the normal species context of Homo Sapiens, had infiltrated the government.

While anatomically Dixie May's people look human, genetically, they would best be described as cousins to the human species. Yet, they existed long before the genetic engineered people called Homo Sapien Sapien (modern-day humans). According to Iranian propaganda, the secret rulers of America were the Tall Whites. At five feet, five inches tall, Dixie May just happened to be the runt of the bunch. Without the distraction her makeup, eye contacts, and grey stranded blonde wig provided, one would easily note that something about Dixie May was different. She had chalk white skin, dazzling blue eyes, and age-spotted skin. Not so easily detected was her bald head.

National Director Gregory read over Edward Snowden's leaked documents multiple times. He was the exiled American, National Security Agency (NSA) whistleblower, who sought asylum in Russia. The Fars News Agency (FNA), along with Snowden's alleged findings, reported that the United States' policies were 'driven by aliens'. The FNA was the English-language news service of Iran. The alleged alien takeover had been revealed in an unverified Russian FSB report. The FSB is a Russian spy agency, whose operations relate to the internal affairs inside the country. According to the alleged report, 'incontrovertible proof' had been found that Extraterrestrials (ETs), and Extraterrestrial Biological

Entities (EBEs) had been driving U.S. domestic and international policies since 1945.

What really interested National Director Gregory about the leaked Snowden report is this: documents leaked by the NSA whistleblower conclusively prove that the United States has been ruled by a race of tall, white space aliens who also assisted in the 1930s rise of Nazi Germany.

The National Director read the above excerpt - which came from investigational material prepared by Michael Peck - two, or three times. While Forbes magazine published Peck's report on January 13, 2014, it made clear to readers that as a Forbes Contributor, the opinions Peck expressed were his own. The title of his controversial article was Iran Says 'Tall, White' Space Aliens Control America. National Director Gregory considered Michael Peck's opinion essential, if not indispensable, because he was noted for covering national security and defense issues.

National Director Gregory also reflected on Grant Cameron's August of 2009, report called, The Disney UFO Connection. That report alleged that Robert Emenegger, documentary film producer and writer, had been approached by the Pentagon to produce an officially sanctioned UFO documentary during the first Nixon administration. In the beginning of National Director Gregory's career, she looked into the rumored allegations. At the time, her unnamed source told her to watch a Disney cartoon feature called, Lilo and Stitch. National Director Gregory didn't appreciate the humor. Needless to say, that unnamed source was found dead a few days later, the result of an auto accident around Fort Mead, Maryland.

Dixie May and National Director Gregory never met. But, they had knowledge of one another. From National Director Gregory's perspective, Dixie May played both sides of the fence. She worked for the three letter group out of Langley, and gave orders to those rumored DC Nazis.

National Director Gregory believed in the power of Badb Catha. So, she felt invincible. Additionally, her Hollywood Order of Good Witches told her, "Nothing will happen to you Nessa, unless the Morrigan sanctions it." Only a very few, and extremely close people knew that 'Nessa' was National Director Gregory's childhood nickname. Even fewer were permitted to use it.

According to Celtic, or Irish lore, the Morrigan was the shape-shifting goddess of magic. Badb Catha appeared in the form of a Battle Crow. She caused fear and confusion to beset her enemies. Nessa believed Badb's wailing cries helped her to win political battles and to carry out unsanctioned police actions. Unsanctioned police action refers to the private wars she engaged, without any congressional oversight.

When it came to the belief in gods, Dixie May's position was that all humans were stupid. From her perspective, humans were pawns ... toys for the gods to play with. Her people - the Tall Whites - said, "The gods fought proxy wars through humans on earth and those same gods also fought one another in the vast regions of space."

The methodology of the gods involved the division of the human species by classification: race, religion, creed, and color. Within their domain, the gods had stables of planets, countries, states, and provinces they'd selected to reign over. Humans fought wars in the name of their gods. But, what the gods would not entertain were human thoughts of insurgency in any of its forms. And, certainly, human rebellion against the gods was not tolerated. These instances were dealt with immediately, even if it warranted the gods joining forces to combat and subdue them. Transgressions, and offenses were met with retribution inflicted through the subtle causation of droughts, wars, famines, diseases, and destruction.

"The humans are easy to manipulate," Dixie May's Tall White parents told her when she was young.

Dixie May knew there was only ONE Universal Source of All Life. The irony is that she failed to acknowledge its incomprehensible presence. Plus, she enjoyed playing with the humans as well. With the exception of her chalk white skin, Dixie May appeared to be human. But, she needed to wear a grayish, blonde wig in order to cover her bald white head. She also wore contacts to help tone down the brilliance of her dazzling blue eyes. In the event Dixie May was required to physically be in her Langley office, she'd warm her skin tone using a spray-on-tan.

Dixie May became acquainted with the intelligence community during President Truman's era. She had been an exchange student from the Nevada desert, north of the Creech Air force base. Dixie May was immediately assigned to the unit that dealt directly with the ETs and EBEs. That controversial agency also consulted demonic forces, Ouija boards, and other disembodied spirits. Some of those otherworldly intelligence(s) exchanged exotic weapons for human souls. National Director Gregory surmised that the Nazis acquired superior knowledge and advanced technology in exchange for their trade. Allegedly, they traded human souls with that otherworldly intelligence during World War II.

Unjustified anger honored the dark forces. Human fear fed the demonic forces. And millions of incinerated humans paid for Nazi intelligence. The rumored bill collector was the infamous Kosmokratōr. The word 'Kosmokratōr' came from the Greeks. Translated, it means, "Lord of the world; prince of this age; the devil and his demons." National Director Gregory knew that in the Christian Bible - Ephesians 6:12 - Kosmokratōr is called the Ruler. She also understood the holocaust served as the Nazis' reprehensible trading post. Interestingly enough, the word 'holocaust' means 'a sacrificed religious animal that had been consumed by fire'.

Dixie May passed every diagnostic the CIA required, except the blood test. Her blood pointed to her non-human origins. When she became a case officer, she understood that this aspect of her true nature had to be safeguarded at all costs. Inevitably, this meant that every scientist, lab technician, and mail carrier involved with the processing, handling, and/or delivery of Dixie May's blood work had to be neutralized. Her term for it was that the aforementioned people 'got dealt with'. Dixie May's preferred method of neutralizing someone was having the individual suicided, meaning their murder was staged, reported, and documented as a suicide.

With that being said, National Director Gregory along with the former Secretary of Defense, former U.S. Senate Majority Leader, former Secretary of State, former Chairman of the Senate Armed Services Committee, former CEO of a major U.S. bank, and former National Security Advisor for two U.S. Presidents, had backed a teen-aged prodigy from a popular California university.

The teenage female prodigy raised billions of dollars for her 'one-drop' blood testing company. Supposedly, they backed her company on the premise it would help the government detect 'the others' - people like Dixie May - who worked for the U.S. government, in private industry, and public arenas. In addition to identifying who was human, and who was not… despite how human looking they might appear, the rumored one-drop blood test also included gene sequencing. This diagnostic feature would help the government determine where a tested individual came from. For example: The Y chromosomes, or paternal genes, as well as the mitochondrial haplogroups, or maternal genes, quickly identified ones ancestral lineage.

The abovementioned blood testing company was discredited by leading investigators and journalists. Quietly, the 'powers that be' welcomed the negative publicity because subliminally it suggested 'there's nothing to see here'. In other words, the 'one-drop' blood test reportedly stated: The hybrid bloodline is easily detectable by checking the test subject's 'Creatine Kinase' level. If, the subject appears to be normal, but, his or her Creatine Kinase is between 1500 - 2500 units per liter of blood, you're dealing with an alien, and/or a human-hybrid (Annunaki).

Now, here's the nerdy section… Creatine Kinase is connected to one's life-force. It's primarily produced by the heart muscle and skeletal muscle. Normal human females have between 10 - 79 units of Creatine Kinase per liter of blood (U/L) and 17 - 148 U/L for human males. A normal human with above average Creatine Kinase levels may experience a heart attack, acute renal failure, and or stroke.

National Director Gregory, along with the other investors, quickly realized that a previously unexpected component existed that was worth exploring, and exploiting. Personalized bio-weaponry was the unforeseen, added bonus of the 'one-drop' blood test. For example: militarized geneticists' created an African bio-weapon targeting the Delta32 positive gene - to help kill thousands of Africans at an alarming rate. That public revelation came through the rumored bio-weapons hunter, Dr. Boyd E. Graves. His rumored research revealed HIV/AIDS along with the enhanced Burkitts Lymphoma cancers were, in fact, militarized bio-weapons created, and used to kill thousands of black folks.

National Director Gregory had knowledge of the African Bio-weapons Program. She had been briefed on the continuous production of cervical cancer cells too. The cells were taken - without permission - in 1951 from Henrietta Lacks, a black woman. By harvesting Henrietta's cancerous cells, and continuing to use them scientifically even today, an immortal cell line remains in existence. At a very fundamental level, Henrietta Lacks lives because of the unceasing use of her intrinsic essence - her cells.

The National Director had also been briefed on the seven European haplogroups. That bit of information interested her because her ancestry was both English and Scotch-Irish. The seven European haplogroups were identified by Brian Sykes, a British geneticist, who pioneered a method of using 'mtDNA' to determine the ancient genetic ancestry of all modern humans. Sykes' research revealed 95% of all modern-day Europeans came from seven clan mothers. Those clan mothers were also known as the Seven Daughters of Eve. Sykes gave each of the seven daughters a name: Ursula (Greece/45,000 years ago); Xenia (Southern Russia/25,000 years ago); Helena (Southern France/20,000 years ago); Velda (Northern Spain/17,000 years ago); Tara (Central Italy/17,000 years ago); Katrine (Northeastern Italy/15,000 years ago); and Jasmine (Middle East/10,000 years ago).

All Seven Daughters of Eve, and another 26 global haplogroups, were traced back to one 'Mitochondrial Eve', an African woman who lived about 140,000 years ago in Africa. According to Sykes, all modern humans are the direct maternal descendants of that black African woman. Rightly, or wrongly, the geneticists who briefed National Director Gregory were skeptical, and questioned Sykes' findings.

"What about that black man from South Carolina?," queried one geneticist. "We traced his DNA back 338,000 years ago."

"Yes, but we focused on his paternal DNA, not his maternal DNA," clarified the other geneticist.

"And his people were the Mbo, from a tiny village located in Western Cameroon. But, what does that have to do with decoding the message of the pulsars?," National Director Gregory rhetorically said to those bewildered geneticists.

"Well? Let's see the pulsars …"

National Director Gregory was snippy when she told those nerdy geneticists "Don't answer that! It was a rhetorical question!"

Pulsars are neutron stars used for signaling messages across the galaxy. An ancient, intelligent, species engineered those pulsars as interstellar radio beacons. Their deliberate signals, or messages, were directed toward earth. Evidence for the existence of interstellar radio beacons of extraterrestrial intelligence (ETI) had been published in the book, Decoding the Message of the Pulsars, authored by astrophysicist, Dr. Paul LaViolette.

"That's strange … why am I thinking about Theranos, the Annunaki, and Dr. Paul LaViolette?," wondered Paradise.

Theranos, Incorporated, was a blood testing company backed by a group of American politicians and military elite. The Annunaki were believed to be the immortal gods, who came to Earth, settled in ancient Sumer, now modern-day Iraq, created and procreated with their human subjects.

Paradise arrived in Nashville, Tennessee over an hour ago. She searched for a gas station in the city's unsavory Bordeaux section.

"I got that Hidden Colors 4 DVD," offered the bootlegger to Paradise.

"What?," a confused Paradise asked.

The eager bootlegger urged her, saying, "Roll your window down."

Paradise looked to her left, discovered a gas station, rolled down the window, and gleefully screamed, "NURSE DAVIS!"

19

SPACEY TRACEY

Bordeaux, Tennessee

Paradise had unknowingly become lost in a section of Nashville called, 'Bordeaux'. In the mid-1800s, that section of Tennessee's capital city was occupied by Scotch-Irish and freed black folk. In modern-day terms, Bordeaux was simply called, 'the hood'.

Paradise had been approached by a 40 year old African-American bootlegger trying to get his hustle on. He attempted to sell her an illegal copy of the documentary, Hidden Colors 4, which told the real and untold history of people of color around the globe. The bootlegger got mad at Paradise because she coldly said, "Keep it push'n. I don't support bootleggers."

"You can't help a brother out?," questioned the bootlegger.

"You ain't my damn brother. So, keep it move'n," Paradise said insensitively, and with a great deal of force.

"Hey Angelina, what are you doing out here? Is everything alright?," asked Nurse Davis.

"You want to buy some DVDs? I got that Gentrified or better yet, what about that 7 AM," inquired the unrelenting bootlegger to Nurse Davis.

"We rented Gentrified online… it's about ethnic cleansing, American style, " Nurse Davis replied.

"Yo, keep it move'n," Malachi commanded.

"It's like that?," the offended bootlegger said defensively to Malachi.

Unconcerned with the bootlegger's agitated state, Marcus was cool when he authoritatively told the brother, "It's like that. Now, step man."

The bootlegger felt their lack of cinematic appreciation. So, he forcefully exhaled, scratched his scrotum, and walked away. Nurse Davis was at the gas station, with her twin grandsons, when Paradise yelled to her from across the street. She recognized 'Angelina' and immediately drove over to her location. After the bootlegger walked away, Nurse Davis looked Paradise up and down. Marcus, the shorter twin asked, "Why do you have blood on your face?"

"Here we go again," said Malachi, the taller twin, to his grandmother.

"Shut-it-up," Nurse Davis said sternly to Malachi. "... and, you too!," she told Marcus.

Shrugging his shoulders, Marcus mumbled, "We didn't say anything," to Paradise.

Nurse Davis was curious. "Angelina, what are you doing in Nashville?," she asked Paradise.

"I'm passing through," said Paradise cryptically.

Now confused, Nurse Davis commented, "I thought you were going to New York."

"It's a long story."

"Well, I've got the time … I'm retired now," Nurse Davis informed Paradise. "Follow us to the hotel. And, I won't take "no" for an answer," she said authoritatively.

Paradise sighed, Malachi exhaled forcefully, and Marcus rolled his eyes, to which Nurse Davis dominantly said, "Angelina, you've got some explaining to do. Malachi, get in the van with Angelina."

With no interest in being cooperative, Malachi's suggestion was somewhat dismissive, "All come on Nana, send Marcus."

"Boy, get your ass in that car," Nurse Davis demanded.

"And Angelina, why do you have blood on your clothes?," asked Nurse Davis of Paradise.

"I …"

"Wait. Don't tell me until we get to the hotel."

"I can't be seen in public," mouthed Paradise quickly to Nurse Davis.

Under his breath, Malachi whispered and rolled his eyes saying, "Aw, here we go again."

"I heard that," said Nurse Davis to Malachi.

"Then, what are you doing driving?," Marcus said under his breath.

"I heard that too Marcus. Now, give Angelina that thing you invented," said Nurse Davis sternly to Marcus.

Marcus' disinterest was also apparent. "Aw, come on Nana," he said in a whining tone.

The look on Nurse Davis' face spoke volumes. "*Don't make me cut you.*"

"Alright, alright … and, it's not a 'thing'. I call it Therianthropy 44," Marcus announced proudly to Nurse Davis.

Only, she was flustered. "I don't care what you call it, take it off, and give it to her," Nurse Davis said impatiently.

Malachi corrected Marcus. He said, "I told you to call it DX 44." "*Didn't I tell you to get your ass in that van?!,*" said the expression on Nurse Davis' face.

Malachi read his grandmother's displeased look. So, he opened the passenger door, got in, and started to sulk. As he began to close the door, his eyes briefly crossed with Paradise's eyes. When they were within each other's view, Paradise smiled. And, Malachi acknowledged her by nodding, "*Hey*."

Looking at Marcus, Paradise asked, "What's DX 44?"

Malachi was gloating. He told Marcus, "See, I told you."

Nurse Davis gave Malachi the 'evil eye'. He understood, and quickly quieted himself. Nurse Davis then directed her attention to Marcus, who proudly said, "I created a device that distorts digital camera images."

"I don't understand," said Paradise confusedly.

"Just give her the necklace Marcus," commanded Nurse Davis.

"See, look," said Malachi to Paradise.

In amazement, Paradise asked Malachi, "Whoa! What kind of magic is this? I see your grandmom; but, where's Marcus?"

"That's cool as shit, ain't it?!," said Malachi, who was also clearly excited.

Nurse Davis snapped angrily at Marcus. "What did I tell y'all about cursing?!"

"I didn't say it!," Marcus said in defense of himself.

Now, thoroughly frustrated, Nurse Davis became terse. "I know who said it! GIVE ANGELINA THE DAMN NECKLACE!!!!," she told Marcus.

"No more talking until we get to the hotel," Nurse Davis stated.

"Do you mind driving?," Paradise asked Malachi.

"Sure, I'll drive," he said happily.

The look on her face reflected Nurse Davis' indignation. "*Oh! Y'all just going to ignore what I said?*"

"Sorry, Nurse Davis," said Paradise apologetically.

Marcus handed Paradise his coveted necklace. She put it on, switched seats with Malachi, and whispered, "I need gas."

"HEY GRANDMOM, ANGELINA NEEDS GAS," Malachi shouted humorously just to aggravate his grandmother. .

"I'm a hurt you, Malachi," said Nurse Davis light-heartedly.

Nurse Davis and Marcus returned to their vehicle, and drove past Paradise's van. Malachi followed behind them.

"Hey Malachi, what inspired Marcus to invent this magical device?," inquired Paradise inquisitively.

"We have family in New Orleans that Twin and I never met. But, Nana said her brother, who's our uncle, followed the tenants of Ma'at. Twin wanted to know more, so he Googled Memphite Theology. That's the ancient Egyptian religious system, just in case you didn't know Angelina," Malachi boastfully teased.

"Boy, don't try and play me. I'm well aware of Memphite Theology and the 42 Principles of the goddess Maat. Truth … balance … and justice … SO, stop joking around and finish the story," said Paradise to a pleasantly surprised Malachi.

"My 'bad' Angelina. Listen, if it ever comes up, DON'T tell Twin I told you. The idea for the DX 44 came from a dream. But, he's going to say he got the idea from reading Dr. Oyibo's explanation of Memphite Theology," said Malachi.

"Who?," asked Paradise.

"Dr. Gabriel Oyibo. He's the Nigerian, who provided the mathematical equation for the Grand Unified Theorem, also known as GAGUT."

"CAT GUTS?," Paradise said in jest.

"So, now you got jokes Angelina. I didn't say, "cat guts" … I said GAGUT. GAGUT stands for God's Almighty Grand Unified Theorem. According to Dr. Oyibo, his Grand Unified Theorem is the African Science of the Universe. He received a Nobel Prize nomination in physics for revising Albert Einstein's Theory of Relativity," Malachi stated impressively.

Paradise worked to digest the information Malachi shared, but found herself in awe. She said, "Whoa. So,

Dr. Oyibo discovered the mathematical equation that proves the existence of God."

"Whoa is right Angelina," said Malachi to Paradise.

Dr. Oyibo said his knowledge was derived from the Maa civilization. Maa meant knowledge of infallible truth and intelligence.

"Hey, Angelina."

"Hey, Malachi," Paradise said light-heartedly.

"My uncle might feel some type of way. But, before Egypt, Africa's first civilization was the Maa, or Fish Confederation. The Maa worshiped the god Amon," said Malachi.

"Dr. Clyde Winters. Very impressive Malachi," said Paradise.

"*You got it going on too,*" nodded Malachi.

"I'm extremely impressed with your brother's Therian-throphy 44," Paradise said to irritate Malachi.

"That name is whack! Call it DX 44 Angelina."

"*DX 44 it is,*" nodded Paradise.

The Therianthropy 44, or DX 44, Marcus Davis invented had two settings: What the Hell?! - and - Where did he go?! Marcus had discovered a way to make harmless harmonics bend light. His necklace made the person wearing it imperceptible, or unseeable.

A few summers back, a stranger appeared in Marcus' dream. He revealed to Marcus the mineral silicate and liquid crystal combination, along with the frequencies needed to bend time and light. Marcus' magical necklace caused a type of interference that inhibited security cameras, smartphone cameras, and facial recognition software, from viewing the targeted image.

For example: when Malachi pointed the lens of his smartphone in the direction of his brother and grandmother, only Nurse Davis appeared on camera. The thin gold wire, along with Marcus' mystical combination, used bio-photons as its battery, or power source. The bio-photons were supplied by the person wearing the necklace. 'Bio-photon' is a word that comes from the Greeks, and is actually comprised of two separate words. Bio, means 'life', and photon means 'light'. In scientific terms, those literal life-lights are produced by the biological system of a human. The light generated by the human biological system appears in the ultraviolet and low visible light ranges.

Marcus, along with the U.S. Defense Advanced Research Projects Agency (DARPA) were inspired to make an invisibility, or cloaking device after watching the film, Harry Potter and the Deathly Hallows. That mythical character wore an invisibility cloak in the movie. An invisibility cloak was a magical garment that rendered whoever wore it, or whatever it covered, unseeable.

On January 4, 2012, the National Post (Agence France-Presse) reported that the cloak of invisibility was developed by Pentagon physicists who had the ability to 'bend time'.

Malachi wanted to call the cloaking device his twin brother created in necklace form, DX 44. The Nama people of Namibia, Africa, called the GOOD and APPROACHABLE GOD 'DXUI'. DXUI also stood for 'TSUI-GOAB'. TSUI-GOAB was the Supreme Shape-shifting Creator God. Marcus called his mystical necklace "Therianthropy 44." Therianthropy means the mythological ability of human beings to metamorphose into other animals by the way of shape-shifting.

The number 44 had been selected in honor of a brother called Blue Pill. Blue Pill - along with his twin brother, Red Pill - hosted Underground Radio, an internet podcast. Blue Pill had a theory called, 'The Law of 44'. His theory encompassed the universal energy of God revealing synchromystic messages through superstars, such as hip-hop artists and other celebrities.

Unknown spell casters created the word 'synchromysticism' when they combined two magical words - synchronicity and mysticism - together. Synchronicity served a coincidence not likely to happen naturally. Mysticism meant the belief in direct experience of transcendent reality or God.

According to the theory of synchromysticism, all symbols have multiple layers of information, histories, and interpretations.

Paradise met Nurse Davis, Malachi, and Marcus in Las Vegas, Nevada. Nurse Davis took great care of Paradise during her inpatient admission at the city's Mountain View Hospital. Paradise was admitted there with serious injuries. As part of her treatment, she underwent a medically induced coma to help reduce the swelling on her brain. The coma also allowed her internal organs time to heal. Although Paradise spent over a month in the hospital under the name 'Jane Doe', her patient file was later updated to list her name as 'Angelina Ferrari Bridgewater'. The hospital staff believed Paradise was Angelina, because of the U.S. Passport her husband, Sin, presented to the facility's admissions office. The hospital staff didn't know that passport belonged to a dead woman named Angelina. Sin was successful with the fraudulent cover, because visually, Paradise was a perfect match to Angelina. Unfortunately, upon her discharge, the hospital officials were required to return Paradise to her abuser, Sin.

Nurse Davis protested the hospital policy that returned Paradise to Sin. But, she was overruled. Paradise begged

Nurse Davis to let her go. Ultimately, Nurse Davis had to relinquish Paradise into the custody of her husband. Nurse Davis couldn't save Paradise because she didn't want to be saved. Nurse Davis took Paradise's situation personally. Afterall, her own daughter … her only child … mother of Marcus, and Malachi, had been killed by the boys' father over a visitation dispute. Following the funeral, the court awarded Nurse Clara Davis custody of her twin grandsons. Malachi and Marcus came to live with her when they were nine years old.

When Paradise met the twins, they were seventeen years old. They'd graduated from Las Vegas High School at the age of sixteen. Marcus and Malachi were the spitting image of their mother and grandmother. The young men had broad features, a few freckles, and light chestnut skin. Those teen twins were only teased once regarding their looks. Their peers' one-time joke was, "Did y'all really have a daddy and granddaddy?"

Malachi responded with the customary middle finger. But, Marcus checked his ignorant classmate, along with his friends, when he said, "Of course, we had a dad and granddad. But, the genes on our grandmother's side were stronger. At least we can trace our lineage … how many dudes been splash'n up in your moms? And what about you? Oh, that's right … you were fathered by your grandfather! "

Marcus and Malachi were never teased again. Plus, they had earned their black belts in the African art of war called, Vita Saana. That extremely effective martial art had been developed by two brothers from Philly over twenty-five years ago.

On the night of Sin's death, Paradise fled the scene and stayed with Nurse Davis, Malachi and Marcus. At the time, Paradise wanted to tell Nurse Davis her real name. But, Nurse Davis wasn't prepared to hear the truth. So, they both silently agreed to withhold their secrets. When Nurse Davis drove Paradise to the McCarran Airport in Las Vegas, they were very emotional. Paradise had become Nurse Davis's surrogate daughter, and Nurse Davis had become Paradise's surrogate mother.

From Nurse Davis' perspective, Paradise was headed to New York. Her intent for going was to start a new life. From Paradise's perspective, she had the same thought. But, their shared perspective would be overridden by another view point. Paradise's flight to New York was re-routed to Devils Lake, North Dakota. After the plane landed, Paradise walked toward the baggage claim section. She read over the flight schedule to identify the next flight to New York. That's when the three limousine drivers caught her attention. Paradise approached the driver in the middle because his small sign read, 'June Spade'.

That's where Paradise officially met Lulu … he was the limousine driver who stood in the middle. After their intense meet and greet, they exited the Devils Lake airport. Lulu made sure he used the security cameras' blind spots to his advantage. In the event the airport's security cameras where unavoidable, he walked with his head held down.

It took some time, but Dixie May found Lulu first. That meant she had a photograph of Lulu and Paradise. They were seen together exiting the Devils Lake airport. Although Dixie May discovered the two had been in St. Louis, Missouri, her team wasn't able to apprehend them there. When they were dispatched to Ms. Mattie's house, they got side tracked while in route. In other words, the thought of arresting Paradise and Lulu had mystically or miraculously slipped their minds. Dixie May figured Paradise was headed to St. Louis because her DHL contact 'jacketed' a large envelope June Spade's mail.

'Jacketed' meant the Post Office, along with the other logistics couriers responsible for the local, and/or global delivery of parcels, freight, and express mail, allegedly photocopied the name and address information written on envelopes and packages they deemed suspicious. Dixie May's contact, who worked inside the American Embassy at Plateau de Serpent, Djibouti, in East Africa, informed her that someone inside the embassy sent a package, via DHL, to the Spiritualist Church in St. Louis, Missouri.

Dixie May didn't need a rocket scientist to help her piece those clues together. Her powers of deduction were more than sufficient. She knew that a little under a year ago, Paradise called the Embassy at Plateau de Serpent, Djibouti, from a pay phone, located on South Rampart Street, in New Orleans … clue number one. Dixie May then linked Devils Lake, North Dakota, to St. Louis, Missouri, because the two locales were in the same region … clue number two. However, it was the Spiritualist Church of God in St. Louis that proved critical in confirming Paradise's whereabouts … bam!, clue number three.

When the federal agents from the local St. Louis office failed to apprehend Lulu and Paradise, Dixie May vectored her anger upon Blurry's mother, Wanda Jackson. She figured Mom Jackson's death was the easiest, and most expedient way to smoke out Lulu and Paradise.

National Director Gregory realized Paradise and Lulu were connected when she personally interviewed the Minnesota Park Ranger at the sand-bottomed pool in New Ulm. The pool was the place where Lulu, Blurry, and Taka recovered Paradise. When asked if he'd seen anything unusual, it wasn't hard for the park ranger to recall, and/or to describe the foursome. They were the only black people at the sand-bottomed pool. National Director Gregory called in a sketch artist to provide a drawing that would illustrate what the park ranger had seen. Based on the level of detail provided, the sketch artist assigned to the task, captured their likeness with unbelievable accuracy.

"Do you have a medical condition?," asked Malachi tender- heartedly.

Paradise became somewhat defensive. "Huh? … NO! … not that I know of? … why?," she said to a concerned Malachi.

"You be straight Spacey Tracy," Malachi rhymed.

"What?"

Paradise was confused. Malachi was perplexed.

"You used to do that at the house. You would just flake out," said Malachi with a straight-face.

Paradise was just as straight-faced. "Well, I'm present now. Besides, I'm a Pisces. We escape. If, we don't have unity, we escape."

Malachi explained. "I don't know what that means. But, I know you be talking to those voices inside your head. It's like you're in communication with another reality. No disrespect; but, you be weird'n me out sometimes. And for-real-for-real, you remind me of that song my pops used to play."

"What are you talking about?," Paradise questioned.

"My Pop used to play this song … but, I forgot who sings it. He used to sing it to my moms all the time. OK, now I remember the words …," Malachi said sadly, reminiscing about better days.

"What words? What song?," demanded Paradise.

"*Your body's here with me … but, your mind is on the other side of town …*"

"Alright Eddie," interrupted an impatient Paradise.

"First of all, my name is Malachi - NOT Eddi … yeah, that's it … Eddie - Eddie Levert … he was with The O'JAYS. Anyway, your body be here. But, your mind be in another world," he said.

"*Yeah, whatever,*" said Paradise's raised eyebrow.

Though Paradise attempted to 'blow off' Malachi's observation, he wasn't willing to be dismissed so easily. He came right back, saying, "Whatever, nothing."

"Well, I'm present now," said Paradise reassuringly.

"Yeah, for the moment," Malachi said sarcastically.

"How long was I out?," questioned Paradise.

Nurse Davis answered Paradise, "Long enough for us to go inside the hotel."

Marcus chimed in too, "Long enough for me to use the bathroom."

"And long enough for Marcus and I to come back for you," Malachi told Paradise, with trepidation.

20

BEER & PIZZA

Cookeville, Tennessee

Paradise and Nurse Davis's family stood in the parking lot of the Hutton Hotel on the west end in Nashville, Tennessee. They waited outside for a moment. Nurse Davis motioned with her head for Malachi to help Paradise with Lulu's luggage.

When Malachi saw Paradise's Flintstone lunch box, he shook his head in disgust. Malachi then looked at Marcus, who frowned. Malachi whispered to his brother, "She too damn pretty to be that crazy ..."

"I'll still hit it," whispered Marcus to Malachi.

Having overheard their hushed remarks, Paradise told the twins, "Y'all like my brothers. So, you'll NEVER get any sex from me." She whispering as she spoke.

"Are y'all coming?," Nurse Davis hollered out to Paradise.

As Paradise trotted toward Nurse Davis, Marcus closed the van's doors and mouthed, "Yo Twin, how did she hear that?"

Malachi's shrugged shoulders answered, "*I don't know.*"

Nurse Davis rented a deluxe suite to celebrate her retirement, their vacation, and the new home that awaited them in Atlanta, Georgia. Paradise looked around the suite, got a cold chill, and walked inside the bathroom.

"Close the door Angelina," Nurse Davis quietly requested.

"I'd rather not. PLEASE tell the guys to turn their backs."

"You heard her. Now, turn around. Look out the window, or something," Nurse Davis instructed Malachi and Marcus.

The twins complied. Marcus looked at Malachi, who said, "Yo that chic is crazy."

Marcus' position had not changed. "I know. But, I'd still hit it," he mouthed to Malachi.

Paradise didn't stink the bathroom up too bad. She misted the room by spraying several squirts of the teen's fancy colognes into the air. It helped mask the odor. Meanwhile, Nurse Davis removed the hotel's menu from the kitchen counter and asked, "Malachi and Marcus what do y'all want to eat?"

"Angelina, are you hungry baby?," said Nurse Davis to Paradise.

"No ma'am,"

Nurse Davis asked, "Marcus, go get me a clean washcloth, run it under some warm water and bring me a fresh bar of soap."

"Okay Nana," said Marcus caringly.

Nurse Davis motioned to Paradise. "Angelina, come sit down baby," she said caringly.

"Hey Nana, I'm ordering pizza," Malachi stated nonchalantly.

"That's fine. Order enough for everybody."

"What's wrong Nurse Davis?," asked Paradise worriedly.

"Just have a seat baby," Nurse Davis said to Paradise, followed by her comment to Marcus. "Thank you, baby," she told him.

Paradise sat, Marcus sat, and Malachi called room service. In a light and tender manner, Nurse Davis washed the blood from Paradise's face. Marcus became sad because, in that moment, Paradise appeared to be a little child. As Paradise took a deep breath, inhaling very slowly, her eyes filled with water. Nurse Davis made a simple sympathetic suggestion, "Let it out baby. If, you have to cry, cry ..."

"What's wrong with her Nana?," Malachi asked.

"She has PTSD," Nurse Davis advised.

Directing his question to his twin, Malachi ignorantly asked, "What war was she in?"

Filled with compassion, Marcus told his brother, "Everything ain't a joke Malachi."

"That's my bad," Malachi said apologetically.

There were questions to be asked and answered. But, to go where they needed to go, emotional diplomacy was required. Initially, Malachi still stumbled, insensitively asking, "What's wrong with you?" Anyone with eyes could see that Paradise was visibly stressed. So, rather than come off as combative, he quickly checked himself, and reset his intention. Modulating both the tone, and pitch of his voice, he proceeded. "Wait … that didn't come out right … I apologize," he said. "Tell me - us … what happened to you? … why is there blood on your clothes and face? … what's wrong with closing the bathroom door? … and, is Angelina your real name?"

A residual amount of the white powdered gold remained inside Paradise's head. It spoke to encourage her. "*Tell the truth and shame the Devil. Tell the truth. Tell the truth. Tell the truth and the truth will set you free.*"

Paradise heeded the advice and set herself free. In a single breath, she spoke her truth. "Turn on the news … I survived that massacre in Big Prairie … either the FBI, or Homeland Security, just took my boyfriend … well, he's not my boyfriend … well, at least not yet … I don't know - who knows what's going to happen between us … but, I know they took him and they didn't say why … the blood on my body came from the active shooter … his blood is mixed with the blood from my grandmother's long time friend, and her family … you asked why didn't I close the bathroom door … well, let's see … this hotel suite reminds me of that hotel suite, where I got beaten within an inch of my life … the bathroom door was closed … he kicked it in … we fought … I slipped and he stomped me … that's why I didn't close the bathroom door … it's just like I said, I had a flashback … up until now, I didn't have any problem closing the bathroom door … and, no my name isn't Angelina … it's Paradise … and, just to put it all out there, my birth name is Isabella Rosemarie Montoyier."

"Did you say Montoyier?," said Nurse Davis shockingly.

Panting and winded, Paradise questioningly replied, "Yes."

Overwhelmed, Nurse Davis gasped before uttering, "Oh my."

"Oh my, is right. Now, I need to be debriefed," said Marcus.

Malachi was hyped. Pointing to the television, he commanded everyone's attention. "Hey y'all look! There goes Angelina, Paradise, Rosemarie, or whatever name she's using," Malachi shouted sarcastically. "She's on TV!"

Paradise, along with Nurse Davis, Malachi, and Marcus appeared to be in shock. They watched the news broadcast with their eyes wide opened, and their mouths gaping. The news report revealed the smartphone footage of Paradise, and the other hostages, walking out of the Missouri Medical Center with their hands up.

"TURN IT OFF," screamed Nurse Davis to Malachi.

"It's off," Malachi nervously responded

Marcus was also anxious. Quietly, he asked everyone, "Who's banging on the door?"

In his customary uncouth fashion, Malachi took the initiative to yell, "WHO IS IT?," to the unknown person on the other side of the door.

"It's room service. Somebody from this room ordered three large pizzas from the kitchen," the concierge announced from behind the door.

"*You ordered three pizzas,*" said the fire in Nurse Davis's eyes.

"Hold on," yelled Marcus.

Malachi opened the door slowly, grabbed the three pizzas and left the concierge waiting for a tip. Nurse Davis gave

Malachi *that* look. He got the message, though he remained reluctant as he reached inside his pocket, removed a twenty dollar bill, and gave it to the concierge.

For that generous tip, he got a happy, "Thank you."

"*You're welcome*," nodded Malachi back.

"How much did you give him?," asked Marcus curiously.

"Oh, I can't tell you that," Malachi said.

"Why not?," Marcus wanted to know.

"Are you trying to mess up my blessing?"

"Nah, never that, I just wanted to know," Marcus said.

"Let's just say, the more you give, the more you receive. Ain't that right Nana?," Malachi proudly proclaimed to Nurse Davis.

"The correct word is 'isn't' … and, "yes" Malachi, that's right," said Nurse Davis.

"*See, I know what I'm talking about*," nodded Malachi to Marcus light-heartedly.

"Just say the blessing," suggested Marcus to Malachi.

"Everybody grab hands. And, that includes you Paradise," said Malachi inclusively.

"*Thank you*," nodded Paradise to Malachi.

The group held hands, bowed their heads, and closed their eyes. Malachi inhaled slowly, Marcus opened his eyes, and Nurse Davis mouthed, "Close y'all eyes."

"Lord, a stranger has reappeared in our midst. And, we've been told people enter our lives for a reason, for a season, and for a lifetime. Father-God, place it upon our hearts to be kind to one another. To bless those who bless us. And, with that being said, thank you for this food," prayed Malachi.

"In Jesus name we say ...," said Marcus for Malachi.

In unison, the group said, "Amen."

Malachi opened the pizza box first. He removed a slice, only to have Marcus grab it. Nurse Davis firmly, and lovingly said, "Boy, I taught you better than that."

"It's okay Nana, at least we know who has manners," said Malachi playfully.

In a tender-hearted tone, Nurse Davis invited Paradise to join them. "If you're hungry baby, come eat something."

"I will … thank you. But, do you mind if I take a shower first? I promise, I'll close the door," Paradise said sincerely.

"You can leave the door open," snickered Marcus mischievously. The next thing he said, "Hey! What did you do that for?," is the result of the sharp smack his grandmother successfully landed on the back of his head.

Malachi shook his head, chewed his slice of pizza and said, "I knew your name wasn't Angelina."

"Will y'all leave her alone!," said Nurse Davis to Malachi.

"Isabella, you can use the shower in my bedroom. Do you have any clothes?," asked Nurse Davis.

"Yes ma'am. And, please, call me Paradise."

"Okay, Paradise. Take as much time as you need baby."

With a straight face, Paradise asked, "Do you have any beer?"

"I don't think you need to be drinking right now baby," Nurse Davis said in a protective tone.

Paradise explained, "I don't want to drink it. I need to cleanse myself spiritually. But, I don't have any Divine Baths with me. So, beer will have to do. I know it sounds weird; but, I need something to wash this negative energy away."

Nurse Davis was sincere when she soberly remarked, "Nothing sounds weird anymore."

"Malachi, get off that phone and get Paradise two, three …"

"Two beers will be fine … and, thank you again," Paradise said to Nurse Davis graciously.

Attempting to lighten things up, Nurse Davis replied, "Child please."

Malachi opened the refrigerator, grabbed two beers, and a large styrofoam cup from the counter. He sucked his bottom lip, flared his nostrils, and handed those items to Paradise.

"Thank you," said Paradise softly to Malachi.

"You're welcome … and, I apologize for offending you," Malachi said remorsefully.

"*Thank you*," nodded Paradise.

"Oh NO!," shouted Paradise.

"What's wrong baby?," said Nurse Davis nervously.

"I've got to get rid of that van," said Paradise.

Nurse Davis calmly directed her, saying, "Okay. Give Malachi your keys."

"I still have them Nana," said Malachi informatively.

"Okay Marcus, go with your brother and take one of those burner phones with you," said Nurse Davis instructively.

"Aw, Nana, I didn't get to eat yet," protested Marcus.

"You can eat when you get back," she retorted sternly.

"Paradise, give Marcus his magical thingy back," said Nurse Davis softly.

"It's the Ther-ron … aw, forget it … come on Malachi," said a hungry and disgusted Marcus.

"Wait. I haven't told y'all what to do. Malachi, I want you and Marcus to wear those light-bender necklaces. And, I need y'all to drive the van four, or five, towns away from here. Marcus, you follow behind your brother in the car. I need y'all to buckle up, obey the speed limit, and use your turn signals. Then, I need you to go to a shopping mall, in a nice neighborhood, and park the van under a well lit light. Matter of fact, drive to the Cookeville Shopping Center," Nurse Davis instructed.

"Come on Nana, that's more than an hour and a half away," pouted Malachi.

"This is not the time, NOR the place to talk back young man! Just, do what I tell you! Malachi, get a pair of those latex gloves out of my nursing bag. I want you to wear them while you drive. Don't take them off until you get back here."

"By the time I get back, my hands will look like prunes," thought Malachi.

Nurse Davis reached inside her bosom, removed her straight razor, placed it on the table, and along with her no nonsense look said, "Boy, don't make me cut you."

Paradise, Marcus, and Malachi read Nurse Davis' vibe. It meant that for the time being, ALL jokes were set aside. Nurse Davis sucked her teeth, flared her nostrils, and sternly said, "Paradise, hand me one of those beers."

Paradise complied speedily.

"Thank you baby," Nurse Davis said politely.

Nurse Davis grabbed the bottle opener from the kitchen counter. She removed the beer cap, took a swig, and instructively told Malachi, "Wipe the inside of the van down. Clean it good. Remove as many fingerprints as possible. When you're satisfied, call the rental company - NOT the cops. Tell them the van broke down at the Cookeville Shopping Center, in Tennessee. Tell them the keys are in the glove compartment … are you still following me?," she asked forcefully.

"I'm following you," said Malachi softly.

"Put that pizza down Marcus! Y'all can eat when you get back," Nurse Davis said authoritatively.

"Now Malachi, listen carefully. Use the burner phone to make the call. After you've made the call, disassemble the phone … break it into three, or four pieces. Wrap the pieces in separate napkins. Remember, the first call from the burner phone will be untraceable. But, the phone pieces are. So, toss each piece into a separate trash can. Do you understand?," said Nurse Davis instructively.

"*I understand*," nodded Malachi.

"I need to hear it," said Nurse Davis commandingly.

"I understand," said Malachi attentively.

"Good. Now, y'all look out for each other. And, be careful. I'll have a real meal prepared when y'all get back," Nurse Davis assured the twins.

"Paradise, go take your shower … and, do what you need to do to feel better … 'cus you and I need to talk," said Nurse Davis.

Paradise walked to the bathroom, the twins walked out the suite, and Nurse Davis drank her beer.

21
UNSEEN REALMS
Atlanta, Georgia

Nurse Davis sent her twin grandsons to Cookeville, Tennessee, to drop off Paradise's van. They complied with every command given to them by their grandmother, including her instruction that Malachi call the rental company. They returned to the hotel in Nashville extremely hungry. Paradise had taken her beer bath, washed normally, and got dressed. Nurse Davis changed her mind about making a home cooked meal, deciding instead to order out. She called Hattie B's Hot Chicken, an eatery in West Nashville, placed an order, and had the twins pick it up. Nurse Davis ordered: two mild fried chickens; two very spicy fried chickens; collard greens; mac 'n cheese; baked beans; potato salad; banana pudding; and peach cobbler.

On the way back to the hotel, Marcus and Malachi talked about the mass shooting in Big Prairie Township. They agreed with the homicide detective on the radio, who said, "I'm NOT speaking for the bureau, this is my personal opinion: those unarmed victims weren't completely powerless. Prior to the active shooter entering the cafeteria, they should have barracked the doors. Then, they should've turned over those tables for added shelter. Everybody in there should have grabbed unopened soda cans. They should have grabbed apples, plastic plates and plastic trays … anything that could become a projectile. That way, when the shooter breached the door, everyone inside should have thrown everything that they had at his head …"

"Whose Spacey Tracey now?," Paradise playfully said to Malachi, who had been in a trance.

"Finish your food Malachi," said Marcus.

"Yo, I'm stuffed bro," Malachi admitted.

"Thanks Nana," they said in unison.

Nurse Davis expressed her gratitude to her grandsons. "You're welcome. And, thank y'all for what you did."

"*It's all good Nana,*" nodded the twins.

Needing to refocus, Nurse Davis turned to Paradise, and recommended, "Now, let's get down to business."

"Where do I begin?," Paradise asked apprehensively.

"What brought you to Nashville?," Nurse Davis inquired.

"An unseen force planned for me to be here. So, our meeting is no accident. It appears there's a higher power writing this story," said Paradise to Malachi.

He supportively nodded, "*I understand.*"

"Nurse Davis, do you mind going first," requested Paradise.

"Sure, we're in Nashville for several reasons …"

Malachi became irritated, and without thinking cut his grandmother's response off. In a rather blunt, curt tone, he told Paradise, "We had to leave Vegas 'cus of you."

"What?," Paradise asked surprised and shocked. She couldn't imagine how her circumstance impacted their situation.

Nurse Davis regained control by saying, "I got this Malachi." "What he said is true. He's just mad 'cus he had to leave that fast girlfriend of his. In my opinion, that was a good thing 'cus that girl wasn't any good for Malachi anyway," Nurse Davis told Paradise.

"Aw Nana, come on," protested Malachi.

"What happened? So, y'all moved to Nashville?," questioned Paradise.

"No. We moved to Atlanta. We're in Nashville to visit my great aunt. She's in a nursing home over in Bordeaux. That's how I know your family name. My great aunt's parents owned a restaurant in Greenwood, Oklahoma …"

"Before the white folks burnt it down," chimed in Malachi, flush with a bad attitude.

"They destroyed 35 city blocks - that's over 600 businesses, and 21 restaurants. Everything got burnt down to the ground," added Marcus angrily.

When Paradise connected what she just heard with the significance of historical fact, she was impressed and saddened. "So, your family was a part of Black Wall Street," she noted.

"The key word is "was" … but, we're getting off topic," said Nurse Davis overwhelmingly.

"We sure are," said Malachi agitatedly.

"Angelina … I mean Paradise, the day after you left, we found a dead cat in our yard," said Marcus aggressively.

"And?," Paradise asked defensively.

"And, it was a black cat with no head, no tail, no organs and no blood," Malachi recalled aloud.

"Is that true Nurse Davis?," asked Paradise.

"Except for the part about it being in the yard, it's true." confirmed Nurse Davis. "Someone deliberately placed the cat on our front step. And, "no", the cat didn't have any blood Paradise. But, that's not the only weird thing that has happened since you left."

"Tell her about the Men in Black," urged Malachi impatiently.

Paradise was astonished. "The FBI came to your house looking for me?"

"They were looking for Angelina … and they weren't from NO damn FBI … sorry Nana … they were the real Men in Black … and not the Will Smith and Agent K version either," rambled Marcus informatively.

"They wore black suits, crisp white shirts, straight black ties, black shoes, black hats, and black shades that looked like ski goggles," clarified Malachi.

The thought that prompted Nurse Davis' request was disconcerting. "Now, tell Paradise how they really looked," she asked Marcus uncomfortably.

"Their skin looked like pale plastic. It was close to chalk white. They were around my height, but were VERY thin. Those Men in Black had bald heads, missing eyebrows and no facial hair …"

"How tall are you?," asked Paradise of Marcus.

"I'm six foot even. Marcus is five foot and six inches," he informed her.

"That's not the only thing," added Nurse Davis.

"Huh … what are you talking about Nana?," Marcus asked curiously.

"How did they sound?"

Marcus thought back, and then remembered, "On yeah, one of them talked like a robot."

"A robot," said Paradise skeptically.

"A ROBOT," Malachi and Marcus repeated loudly.

"Okay, okay, I believe you," said Paradise.

"So, they weren't FBI agents," Nurse Davis reiterated.

In one of those characteristic traits of being a twin, Marcus began to say, "Malachi got sick about an hour after they left. But, Nana worked her magic and …", only to have Malachi finish by saying, "… and, I felt better in the morning."

"But, it felt like they were draining my energy," said Marcus.

"That's real talk," Malachi told Paradise.

"I said I believed you," Paradise said truthfully.

"Now, will you believe me? If, I told you my great aunt talked about your legendary grandmother …"

Attempting to be humorous, Malachi - in an animated ringmaster's voice - interrupted Nurse Davis with, "Madame Montoyier, the feared New Orleans mystic … "

"SHUT IT UP Malachi, I'm NOT talking to you," Nurse Davis demanded angrily.

"Sorry Nana," Malachi said remorsefully.

-"You're not sorry! STOP TALKING OVER ME."

"Now, Paradise, I need you to tell me the truth."

"I'll try," said Paradise.

In one of those life-learning moments, Nurse Davis cut to it 'quick'. Serious and sober, she firmly snapped, "Don't try. Just do. You either pick-up the pencil, or you don't pick-up pencil." And, as if she hadn't been clear enough, she drove the point home. This time, however, she laced her comments with loving regard. "So, there's no trying. Either you do, or you don't. I need you to tell me the truth."

"Ok. I'll tell you the truth, as I know it," said Paradise sincerely.

"I respect that. Now, from your grandmother's teachings, who really killed that black cat? I'm asking because the Washington Post published their sanitized viewpoint, for public consumption," Nurse Davis informed Paradise.

Paradise was genuinely unaware - and, was genuinely confused. "I don't know who killed your cat … you said the Washington Post wrote a story about the dead cat on your porch?"

Still squeamish at having to recall the incident, Nurse Davis advised, "The paper wrote a story about several cats that had been found dead and mutilated; but, never reported on the one we found on our porch."

"Now, you can do something Malachi," Nurse Davis said. "Go, on your phone, and read that Washington Post headline to Paradise."

"Okay Nana, finally ...," remarked Malachi enthusiastically.

"The headline read, 'This is the stuff of nightmares' Sadistic cat killer terrorizes London pet owners ..."

"Wow," said Paradise shockingly.

"And, what else?," asked Nurse Davis of Malachi.

"I'll paraphrase it Nana. The authorities in Croydon, that's a large town in south London, were convinced a deranged person was killing more than cats. Authorities have found hundreds of mutilated foxes, birds, rabbits, and puppies. Those furry victims were discovered in multiple communities across England."

"Now - Marcus, tell Paradise the rest," requested Nurse Davis.

"The community pressure was so great Scotland Yard was forced to investigate the matter. Scotland Yard is England's po-po department, just in case you didn't know," explained Marcus light- heartedly.

In a smart-alecky tone, Paradise smirked when she said, "really."

"Go on Marcus, and stop joking around," said Nurse Davis.

"Scotland Yard said a deranged individual did it. But, they never found human DNA on any of those animals. The poor creatures didn't have a chance. And, don't get me started on the human mutilations," Marcus said angrily.

"Marcus and I called the Vegas police department about the headless cat on our porch," said Malachi excitedly.

"They were indifferent and uncaring. They blew us off, telling us to call animal control," injected Marcus. "So, I went on the internet searching for information about mutilated cats. During my search, I discovered the same thing has happened to cattle. I also came across a reference to a documentary on the subject called, A Strange Harvest. It was directed by Linda … oh, damn! … what's her last name?! … damn, I can't remember her last name right now. Well, anyway, that video scared the cheese-its out of me. A retired Logan County Sheriff, from Northeastern Colorado, said he personally investigated the carcasses of 200 mutilated cattle. And, in his opinion, none of the bovine died of natural causes. Based on his findings, the animals were paralyzed and were alive while they were being mutilated …"

"What year was that?," Paradise abruptly asked Nurse Davis.

"Around 1979. Oh … Tex Graves was his name … the name of the sheriff. Funny, how I can remember his name and can't recall Linda's last name. Well anyway, I want you to know I was raised in the church. But, something ain't right

Paradise. That shit shook me so bad I had to call my old Pastor …"

"But, he wasn't any help," said Malachi and Marcus in unison. He really wasn't. But, I remember something my great aunt-*tee* told me when I was a little girl," shared Nurse Davis.

"Which one Nana?," inquired Marcus.

"She's the one in the Bordeaux nursing home. She'd say, "Clara, there's an awful wickedness in this world." At the time, I thought she was talking about toubab, and what he'd done to Black Wall Street. But, after seeing that poor mutilated cat, I now KNOW what my aunt-*tee* was talking about. Over and over again, she'd repeat, "… for we wrestle not against flesh blood, but, we wrestle against wickedness in high places."," recalled Nurse Davis.

"Ephesians 6:12," said Paradise to Nurse Davis.

"That's right, Ephesians 6:12. You know your Bible. So, Paradise what's really going on?," asked Nurse Davis nervously.

"I can only speak on the cats. It appears the entity who harvested those poor animals has been doing it for generations with impunity," said Paradise.

"*That appears to be true,*" nodded Nurse Davis.

In a half serious, half joking tone, Paradise quipped, "Do you know what 'impunity' means Marcus?"

"Oh, you try'n to play me! Malachi and I graduated from high school two years early, with a 4.0 GPA. Since you're coming for me, you need to know I'm a member of iGem …"

"Stop stalling. Either you know it, or you don't. And, what's iGem?," Paradise asked Marcus.

"Stay focused Paradise," advised Nurse Davis.

"Impunity means exemption from punishment, or freedom from the injurious consequences of an action. And, regarding iGem, wouldn't you like to know. Nah, I'm just playing … iGem is …"

"Don't provoke her Marcus. She's a Pisces," Malachi told Marcus. "Pisces want unity. They're connected to the unseen world. They also love retreating into their private fantasy worlds. They often escape through drugs, alcohol, or the arts, and entertainment."

"Oh, you're coming for me too Malachi?," questioned Paradise with an attitude.

Nurse Davis was becoming intolerant. "WHAT, ARE Y'ALL - TWELVE?! Stay on point Paradise! This is important," Nurse Davis said impatiently.

"Wild cats lived among people in Mesopotamia over 100,000 years ago. Domesticated cats lived with the ancient Egyptian royal family more than 4,000 years ago. The penalty for killing a cat in ancient Egypt was death. The ancient

Egyptian goddess Bastet is depicted as a black cat, or as a black woman with a cat's head. In my opinion, Bastet represented those beings from the Lyra star system. IF, she was real, she may have been like a Satyr, or some other transgenic creature. Nevertheless, Bastet is the keeper of hearth and home, the protector of women's secrets, the guardian against evil spirits and disease, and the goddess of cats. Her ritual center had been the City of Bubastis, also known as the House of Bastet. Malefic Rootworker's would give aspiring 'Blues' singers and musicians, a 'black cat bone' to be successful. Now, we need to focus our attention on Bastet, or cats in general, because they're the Guardians against Evil Spirits …"

"What does that mean?," said Malachi.

"It means cats are the bridge between our world and the unseen world. And, whatever mutilated those cats just sent humanity a warning," said Paradise truthfully.

"What type of warning?," asked Marcus.

"What's a Satyr?," whispered Malachi to Nurse Davis.

"I'll tell you later," mouthed Nurse Davis in response.

"An evil force has chosen to kill mankind's warning system," Paradise told Marcus with a straight face.

"What does that mean?," Malachi asked.

"Cats are like smoke detectors. They alert us to any unseen presence, entering the room. That presence may be good, or that presence may be bad. But, hundreds of mutilated cats in England …"

"That means that presence is bad," surmised Nurse Davis.

"That makes sense 'cus England is the home of Harry Potter, witches, warlocks and wizards," said Marcus to Nurse Davis.

"They got white magic and black magic," said Malachi.

"Whatever magical system they're using, I agree with your grandmother, that other worldly cat killer is pure evil. And the deliberate killing of those guardians of the gate is an evil omen," Paradise said insightfully.

In addition to clarifying things, her insights raised new questions.

"What does that mean?"

"What gateway? … like the gates of hell?"

"Like the gates of hell, and other unseen gateways too. Those gateways serve as portals between our realm and the unseen realms," said Paradise instructively.

"That's just what I thought," Nurse Davis said sincerely.

"So, what are we going to do about it?," Marcus asked.

"In addition to praying … ," Malachi added.

"Malachi's right Paradise, the Bible says to pray and DO. So, what can we DO about it?," asked Nurse Davis.

Paradise was direct in her response. "At this moment, I don't know. But, that's why I have to get back to New Orleans as soon as possible. I have to find my grandmother's things." She was careful, and thoughtful about what she said next. "Now, what I'm about to say isn't Sunday school material … "

"Go on baby," encouraged Nurse Davis.

"Okay. My grandmother hid some magical manuscripts and mystical objects in New Orleans. That supernatural technology came from the old world," said Paradise without cracking a smile.

Genuinely befuddled, Malachi also didn't crack a smile when he said, "What old world? I only know this world."

"The world before the world Adam and Eve replaced. I'm talking about an ancient magic from eons ago. Most of my family's magic is archaic … it came from a world that has been long forgotten," said Paradise hypnotically.

Marcus was getting a little ahead of himself. With an impatient, curious excitement, he mindlessly asked, "Do you know where your grandmother hid those magical manuscripts?"

"Why? You trying to thief me?!," snapped Paradise.

"No, never that, we just want to help," said Malachi sincerely.

"Oh. Okay. So, let's do this in order. We got spirit, mind, and body. Our spirits need our bodies to feed our minds' electrical edibles," Paradise stated.

"Electric what?," said the twins at the same time.

"For optimal physical, emotional, and spiritual health, our kind needs to consume more alkaline foods then other folks," advised Paradise.

As a retired registered nurse, Nurse Davis easily related to the information Paradise was sharing. To help the twins grasp it, she confirmed her understanding aloud. "Okay, that makes sense. We're electrical beings that require a good quantity of electrical edibles, also known as alkaline foods."

In acknowledgement, Paradise smiled, "*That's right.*"

"Speaking of spiritual, I'm being led to tell you, this is how you can help. On the third hour, do this when you pray," Paradise instructed Malachi, Marcus, and the very attentive Nurse Davis.

Paradise began to twirl her right thumb clockwise around the tip of her right index finger. Nurse Davis, along with Marcus, watched Malachi do it first. When he failed to turn into a bird, or to disappear, they quickly realized it was safe to 'walk the circle' along with him.

"Yes, that's it … y'all got it," Paradise said happily.

Inquisitively, Malachi said, "Now, that we got it, what do we do with it? And, what's the third hour?"

"The third hour actually references every third hour of time. Using either 12 noon, or 12 midnight, as a starting point, every third hour that follows will be 3, 6, or 9 o'clock, regardless of whether it's AM, or PM. Just remember 3, 6, 9, 12. What's it for? This is one way you open a channel to get to God. So, do what you're currently doing the next time you pray … go heavy on the gratitude too," explained Paradise.

"*Huh?*," said the expression on Nurse Davis' face.

"Tell God everything you're thankful for … and, don't forget to ask God to send his holy angels along with your specific ancestor to help you obtain what you want. Oh yeah - last thing - make sure you tell them what you want it for," Paradise told the very attentive Davis family.

"Okay, that makes since," Marcus told Malachi.

"*Right, right,*" nodded Malachi.

"When you've finished praying, twirl your thumb counter- clockwise ONE TIME around the tip of your index finger. That will close the spiritual gate you opened. Also, you can assist me, by thanking God for helping me find my Mom-Mom's magical manuscripts. For humanity's sake, there's one more thing … I need to find my grandmother's things as soon as possible," Paradise said with urgency.

Wanting to contribute, but unsure how she could assist, Nurse Davis sought answers to her question, "How do we help you look?"

Paradise recommended, "If, you don't have an altar in your home, you need to erect one. 'Cus that's the place where you go to meet God. You can put your altar in any room in your house, other than the bathroom," said Paradise.

"Why? … why not the bathroom?," Malachi asked sincerely.

"You don't pray to God where you move your bowels. My Mom-Mom would say, "Is-ah-Bell-Lah, that's mad disrespectful," …"

"She would say, 'MAD disrespectful'?," questioned Marcus.

"OK … ok … no, she wouldn't have said 'mad', she would have used words like 'extremely', or 'very disrespectful'. However, my friend Lulu, now he would say, "mad disrespectful"," said Paradise light-heartedly.

"*Oh, okay. I'm glad that's cleared up,*" nodded Nurse Davis.

Paradise shared one last bit of info about erecting an altar. She said, "If you can't afford a solid gold altar, an empty shoebox will do. If you have to go the shoebox route, just paint it gold, or red, if you're able to."

"Whoa … a shoebox altar," said Marcus to Nurse Davis.

Concerned, Malachi asked, "What's wrong Nana?"

"Isn't that idol worship?," questioned Nurse Davis.

Paradise was well prepared to respond.

"No," she stated, before offering clarification. "Another angel came and stood at the altar, holding a golden censer; and there was given unto him much incense, that he might add it to the prayers of all the saints upon the golden altar which was before the throne - Revelations 8:3."

"So, we're not praying to a shoebox," said Marcus playfully.

"No. We're not praying to a shoebox. Your golden altar is your smartphone to God. God answers calls at anytime. But, you're more likely to get thru on the third hour. From what I've been taught, divine forces are attracted to candles, flowers, food, and liquor. Oh yeah, and plenty of sweet smelling incense smoke too."

Paradise hit the rewind button, wanting some clarity of her own. She turned to Marcus and asked,

"Now, what's iGem?"

"I'll tell you later," Malachi replied.

Marcus wanted to know, "What's a Satyr?"

"I'll tell you later," Nurse Davis advised.

22

HALF-GOAT

Las Vegas, Nevada

Paradise, along with Nurse Davis, Malachi, and Marcus continued to discuss the fate of humanity. According to that Washington Post article, a deranged individual had been killing defenseless pet cats. From the most fringe of the fringe perspective, those furry creatures were thought to be alien scouts, or guardians. Spiritually, cats are essentially charged with protecting the secret doorway.

After Paradise's appearance in Nurse Davis's Las Vegas home, she and her grandsons fled the city to get away from the paranormal activity. They relocated to Atlanta, Georgia. Marcus, who was the shorter grandson, invented a device that made its wearer invisible to digital cameras and software.

Malachi bragged about being a proud member of iGem. Paradise told the Davis family that her grandmother - Madame Montoyier - had hidden some magical manuscripts. The Montoyiers' supernatural information had come from a time long forgotten. In addition to those documents, Paradise also needed to find her estranged Aunt Ida because she was the keeper of those ancient secret, magical manuscripts.

"Hey, Spacey," Malachi jokingly said to Paradise.

"STOP calling me Spacey, because I'm very present," said Paradise sharply.

"My bad … I was trying to get your attention."

Paradise was now extremely annoyed. "I'm paying attention! You're the one who needs to pay attention … stop playing around so much!"

"I said, "My bad"."

"I guess she checked you," Marcus teased.

"Why don't you shut up!," snapped Malachi to his brother angrily.

Nurse Davis stepped up to shut the whole thing down. "What are y'all - nine? That statement includes you too Paradise, how are you going to help our people, if you're so easily distracted? You need to exercise better control over your emotions. If, you're easily rattled by two seventeen-year olds, what happens when something wicked comes your way? Get a grip. In my opinion, you need to meditate," she said, administering the constructive criticism Paradise needed to hear.

Paradise acknowledged and appreciated the merit of what Nurse Davis said. "You're right," she told her. "And I apologize."

"Apology accepted Paradise. Now, let's get down to business," Nurse Davis suggested.

Then, as though everything went in one ear and out the other, it started up again …

From Malachi to Paradise: "What's a Satyr?"

From Marcus to Paradise: "And who's in New Orleans?"

From Paradise to the twins: "What's iGem?"

"Alright. Alright!. Are we starting this all over again? One at a time!! I feel like I'm the only adult at the table!!!," Nurse Davis said exasperatingly.

"*You got that,*" nodded Paradise to Nurse Davis.

"I'm hoping my aunt-*tee* is still there. Nevertheless, I need to be in New Orleans. But, I need to figure out a way to get there without getting caught," Paradise told Marcus.

"Well, I'll loan you my Therian-tro … aw, never mind. I'll loan you my DX 44, if you promise to give it back. And Twin and I will drive you to the bus station tomorrow afternoon," said Marcus to Paradise.

"We'll do no such thing," Nurse Davis injected boldly.

"Paradise, we'll drive you to New Orleans in the morning," said Nurse Davis to a happy Paradise.

"*Thank you,*" nodded Paradise tearfully.

"You're welcome baby. And, your aunt-*tee* is still in New Orleans," said Nurse Davis, leaving Paradise perplexed.

"How do you know that?,"Paradise asked curiously.

"I remember talking to her. We spoke two, or three times. If, I remember correctly, she has an issue with her throat," remarked Nurse Davis.

"That's funny, 'cus she said y'all only spoke once," commented Paradise.

"So, you've spoken to her?," questioned Nurse Davis.

"Yes, and no," said Paradise cryptically.

"What does that mean?," chimed Marcus and Malachi.

"It means I haven't seen my Aunt-*tee* Ida for years. I've received a letter from her when I was staying at the Mardi Gras Inn," Paradise informed the group.

"That's the motel over there on Paradise Road in Sin City," Marcus mentioned nonchalantly.

Before she realized it, Nurse Davis raised an eyebrow and in terse tone asked, "What do you know about that Vegas motel Marcus?"

Marcus was guarded as he began to explain. "Well, …"

Obviously, disturbed and disappointed, Nurse Davis cut her grandson off. She was serious and quite curt when she said, "Don't answer that Marcus." She then took the time to revisit an earlier point. "See how easy it is, to get sidetracked?" Returning to the issue, Nurse Davis told Paradise, "Your aunt-*tee* and I definitely talked more than once. She told me what happened between her and your family. That's a very sad story. But, I digress. She told me your name wasn't Angelina. She also said whatever you were into had to be serious."

Based on what he just heard, Malachi spoke his speculation aloud. "So, you knew Paradise wasn't Angelina," he asked his grandmother.

"I did," she replied.

Wanting to be truthful, and transparent, Nurse Davis looked at Paradise in earnest and said, "I needed to know if you could be trusted."

"Wait … there's a missing piece," said Marcus. Sounding more like a prosecutor, he questioned, "How did you know Paradise's aunt-*tee*?"

"When I was in the hospital, your grandmother let me use her cell phone. I called my Aunt-*tee* back in New Orleans. But, she wasn't working on the day I called. So, I left a message," Paradise told Marcus and Malachi.

"Remember that night? I asked you, and Malachi, to walk up and down the strip," said Nurse Davis to Marcus.

"Yes, I remember Nana," Marcus recalled. "You wanted us to find Angelina."

"We spoke to all the prostitutes who walked the track that night," Malachi told Nurse Davis matter-of-factly.

The unpleasant look on Paradise's face said, "*Wow. Really?*"

"But, none of those hookers heard of Angelina."

"Now, I didn't tell y'all to go talk any prostitutes!," Nurse Davis clarified. "I told y'all to go inside the Golden Nugget Hotel and Casino, and to ask the man at the front desk to call Angelina's hotel room."

The latter peaked Paradise's curiosity, and prompted her to ask, "What made you think I was there?"

"The young man who took the blame for beating you up, said y'all argued and fought on the Vegas strip. I had a friend who worked at the Clark County Courthouse. She said his street name was Charlie-Boy. You know I had to pay that heifer to tell me where he worked," said Nurse Davis agitatedly.

"So, that's how you knew about the Golden Nugget … 'cus that's where Charlie-Boy worked. But, I was only there for an hour. Remember, I spent nearly a month in the hospital. What did Charlie-Boy say?," inquired Paradise.

"I only saw him once, and that was the night he brought you into the emergency room. Prior to that, I didn't know he existed. And, I didn't know that heifer from the courthouse was going to charge me either. But, I digress. She pulled up his case number and told me where he worked. Well anyway, I went to the Golden Nugget looking to question him. Someone said he either quit, or got fired … and, he'd left town with a large sum of money. I put two-and-two together and figured your sadistic husband paid him off," Nurse Davis advised. "Now, what's a Satyr, Lyra, and transgenic?"

Paradise flinched.

"Okay … wow … that was a mouthful. Have you ever heard of an alien hunter?," asked Paradise with a straight face.

"No, I haven't," replied Nurse Davis with a straighter face.

"Okay, let's do this a different way … have you ever heard of the UFO community?," questioned Paradise.

"Now, of course I've heard of that. We lived in Nevada remember? Area 51, Papoose Lake, tin foil hats, and UFO conventions," Nurse Davis stated confidently.

"Okay … we'll go with that angle. You asked what's Lyra? Well, some people in the UFO community believe humans started in the Lyra Star system. Is it true? Who knows. Well, a subgroup of Lyrans were humanoids, with cat-like features. They weren't furry like the cats on earth, they had a fine layer of hair to help protect them from the ultraviolet light on their planet," explained Paradise.

"So, is that why you said, "Bastet"?," Marcus asked curiously.

"Yes. The ancient Egyptian goddess Bastet, reminded me of those alleged feline people on Lyra," said Paradise.

"In your opinion, did they really have pointy ears, large eyes, and vertical eye slits?," Malachi asked Paradise.

"Did they have cat noses and little cat mouths?," Marcus added humorously.

"I don't know … I've never seen one … and, who knows if that Lyra story is even true? What I do know is 1 Chronicles 12:8," said Paradise honestly.

Nurse Davis' curiosity was aroused. "What's it say?"

"My mom used to read it to me," said Paradise.

Even as Marcus began accessing the scripture on his smartphone, Malachi still asked his brother, "What does it say?" "Some Cats from Gad … no pun intended … they left the tribe of Gad to fight with King David. Those men were skilled fighters, who knew how to handle their spears and shields. Their faces were like lions, and they were as swift as gazelles," Marcus told his twin, and grandmother.

"Whoa. I never learned that in Sunday school," said Malachi to Paradise.

"We sure didn't," said Marcus to Nurse Davis.

"Now, you asked what's a Satyr," said Paradise to Nurse Davis.

Sitting up, Nurse Davis eagerly confirmed, "I sure did."

Paradise asked her, "Do you have your Bible?"

"I sure don't."

Paradise directed Marcus saying, "Can you look in one of those dresser drawers and give your grandmother the Bible."

"Sure … no problem," said Marcus.

Malachi added, "This should be interesting."

"I was curious before … but, I'm really curious now!," emoted Nurse Davis.

As everyone waited for Marcus to retrieve the Bible, Malachi asked Paradise, "What's an alien hunter?"

"Alien hunters were brave humans who worked for various governments. They hunted aliens who hunted humans," Paradise explained.

"Wow. That was a mouthful," said Nurse Davis light-heartedly.

"*That makes sense to me,*" nodded Malachi to Nurse Davis.

"Here you go Nana," Marcus said, as he handed his grandmother the Bible.

"Thank you baby," she replied kind-heartedly.

Nurse Davis was now 'armed' and ready. Excited, she asked, "Now what Paradise?"

"Turn to Isaiah 13:21," Paradise instructed.

"Okay, let's see here. We got Proverbs … Ecclesiastes … Song of Solomon … and, Isaiah. Okay, Isaiah the thirteenth chapter - what verse Paradise?"

"The twenty-first verse," advised Paradise.

"Okay. I found it. It says, "But wild beasts of the desert shall lie there; and their houses shall be full of doleful creatures; and owls shall dwell there, and Satyrs shall dance there," said Nurse Davis. However, what she read confused her.

"I don't have a clue about what you said Nana. But, I heard you say "Satyrs", which tells me there's more than one," stated Malachi.

Equally confused, Marcus questioned Malachi, "More than one of what?" He then commented to his grandmother, "We don't even know what one Satyr is, let alone two, or three."

"He's right Paradise. You've been stringing us along," said Nurse Davis, who desired a satisfactory answer.

"Some Bibles may say 'wild goat', but, the correct word is Satyr. Some Bible scholar said a Satyr was a he-goat possessed by a demon. In my opinion, that's partly true. However, it's possible the situation may be a lot deeper than that," Paradise told Nurse Davis.

"What do you mean?," Malachi asked.

"In Greek mythology, the demigod Dionysus had a troop of male companions called Satyrs. Dionysus' equine friends were his …"

"His what?," Marcus questioned.

To aid their comprehension, Paradise provided a description. "His equine companions were guys who had horse-like features. They had horse-tails, horse-like ears, and horse-like penises that stayed erect."

Her face scrunched, Nurse Davis squeamishly said, "That's just nasty."

"Why's the son of a god hanging out with horse-dudes with permanent hard-ons?," Malachi asked Paradise.

"What did you say?," Nurse Davis asked in regard to Malachi's colorful question and choice of descriptive language.

"Sorry Nana. But, I'm just say'n …"

Concerned, she worriedly said, "That's blasphemy."

In an effort to shift her thinking, and in defense of his brother, Marcus said, "We're not Greek Nana. So, I'm pretty sure Twin wasn't mocking our God. Dionysus was the son of the Greek god, Zeus."

"Thanks Twin. Plus, guess what Nana … Dionysus' mother was Semele. She was a human being like Mary, the mother of Jesus. Dionysus was also known as the god of the resurrection …"

"The one of rebirth after death," said Marcus to Nurse Davis.

"That's not all. In Roman mythology, the satyrs are called fauns. Unlike its Greek counterpart, the fauns of Roman mythology had goat-like features. They were half-man, half-goat, and roamed the woods and mountains. The satyr also carried a musical pipe and a pipe case," Paradise told Nurse Davis.

"So, we know those are myths. 'Cus there's no way in hell mankind can blend a man with a beast," said Nurse Davis emphatically.

"That's not necessarily true Nana," Malachi said.

"There is nothing you can say, or do, to convince me otherwise," said Nurse Davis staunchly.

"You said you wanted to know Nana," warned Marcus.

"Alright, alright, alright," said Nurse Davis nervously.

"That's what I meant by transgenics. It's also called Transhumanism," said Paradise to Nurse Davis.

"What do you think we are learning at iGem?," Malachi asked Nurse Davis.

"I'm not really sure to be honest. All I know, y'all got good grades, y'all graduated early, and y'all got four year scholarships," said Nurse Davis proudly.

"We're learning about BioSecurity, using FBI protocols Nana," Malachi explained.

"I don't know what that means either. Talk regular, so we plain folk can understand," suggested Nurse Davis.

Marcus broke it down. "Ok Nana, trans-humanism means that some people will evolve beyond their physical and mental limitations, with the help of science and technology."

Nurse Davis sat overwhelmed.

Malachi excused himself from the table with a strange look. He went into his bedroom, returned with his bug-out bag, unzipped it, and proudly said, "Here, look Nana."

"What's that?," Paradise and Nurse Davis chimed in at the same time.

"It's a CRISPR CAS 9," Marcus announced proudly.

Nurse Davis was bewildered, unsettled, and agitated, when she asked Malachi, "It's a what? And, didn't I say talk 'regular'? So, we plain folk can understand."

23
WHO'S MARDUK?
Faubourg Tremé, Louisiana

Nurse Davis had a slight attitude caused by her grandson Malachi. He told her about his CRISPR/CAS 9 that he purchased online. Paradise was equally confused. She wondered why he had that tiny kit as well. Paradise wasn't disturbed by his bug-out bag. She wished she had one in 2005, during Hurricane Katrina. The mind can sometimes be a trickster. It will minimize, or exaggerate a past experience. The truth is that in 2005, thirteen year old Paradise didn't need one, because Madame Montoyier's Tremé home only received minor damage. Tremé stood for the Faubourg Tremé section of New Orleans. The flooding from Hurricane

Katrina wasn't high enough to damage those old raised homes in Madame Montoyier's neighborhood.

"Why do you have a bug-out bag?," Paradise asked Malachi.

"Nana, Twin, and I have bug-out bags just in case anything pops off, we're prepared to fight and escape. We got enough supplies to last us a week," Marcus proudly informed Paradise.

"We have the standard survivalist gear, and a few other goodies," said Malachi enthusiastically.

Paradise was curious. "Like what?," she asked.

"We've got your standard marine raider Bowie knife, glock shovel, compass, quickclot first-aid kit, hygiene products, and iodine pills to slow down radiation poisoning," Marcus advised.

"We've got water bottles, Lifestraw filters, Berkey water bottles with the filter, fire starter tools, a 3D printed gun with 3D bullets, extra flash lights, and duck tape," added Nurse Davis.

"How'd you get a 3D printer?," questioned Paradise.

"Nana bought it," said one twin.

The other twin added, "It was one of our many graduation gifts."

Both young men were clearly grateful to their grandmother.

"I didn't know what a 3D printer was. But, I assumed it was something they needed for their online computer coding class," Nurse Davis told Paradise.

"Well, that was progressive thinking on your part," Paradise said kindly to a most receptive Nurse Davis.

"What else do you have?," asked Paradise.

"Well, let's see …," Malachi said recalling the punch list. "We have a hand crank AM/FM radio, the size of a dollar bill. We've got sewing kits, lightweight work gloves, extra socks, as well as cooking and eating utensils," he rattled off.

"I went online and the Department of Homeland Security suggested we have light weight foods. So, I searched the web for light weight foods heavy in essential minerals and nutrients," said Nurse Davis thoughtfully.

"Such as?," inquired Paradise.

"Well, I went online, checked out the Sister Maa's 'Alkaline for Life' series on Youtube, as well as any video posts from the world renowned healer, naturalist, and herbalist, Dr. Sebi. You know Dr. Sebi, proved he cured our people of AIDS, cancer, and diabetes in the Supreme Court of New York, with herbs, roots, and other vegetable compounds. That was back in '87, and I think it's just awful what the 'Powers-That-Be' did to that brother. But, I digress. Dr. Sebi talked about the nutritional benefits of Irish Sea Moss … the powdered kind, not the wet version. So, we bought a few pounds of it. Now, I have a friend, who had a friend, who lived in South Africa. My friend's friend was able to smuggle some Hoodia root into the country. So, we have Hoodia root too, in addition to your standard granola bars, and MREs," said Nurse Davis.

"MERs?"

"No, its MREs, which means Meals Ready to Eat," Marcus told Paradise.

"Yes, I know what it means," Paradise said. She went on to give the family kudos, proudly telling them, "I'm just surprised y'all got it going on like that."

"After meeting Angelina … I mean you Paradise, our whole world changed," Malachi said sincerely.

That comment left Paradise dangling. "I don't know how to take that," she said with uncertainty.

Nurse Davis didn't hesitate to assure her, "It's a good thing."

"Thanks. That makes me feel a lot better," nodded Paradise. Thinking aloud, Paradise thoughtfully said, "Hey, y'all didn't say batteries."

"No, no, we have batteries," Marcus told Paradise.

"Plus, Twin got us a couple of Tesla flashlights, AND he made some crystal power battery cells too," Malachi noted proudly.

"What are crystal power cells?," questioned Paradise.

In an uncomprehending manner, Nurse Davis injected, "And what does that crispy cream thing do again?"

"Nana got jokes," snickered Marcus to Malachi.

Nurse Davis was truly perplexed now. With real concern, she asked, "Did I say it wrong?"

"Yeah Nana, but it's alright. It's called a CRISPR CAS 9," said Marcus helpfully. "Crystal power cells are long lasting batteries. We use them to power our LED flashlights. We can generate 15 Volts of electricity with 10 copper end caps, a magnesium core, and powdered crystals," he informed Paradise.

Paradise wondered to herself before saying anything. When she couldn't satisfy her own curiosity, she asked Marcus, "What kind of crystals? Quartz, Pyrite, and Garnet?"

Malachi responded, "No Paradise, not those kind of crystals."

"Think borax, epson salt, alum, and the sodium substitute, No Salt," Marcus explained.

"No Salt? No Salt, No Salt as in potassium chloride No Salt," pondered Paradise.

"Alright Dr. Spock and Uhura," Nurse Davis quipped to Marcus and Paradise light-heartedly.

"You can call me Mansa Musa, Nana," said Marcus.

"If he's the world's richest man, you can call me Oprah's forgotten stepchild," jested Paradise to Nurse Davis playfully.

Paradise stood, stretched, inhaled deeply, sat back down, and interrogatively said, "Look here Malachi, start talking!"

Malachi looked confused. He wiped his mouth and cautiously said, "About what? … Nah, I'm just playing. The CRISPR is a gene editing tool. They are scissors used to cut DNA. If, you see a gene you don't like, you simply cut it out."

"Give me an example," Nurse Davis asked inquisitively.

"Okay Nana. You retired from the hospital, so, I'm pretty sure you've seen a few patients with hepatitis," said Malachi.

"A few," said Nurse Davis engagingly.

"Well, those CRISPR scissors can inhibit Hepatitis C in human cells, and defy Mendel's law of inheritance," Malachi said informatively.

"You can do that?," inquired Nurse Davis impressively.

"I can't. But, the synthetic biologists at the University of California can," Malachi told his grandmother.

"Aw, come on Malachi, that scissor kit is no bigger than a pack of cigarettes," observed Nurse Davis.

Malachi was serious when he replied, "Well, it's a little bit bigger than that."

"You know what I mean," Nurse Davis said sarcastically.

Paradise asked Malachi, "What's Mendel's law, and what's a synthetic biologist?"

Before he could answer, Marcus responded. "The hood version of Mendel's law says mutated genes get passed down from parent to child."

"But, with these scissors, you can remove the mutated genes at the germ line," inferred Paradise academically.

"Okay, the germ line is when the sperm and egg meet. So, they cut out the disease, or mutated gene, at the germ line," said Nurse Davis engagingly.

"That's right Nana," said Malachi impressively.

Paradise's awareness was striking. Her capacity to grasp unfamiliar information and to then relay that information comprehensively was impressive. "And since they removed the mutated genes, they can't be passed to the next generation, 'cus there aren't any mutated genes to pass on," Paradise said confidently.

Amazed, Marcus proudly said, "You got it Paradise!"

"So, a synthetic biologist must be a person who makes new biological systems and artificial life forms," Paradise continued.

"Wow," said Malachi, in admiration and awe.

"I graduated early too," admitted Paradise proudly.

Nurse Davis was drawing conclusions too. Though the thought was terrifying, she deduced that, "If you can edit genes at the germ line, that means cloning is possible … and, if cloning is possible, that means blending human matter with animal matter is too."

"They're doing all that Nana," said Marcus enthusiastically.

"They're called Chimeras," Malachi advised.

"Chimeras?!"

"Yeah," Marcus said. "They're human-animal hybrids. They're made at the germ line using two, or more different species. Why are you looking at me like that Nana?," he nervously asked Nurse Davis.

"Remember the movie, Splice?," asked his grandmother.

"Never heard of it."

Paradise frame of reference left her feeling curious and conflicted. Seeking clarity, she asked Marcus, "I thought Chimeras were vicious monsters, like that ancient Babylonian Mušhuššu?"

"A WHAT?!," thundered Malachi, Marcus, and Nurse Davis.

"It's Akkadian for Sirrush. That mythological hybrid on Ishtar's reconstructed gate can be seen at the Pergamon Museum in Iraq," Paradise stated causally.

"And, you just happen to know that," Nurse Davis commented soberly.

"*Yep*," conveyed the gleam in Paradise's right eye.

In marvel, Marcus' eyes begged to know, "*What's it look like?*"

"At first look, the Sirrush looked like a scaly dragon; however, upon closer observation one would note it had the back legs and talons of an eagle. Its front legs were feline; it had a long scaly neck, a snake-like tail, a horned dragon-like head, and a snake-like tongue. And he, she, or it, wore a crest. It may be the crest of Marduk, because the Mušhuššu, or Sirrush, was Marduk's sacred animal," said Paradise, who spoke like the museum's tour guide.

Marcus was fascinated. "Who's Marduk?," he asked Paradise.

"He was an ancient Babylonian god credited with deliberately exploding the planet Tiamat, named after the goddess Tiamat, millions of years ago."

"Tia-who, Tia-what?," humoured the twins.

Paradise informed her captive audience, "According to the story, an ancient cosmic war took place within our solar system, causing the gods to fight the war in heaven. During the conflict, Marduk blew up the water planet, Tiamat. Evidence of that destroyed planet happens to be our asteroid belt."

"The asteroid belt is between the planets Mars and Jupiter," Marcus told Nurse Davis remedially.

Nurse Davis was a little testy when she replied, "I know where it is Marcus."

"Now, I heard of Marduk 'cus he's mentioned in the Bible. But, Paradise is talking fantasy and I'm not interested in Babylonian fairytales. So, can either of you provide me with some tangible evidence that supports your chimera, or hybrid theory?," Nurse Davis asked the twins.

"This is all in fun. But, since you come'n at me, I've got to come for you," said Paradise light-heartedly.

Nurse Davis jovially bantered back, "Bring it."

"I bet you Marduk isn't even mentioned in the Bible," Paradise stated skeptically.

Head slightly lifted, and completely self-assured, Nurse Davis spoke like a professor, as she delineated her answer, "Marduk is broken in pieces - Jeremiah 50:2, in the the King James version of the Bible."

"*And, you just happen to know that*," smugged Paradise's raised eyebrow.

"Go head Nana! … talk that talk!!," the twins cheered enthusiastically.

Marcus decided it was time to enter the ring. He cracked his knuckles, sat back, and playfully said, "Now, it's time for me to do my thing! You wanted tangible proof regarding those human-animal hybrids. Well, according to the Journal of Nature, Chinese scientists at the Shanghai Second Medical

University successfully created 100 human-rabbit embryos. The Chinese scientists told the reporters they destroyed the hybrid embryos before they became babies."

"*Thank you Marcus*," nodded Nurse Davis.

"But, I asked the two of you," Nurse Davis informed Marcus. "Malachi, what evidence do you have to offer?"

"Scientists in England make human-mice," briefed Malachi.

Appalled at the thought, and disgusted at the reality, Nurse Davis could only repeat, "Human mice?"

"Think Pinky and the Brain cartoon," said Malachi.

Shifting in another disturbing direction, Marcus told Paradise, "You, think that's someth'n, we also got three-parent teenagers running around too."

"Three-parent teenagers?" Paradise was dumbfounded.

"Yeah, some scientists have made designer babies. At the germ line, they taken some dude's sperm, and combined it with the biological matter retrieved from the eggs taken from two different women," said Malachi nonchalantly.

"And, they successfully made three-parent babies," reiterated Marcus.

"Some people in the transhumanism community are hoping they can self-replicate."

"Self-replicate?," said Nurse Davis shockingly.

"Yeah Nana, it's rumored that the FBI calls those self-replicating cells 4D printing," advised Malachi.

Paradise founded the subject riveting. Completely enthralled, she asked, "So, what's 3D printing?"

"3D printed organs, or organisms, are made with an ink-jet printer," said Marcus.

"Instead of using colored ink, geneticists and synthetic biologists use human DNA, or modified bacteria, as biological ink," Malachi told Paradise and Nurse Davis.

"You enter the person's genetic blueprint, or DNA sequence, into your computer, and press the 'enter' button on the keypad," said Malachi.

"After which, you can watch the 3D printer print a functional bladder, kidney, or heart," said Marcus to Paradise admiringly.

"And the organs actually work?," Nurse Davis asked skeptically.

"Yeah Nana, as long as the DNA is supplied by the person who needs the kidney, liver, or heart," Malachi clarified.

" If they can do that, what's stopping some psycho from emailing a DNA sequence of the Ebola virus to another nut?," Nurse Davis horrifyingly asked the twins.

"That's why the three letter groups have a bio-security protocol in place," Malachi told Nurse Davis and Paradise.

"Whatever that means? Biology is information. That biological information is DNA code. In theory, that DNA code can be emailed from a college dorm room to a bio-terrorist in New York," said Nurse Davis, still uneasy - if not frightened at the possibilities.

"Sure, that's possible Nana, but they got that Draco Nano trap," said Malachi enthusiastically.

24
FALLEN GODS
London, England

Paradise shared mythological stories with the Davis family, and they, in turn, kept her entertained with their stories, insights, and experiences. The combination took everyones' mind off of the Big Prairie Township Medical Center shooting. Nurse Davis expressed her justified concerns regarding weaponized viruses to her grandsons. Paradise shared the same concerns, scratched her head, and asked, "Hey Malachi, can you repeat what you said?"

"Sure. I said they got that Draco Nano trap."

Nurse Davis remained confused. "They got that what?!"

Excited to tell them, Marcus stated, “It’s called Draco Nano trap. It was developed by some college students in Cambridge, Massachusetts.”

“What does the dragon do?,” Paradise asked in earnest.

Malachi corrected Paradise, “It’s Draco Nana, not dragon.” Then he explained, “The Draco Nano trap was designed to kill all known, and unknown viruses.”

“What’s the science?,” questioned Paradise.

“In reality, the Draco vaccine causes apoptosis, or cell suicide. Here’s how it happens: once injected, Draco deceptively presents itself to the human body’s immune system as the offending virus via the vaccine. When the artificial virus (Draco) mingles with the offending virus, it triggers a signal that unleashes its destructive properties. The result is the activation of apoptosis, or cell suicide.”

“Even if I believed that story was true, which I don’t, the ‘Powers-That-Be’ would never give that particular vaccine to the common folk,” proposed Nurse Davis, speaking to Malachi. “After all, that would be man playing God,” she said to Paradise.

“That may be. But, nevertheless those fallen gods did the same thing,” Paradise told Nurse Davis.

“What do you mean?,” Malachi asked.

Nurse Davis notified the twins, “This is the last scary story for the night. ‘Cus it’s time we went to bed. Plus, we have to get Paradise back to New Orleans, 'cus she's got things to do."

"*Okay, Nana,*" nodded Marcus and Malachi in unison.

"According to the story, there was a war in heaven. God's military led by the Archangel Michael kicked Draco out of heaven. Draco, along with a third of his army, was forced to live on earth," said Paradise informatively.

"The Bible says it was a dragon, not Draco," said Nurse Davis.

"Yes, you're right. I stand corrected. But, the section of heaven the dragon fought from was called Ouranos. Ouranous is Greek for Uranus. And, in Greek mythology, Uranus and Gaia were the parents of the first Titans. Gaia was the earth mother. Uranus was the sky father, and the Titans were their giant children. Those giant offspring had incredible strength and they ruled heaven and earth during the golden age. It's claimed by the ancient Greeks, there was a war in heaven between the gods. The Olympian gods fought the Titan gods in a war called the Gigantomachy. The Olympian gods sought to overthrow the Titan's old religion. In addition, they also wanted to establish themselves as the new rulers of the cosmos. But, I digress," said Paradise.

Although the hour was late, and there was much to do, Nurse Davis urged Paradise to continue. "No, go on 'cus this is interesting," she said.

"According to Hebrew mythology, 200 fallen Watchers left their first estate," Paradise advised.

"What does that mean?," questioned Marcus.

Malachi looked at his grandmother and asked, "What's a Watcher?"

"*I don't know,*" shrugged Nurse Davis.

Paradise recounted the tale, "The Watchers are ambassadors, or messengers. They're what people today call angels. The Watchers are dispatched by God, and their duty is to watch over the humans who live on Earth. That phrase - 'they left their first estate' - refers to the 200 Watchers that rebelled against God. They were kicked out of heaven and thrown to Earth. Their leader, Samyaza, instructed the fallen Watchers to teach mankind the arts, weaponry, cosmetics, mirrors, sorcery, and other heavenly technology."

"Hold that thought Paradise," Nurse Davis recommended, as she scooted off.

"Where you going Nana?," asked Malachi.

"I'm going to the bathroom … I'll be back."

Nurse Davis returned from the bathroom, as quickly as she left. She was visibly tired; but, the Spirit of Curiosity pushed her to stay awake. The Twins warmed up the remaining food, sat back down, and got real comfortable. Paradise poured herself some water to drink. Prior to Nurse

Davis' departure, she had been telling the story about the 200 fallen Watchers, who were forced to live on earth.

Nurse Davis made sure Paradise picked up where she left off. "Now, what were you saying about those fallen 200?"

"Those fallen 200, along with some other gods, corrupted mankind's gene pool," Paradise told Nurse Davis.

Her response was, "That sounds like fairy tales."

"That may be. However, Hebrew lore says those fallen gods and angels pro-created with human women, animals, sea creatures, even plant life," Paradise said with a straight face.

"Where's your supporting evidence?," challenged Malachi, who played the role of a federal prosecutor.

"A few years ago, on the Discovery Channel, they aired an episode called, Into the Unknown Sideshows and Skeletons. That particular episode featured the Naree Pons, or Flower Pod People, of Thailand. Naree Pons are tiny humanoid creatures rumored to be comprised of both plant and human DNA. Generally, they're about six inches long, and look like skinny humans, with elf ears, distorted faces, and brown vine-like skin," said Paradise informatively.

"Weird, weird, weird," Nurse Davis said skeptically.

"When I was a little girl, Avi Weinberg, who was my grandmother's lawyer, told us a story. He said his Rabbi talked about the plant people too," said Paradise.

"Is that true?," questioned Malachi.

"I don't know. I'm only repeating what he said. He told us that a long time ago; plant-like creatures lived in the oasis of the Middle East …"

"You mean Northeast Africa," said Marcus in a scholarly tone.

"Okay, Northeast Africa. Well anyway, those weird humanoid plant creatures were extremely intelligent. They grew like pumpkin gourds according to the legend," Paradise told Marcus.

"What does that mean?," asked Malachi curiously.

"That means they were attached to the earth by a long vine. According to Avi's Rabbi, those tiny plant-men were extremely quick, and were not pleasant. There was only one way humans could kill those plant-like creatures," Paradise said creepily.

"What way was that?"

"They needed to use an anointed machete."

Malachi inquired, "How was it prepared?"

"It's an unspoken process … in other words that's not book writing material," Paradise jokingly said.

"What? I'm confused," said Marcus.

"I'm just playing. Those Jewish swords, or machetes, were forged in a fire fueled in part with human bones," Paradise reported nonchalantly.

Nurse Davis remarked, "That's creepy."

Concerned, Marcus commented, "And, you're a little to calm too Paradise."

"Look Nana!," Malachi said, excited to get his grandmother's attention.

Nurse Davis asked him, "What am I looking at?"

"I went on Pinterest, and looked up 'magical creatures' ..."

"What does it say Malachi?"

"'Faduah' is the name of the humanoid plant-man mentioned in Jewish mythology. The creatures were rooted into the earth via a stem ran from their belly buttons into the soil. The site also says they were extremely aggressive, attacking, and killing anything that got in their way. The creatures only died when their stems were severed," Malachi read, with a straight, yet mystified face.

Curious, Paradise asked, "Does it say anything else?"

"Okay ... hold on ... I'm going onto another site. Okay, this one says, according to the Jewish Talmud, the mythical plant-man was based on the legendary Vegetable Lamb of Tartary," read Malachi.

Thoroughly perplexed, Marcus blurted out, "The what?"

"Hold on Twin. It goes on to say that around 436 CE (Christian era), or prior to God's creation of Adam, God constructed a human-like plant-man in the Garden of Eden called Faduah, or Adne Sadeh. Reference source <u>Tree of</u>

Souls: The Mythology of Judaism, by Howard Schwartz," Malachi read informatively.

"I'm all 'in' Paradise," Marcus said. "But, what about those fallen angels and gods having sex with animals and women?"

"Get your mind out of the gutter!," snapped Nurse Davis angrily.

"If its Bible based, is Twin's mind really in the gutter?," Malachi argued in defense of his brother.

Nurse Davis thought for a moment, rubbed the back of her neck, and in an exasperated sigh, muttered, "Please continue Paradise."

"In the sixth chapter of Genesis, verses one through six, it says the Ben Elohiym …"

A bit fatigued, Nurse Davis timidly asking Paradise, "Who?"

"'Ben Elohiym' is Hebrew for the 'Sons of God'. Since, the word 'Elohiym' means the 'divine ones' - the gods and goddesses, technically speaking, the 'Ben Elohiym' are the 'sons of the gods and goddesses'. But, I digress. According to the Biblical story, the sons of the gods impregnated a lot of human women," Paradise explained.

"SHUT THE FRONT DOOR!," shouted Nurse Davis.

"Stay with me Nurse Davis … the Bible also says that those women bore children with those gods. The ancient

Hebrews called those half-human children the Nephilim. That word 'Nephil' in Hebrew means 'giant bullies'. Those giant tyrants terrorized mankind according to the story. I listened to an interview where Mauro Biglino, an Italian essayist and translator, was the guest speaker. From his research, Biglino said he discovered that the word 'Nephil' - as a noun in the Aramaic language, meant 'Orion' …"

Marcus said a confusing mouthful when he asked Paradise, "Orion, as in the mighty hunter Orion, or Orion, as in Orion's belt Orion?"

"Who's Mauro, the Big Lino?," said Malachi to Paradise.

"It's Mauro Biglino, and I was referring to Orion's Belt, as in the star system Orion," Paradise told Malachi and Marcus.

"Now, what's Lino Bigg's claim to fame?," questioned Nurse Davis.

"It's Biglino, and he translated 23 books of the Bible for the Vatican. But, they felt some type of way and let him go. 'Cus the original Hebrew words in the Bible state that Jehovah, the God of Israel, traveled in a spaceship," said Paradise non-combatively.

Ready for all takers, Nurse Davis combatively, responded, "Aw, hell! I don't believe that!"

"Well, the Vatican did," said Paradise.

"And, they let him go?," asked Marcus.

"I said they felt some type of way," Paradise reminded Marcus.

"How about Steven Spielberg's movie called the BFG?," Malachi injected nonchalantly.

Still in combative mode, Nurse Davis winced as she asked Malachi, "The what?"

"It means 'Big F'n God'," Marcus said jokingly.

"WHAT?!," growled an angry Nurse Davis to Marcus.

"BFG stands for the 'Big Friendly Giant' Nana. He's 24 feet tall, and he befriended a little white boy," Malachi explained.

He was excited to continue on, and to tell everyone, "How about in 2002, the National Geographic Magazine reported they found a dozen cyclops skeletons in Greece. The skeletal remains of those one-eyed giants stood 12 to 15½ feet tall."

"Oh, that ain't nothing. Back in 2004, some guy from Riyahd, called Saalim Alvi, published an article titled, Giant Human Skeleton found in Saudi Arabia. According to the story, the Saudi Arabian military allegedly found evidence of the Aad people. The Aad people are mentioned in the Qur'an, and were a rumored race of giants. As stated in Islamic tradition, Allah destroyed the nation of Aad. Anyway, some explorers from the ARAMCO oil company supposedly discovered a large skeleton in the desert region they call the

Empty Quarter. What they uncovered was a humanoid skeleton, whose head was five feet long. So, that puts their Big F'n Giant at 25 to 30 feet tall," Paradise informatively told an intrigued Malachi, and Marcus.

"Is there a point?," Nurse Davis asked aggressively.

"I know you're tired Nurse Davis, but there is a point. In the Book of Enoch, around the seventh chapter, it says the fallen angels sinned against birds, beasts, reptiles, and fish too. That's where the mermaid myth comes from," Paradise said quickly.

"Take your time Paradise. What do you mean they sinned against those animals?," questioned Marcus.

"They impregnated those creatures, and those creatures produced forbidden life forms."

Malachi was genuinely fascinated. "Like what?," he asked Paradise.

"You better not say fairies and gnomes," ribbed Marcus.

"Oh, I don't believe this nonsense!," Nurse Davis gasped.

"Wait Nana," Marcus pleaded.

"Okay … this better be good Paradise," warned Nurse Davis.

Paradise announced, "Alright, this is the last story for the night."

"You promise?"

"I promise."

Despite his apparent crush, Marcus decided to take a mature approach. He sat up, and assuringly told Paradise, "Okay, you have my full and undivided attention."

"Around 1960, a demolition team prepared to knock down an old mansion in London, England … "

"Here we go with England again," Malachi said abruptly.

"Shh, let her tell the story," agreed Marcus and Nurse Davis.

"Before the old mansion was converted into an orphanage, it had been the private residence of Lord Thomas Theodore Merryln, an English aristocrat. In addition to being a high society property owner, Merryln also worked as a Cryptozoologist," said Paradise intriguingly.

"What's that?," Marcus asked curiously.

Paradise wasn't given an opportunity to respond. Nurse Davis took the initiative and hijacked the moment. With a measurable amount of hateration oozing from her voice, Nurse Davis began to speak. "It's FAKE, or pseudoscience, that involves the search for creatures that never existed. OR, for Paradise's sake, let's just say there's a lack of evidence supporting those alleged creatures ever existed."

"Why you hate'n Nana?," asked Marcus, in defense of Paradise.

"Ain't nobody hate'n … I'm just tired … go on Paradise," said Nurse Davis exhaustedly.

"Lord Merryln collected strange creatures from all over the world," Paradise told Marcus.

"Alright, I'll bite. What kind of creatures?," Nurse Davis asked.

"The demolition team discovered thousands of small wooden boxes in the basement of the mansion. A great number of those boxes were covered with scriptures, wooden crosses, and Catholic Rosary beads."

"What was inside those boxes Paradise?," questioned the twins.

Paradise described the eerie contents found within those boxes. "Bizarre creatures that resembled those depicted in fairy tales. Lord Merryln collected the real-life skeletal remains of tiny humanoid creatures. Some of them looked like evil fairies, with busted butterfly wings. In other boxes, he had mummified elves that looked like Snap, Crackle, and Pop. Only, those creepy creatures weren't selling breakfast cereal. At eight inches in length, the elves had red hair, slanted eyes, pointy ears, and razor sharp teeth. They were anything but cuddly."

Nurse Davis was clearly disappointed. "I almost believed you," she told Paradise, who was slightly offended by her disbelief.

Paradise was firm, serious, and sincere when she responded, "I have no reason to lie to you."

The twins may have said, "Be nice Nana," but what they really meant - *"temper, temper Nana"* - went unspoken.

Nurse Davis' stare was ice cold. Her face, deliberately twisted in displeasure. The message her demeanor displayed bespoke her feelings well. *"Now, I love Paradise. She's like a daughter to me. But, y'all know what she just said is some bullshit."*

Paradise had no intention, or desire to get caught up. She chose to keep it moving. Speaking to Malachi, she went on to explain that, "The curators at the Merryln Cryptic Museum also had on display, a mummified creature that was part white rabbit, mixed with a deer-like animal. It was a tiny creature with long antlers."

Still perturbed, Nurse Davis sarcastically asked, "Are you serious?"

Paradise looked Nurse Davis directly in her eyes, and with a straight face told her, "Your snide remark about my seriousness is premature Nurse Davis."

"There's more?," said Nurse Davis frustratingly.

"Yes, there's more … Lord Merryln was born in England around 1782. In addition to collecting bizarre species from around the world, his youthful appearance freaked people out. When he was in his mid-80s, he looked like he was forty years old. Lord Merryln also toured America with his strange collection of bizarre creatures. The scientific community called him a fraud. They also called him a witch, a wizard, and a dark magician. Lord Merryln discontinued his American tour abruptly, returning immediately to England with his feelings hurt. Out of frustration, he wrote a scientific paper on time travel. Allegedly, his colleague stole the paper, furthering Lord Merryln's plummeting confidence and emotional descent …"

"What does that mean Paradise?," inquired Nurse Davis.

"That means he felt some type of way," clarified Marcus.

"He had a temper tantrum," said Paradise.

"I know, he lost a lot of cool points," Malachi told Paradise.

"He did. So, he dropped out of English society. According to newspaper clippings, he re-appeared in London society in 1942. He returned to sell his old home, which later became an orphanage. But, Lord Merryln had one stipulation …"

"What stipulation?"

"No one was allowed to go in the basement. That had been Lord Merryln's only requirement."

"Wait!, wait!!, wait!!!," shouted Nurse Davis excitedly.

"What Nana?"

"Marcus, what's 1942, minus 1782?," Nurse Davis asked.

"160," said Marcus quickly.

"He was 160 years old!," Malachi told Paradise in shock.

"Now, you can ask, "Are you serious?"," mocked Paradise playfully.

"I'm not fool'n with you Paradise. I'm going to bed," yawned Nurse Davis light-heartedly. As soon as Nurse Davis said, "I'm going to bed," they heard a light knock on the door.

Marcus gloated, "Hey Nana, no worries. Snopes.com says Paradise's Merryln story is false. It also says, some artist dude named Alex CF made those creepy creatures."

Nurse Davis looked relieved, Paradise appeared confused, and Marcus switched gears by saying, "Shhhh… Everybody be quiet."

"Don't tell me to be quiet!" barked Nurse Davis.

"I guess Snopes will say those 6-inch humanoids living in Atacama Chile, are fake too," thought Paradise.

"You don't hear that Nana?" Marcus calmly whispered.

"Her what?" mouthed Nurse Davis to Malachi.

"I hear it too," squinted Paradise to Nurse Davis.

"Who's knocking on our door at this hour," Malachi's flared nostrils asked Nurse Davis.

"Ut. Oh,"

"Ut. Oh, what," mouthed Marcus to Paradise.

"How'd they find me?"

"Who's looking for you?" whispered Malachi to Paradise.

"Will y'all be quite! Now, get in position," squinted Nurse Davis to Malachi.

"I dare you," mouthed Malachi to Marcus, who aggressively yelled, "WHO IS IT?!"

Book 3 of 'THE RITUAL' series by

Shema'yah Bey is

'SOUL HUNTER'S PRAYER'.

ABOUT THE AUTHOR

Shema'yah Bey is an author, astrologer and screenwriter. He's also a BioAcoustic Researcher. Born under the planetary influence of Uranus in Aquarius, he has always had a natural attraction to ancient technologies, esoteric science, and other mystical arts.

After a life altering encounter with a triangular UFO, Shema'yah jumped down the metaphoric 'rabbit hole' ... a conscious decision that introduced him to the world of paranormal activity, exorcisms, and the teleporting man.

Shema'yah wrote 'THE RITUAL' book series to keep the esoteric stories of his mentor, Dr. Clifford E. Hazel, alive. As a result of Dr. Hazel taking the method of bending a twig* back to the 'World of Spirits' - Shema'yah created the Montoyier family, to help preserve his magical memories and otherworldly secrets.

*A rumored preternatural technique - that involves unseen forces killing ones enemy at daybreak (dawn).

Made in the USA
Middletown, DE
09 April 2024

52654602R00195